Louis Figuier

The Day After Death

Our future life according to science

Louis Figuier

The Day After Death
Our future life according to science

ISBN/EAN: 9783337387952

Printed in Europe, USA, Canada, Australia, Japan

Cover: Foto ©Andreas Hilbeck / pixelio.de

More available books at **www.hansebooks.com**

THE

DAY AFTER DEATH;

OR,

Our Future Life according to Science.

TRANSLATED FROM THE FRENCH OF
LOUIS FIGUIER.

ILLUSTRATED BY TEN ASTRONOMICAL PLATES.

A NEW AND CHEAPER EDITION.

LONDON:
RICHARD BENTLEY AND SON,
Publishers in Ordinary to Her Majesty the Queen.
1889.

CONTENTS.

THE DAY AFTER DEATH.

INTRODUCTION.

READER, you must die. You may perhaps die to-morrow. What will become of you? What shall you be, on the day after your death? I do not now allude to your body; that is of no more importance than the clothes which it wears, or the shroud in which it will be buried. Like these garments, like that cere-cloth, your body must be decomposed, and its elements distributed among Nature's great reservoirs of material, earth, air, and water. But your soul, whither shall it go? That which was free within you, that which thought, loved, and suffered, what shall become of it? Of course you do not believe that your soul will be extinguished with your life on the day of your decease, and that nothing will remain of that which has palpitated in your breast, vibrating to the emotions of joy and sorrow, to the tender affections, the numberless passions and disturbances of your life.

Where shall that sensible, existing soul, which must sur-

vive the tomb, go to? What will it become, what shall you
be, my reader, the day after your death?

To the consideration of this question this book is devoted.

Almost all thinkers have declared that the problem of the
future life defies solution. They have argued that the human
mind is powerless to foresee so profound a mystery, and that
therefore the only rational course is to abstain from the endeavour. This is the reasoning of the majority of mankind,
partly from carelessness, or partly from conviction. Besides,
when we venture to look at this tremendous question closely,
we find ourselves immediately surrounded with such thick darkness that we lack courage to pursue the investigation. And thus
we are led to turn away from all thought of the future life.

There are, nevertheless, circumstances which force us to reflect on this dark and difficult subject. When one finds
oneself in danger of death, or when one has lost a dearly
beloved object, there is no escape from meditation upon the
future life. When we have dwelt long and earnestly upon
the idea, we may be brought to acknowledge that the problem
is not, as it has so long been believed, beyond the reach of
the human mind.

During the greater portion of his life, the author of this
book believed, in common with everybody else, that the problem of the future life is out of our reach, and that true wisdom consists in not troubling our minds about it. But, one
dreadful day, a thunderbolt fell in his path. He lost the son
in whom centred all the hope and ambition of his life. Then,
in the bitterness of his grief he reflected deeply on the new

life which must open for each of us, above the tomb. After
long dwelling on this idea in solitary meditation, he asked of
the exact sciences what positive information, on this question,
they could furnish him with, and subsequently, he interrogated
ignorant and simple people, peasants in their villages, and
unlettered men in towns, an ever precious source of aid in
re-ascending towards the true principles of nature, for it is
not perverted by the progress of education, or by the routine
of a commonplace philosophy.

Thus the author of this book succeeded in constructing for
himself an entire system of ideas concerning the new life of
man, which is to follow his terrestrial existence.

But his system is all contained in nature. Each organized
being is attached to another which precedes, and another
which follows it, in the chain of the living creation. The
plant and the animal, the animal and the man, are linked,
soldered to one another; the moral and physical order meet
and mingle. It results from this, that any one who believes
himself to have discovered the explanation of any one fact
concerning this organization, is speedily led to extend this explanation to all living beings, to reconstruct, link by link, the
great chain of nature. Thus it was with the author of this
book. After having sought out the destination of man, when
dismissed from his terrestrial life, he was led to apply his views
to all other living beings, to animals, and then to plants.
The power of logic forced him to study those beings, impossible
to be seen by our organs of vision, by which he holds the
planets, the suns, and all the innumerable stars dispersed

over the vast extent of the heavens, to be inhabited. So that you will find in this book, not only an attempt at the solution of the problem of the future life by science, but also the statement of a complete theory of nature, of a true philosophy of the universe.

It may be that I am deceiving myself; it may be that I am taking the dreams of my imagination for serious views; I may lose myself in that dark region through which I am trying to grope my way; but at least I write with absolute sincerity, and that is my excuse for writing this book at all. I hope that others may be induced by my example to attempt similar efforts, to apply the exact sciences to the study of the great question of the destinies of man after this life. A series of works undertaken in this branch of learning, would be the greatest service which could be rendered to natural philosophy, and also to the progress of humanity.

After the terrible misfortunes of 1870 and 1871, there is not a family in France which has not had to mourn a kinsman or a friend. I found, not indeed consolation for my grief, but tranquillity for my mind, in the composition of this work; and I have therefore hoped that, in reading its pages, they who suffer and they who grieve might find some of the same hope and assurance which have lifted up my stricken heart.

Society is in our day the prey of a deadly disease, of a moral canker, which threatens it with destruction. This disease is materialism. Materialism, which was preached first in Germany, in the universities, and in books of philosophy, and the natural sciences, afterwards spread rapidly in France.

With brief delay, it came down from the level of the *savans* to that of the educated classes, and thence it penetrated the ranks of the people; and the people have undertaken to teach us the practical consequences of materialism. Little by little they have flung off every bond, they have discarded all respect of persons and principles; they no longer value religion or its ministers; the social hierarchy, their country, or liberty. That this must lead to some terrible result it was easy to foresee. After a long period of political anarchy, a body of furious madmen carried death, terror, and fire through the capital of France.

It was not patriotism which fired the illustrious and sacred monuments of Paris, it was materialism. Nothing can be more evident than that, from the moment one is convinced that everything comes to an end in this world, that there is nothing to follow this life, we have nothing better to do, one and all of us, than to appeal to violence, to excite disturbance, and invoke anarchy everywhere, in order to find, amid such propitious disorder, the means of satisfying our brutal desires, our unruly ambition, and our sensual passions. Civilization, society, and morals, are like a string of beads, whose fastening is the belief in the immortality of the soul. Break the fastening, and the beads are scattered.

Materialism is the scourge of our day, the origin of all the evils of European society. Now, materialism is fiercely fought in this book, which might be entitled, " Spiritualism Demonstrated by Science." Because this is its aim, and its motive, my friends have induced me to publish it.

CHAPTER THE FIRST.

MAN THE RESULT OF THE TRIPLE ALLIANCE OF THE BODY, THE
SOUL, AND THE LIFE. WHAT CONSTITUTES DEATH.

ARTHEZ, Lordat, and the Medical School of
Montpellier have created the doctrine of the *human aggregate*, which, in our opinion, affords the
only explanation of the true nature of man.
This doctrine, of which we shall avail ourselves, as a guide in
the earlier portions of this work, may be defined as follows :—

There exists in man three elements :—

1. The body, or the material substance.

2. The Life, or as Barthez calls it, the *Vital Force.*

3. The Soul, or as Lordat calls it, the *Intimate Sense.*

We must not confound the soul with the life, as the materialists and certain shallow philosophers have done. The
soul and the life are essentially distinct. The life is perishable, while the soul is immortal ; the life is a temporary
condition, destined to decline and destruction ; while the
soul is impervious to every ill, and escapes from death. Life,
like heat and electricity, is a force engendered by certain
causes ; after having had its commencement, it has its termination, which is altogether final. The soul, on the contrary,
has no end.

Man may be defined as *a perfected soul dwelling in a living body*.

This definition permits us to specify what it is that con-stitutes death.

Death is the separation of the soul and the body. This separation is effected when the body has ceased to be animated by the life.

Plants and animals cannot live except under certain condi-ditions : plants in the air or in the water, animals in the air, fish in the water ; and if they are deprived of these condi-tions, they perish immediately. Again, there are existences which require special conditions for their support within the general ones.

Certain polypoid-worms can live only in carbonic acid, or azotic gas ; the germs of cryptogams produced by damp can be developed only in aqueous infusions of vegetable matters ; the fish which live in the sea, die in fresh, or only moderately salt, water.

Every living being has then its special *habitat*. The soul does not form an exception to this rule. The place, the *habitat* of the soul is a living body. The soul disappears from the body when this body ceases to live, just as a man forsakes a house when that house has been destroyed by fire.

Such is the doctrine of the triple alliance of the body, the soul, and the life, as formulated by the School of Montpellier, and such, as a consequence of this doctrine, is the mechanism of death.

It must be added that this triple alliance of the body, the

soul, and the life, is not peculiar to man; it exists also in all animals. The animal has also a living body, and soul; but the soul in animals is much inferior to the soul in men, in the number and extent of its faculties. Having few wants, the animal has a very small number of faculties, which are all in a rudimentary condition. It is only in the very considerable development of the faculties of the soul that man differs from the superior animals, to which he bears a strong resemblance in his physiological functions, and his anatomical structure.

It must be remarked that the Montpellier School does not admit this view of the condition of animals. In another part of this work,* a fuller explanation of the distinctions which divide man from animal will be found.

* Ch. XV.

CHAPTER THE SECOND.

WHAT BECOMES OF THE BODY, THE SOUL, AND THE LIFE, AFTER DEATH.

AFTER death, the body, whether of a man, or of an animal, being no longer preserved from destruction by vital force, falls under the dominion of chemical forces. If the body of a dead animal, or a human corpse be kept in a place where the temperature is below 0°, or if it be shut up in a space entirely air-tight, or if it be impregnated with antiseptic substances, it will remain intact, as at the moment at which life has abandoned it. Such is the process of embalming. The effect of the various chemical substances with which a corpse is impregnated, is to coagulate the albumen of the tissues, and thus to preserve the animal substance from putrefaction. A similar result will be obtained if the corpse be placed between two layers of ice, or in a coffin entirely surrounded with ice constantly renewed. If kept at a temperature of 0°, the body will not be subject to decomposition, because putrid fermentation cannot take place at so low a temperature.

This was the process by which the entire carcasses of the mammoths, or extinct elephants, which belonged to the qua-

ternity period, were preserved.   In 1802 a perfectly preserved carcass of this gigantic pachyderm was found on the
bank of the Lena, a river which runs into the Arctic Sea,
after traversing a portion of the Asiatic continent in the vici-
nity of the North Pole.   The frozen earth and the ice which
covers the banks of the river into which the mammoth had
plunged, had so effectually preserved it from putrefaction, that
the flesh of the huge creature, dead for more than a hundred
thousand years, made a feast for the fishermen of that desert
place.   In northern countries, if one would preserve the body
of a man, it could be effectually done by simply keeping it
constantly wrapped in ice.

When the body of a man, or of an animal, is exposed to
the combined influences of air, of water, and of a moderately
high temperature, it undergoes a series of chemical decompo-
sitions, whose final term is its transformation into carbonic
acid gas, and some compounds, gaseous or solid, which represent the less advanced products of destruction.   Gases of
various kinds, carbonic acid, hydrosulphuric, and ammoniac,
and the vapour of water, spread themselves through the atmosphere, or dissolve into the humidity of the soil.   At a later
stage these compounds, thus dissolved into the water which
bathes the earth, are absorbed by the little roots of the plants
which live on it, and aid in their nutrition and development.   As for the gas, it begins by spreading through the
air; and then falling to the earth again dissolved in the rain-
water, it also equally supplies the needs of vegetable life.
The ammoniac and carbonic acid in the water which pene-

trates the soil, is absorbed by the roots, introduced into the tubes of the plants, and supplies them with nourishment.

Thus, the matter which forms the bodies of men and animals is not destroyed; it only changes its form, and under its new conditions it aids in the composition of fresh organic substances.

In all this the human body does but obey the common laws of nature. That which it undergoes, every organized substance, vegetable or animal, exposed to the combined influences of air, water, and temperature, equally undergoes. A piece of cotton or woollen stuff, a grain of wheat, a fruit—they all ferment, and reduce themselves to new products, exactly as our bodies do. The cere cloth which enfolds a corpse is destroyed by precisely the same process which destroys the corpse.

But, if the material substance which forms man's body does but transform itself, journeying through the globe, passing from animals to plants and from plants to animals; it is quite otherwise with life. Life is a force. Like the other forces, heat, light, and electricity, it is born, and it transmits itself; it has a beginning and an end. Like light, heat, and electricity—the physical agents which make us comprehend life, and which have certainly the same essence and the same origin—life has its producing causes, and its causes of destruction. It cannot rekindle itself when it has been extinguished; it cannot re-commence its course when its fatal term has arrived. Life cannot perpetuate itself; it is a simple condition of bodies, a fugitive and precarious condition, subject to count-less influences, accidents, and chances.

The life is therefore greatly inferior in importance to the soul, which is indestructible and immortal. The soul is the essential element in all nature. It has active and positive qualities in all respects where the two other elements, the body and the life, have only negative qualities. Whilst the body dissociates itself and disappears, while the life becomes annihilated, the soul can neither disappear nor become anni-hilated.

We have seen what becomes of a man's body after his death, and also of his life; let us now examine into the con-dition of his soul.

No philosopher, no learned man, none of those who know the immensity of the universe and the eternity of the ages, can admit that our existence on the earth is a definite thing, —that human life has no link with anything above or beyond itself. Man dies at thirty, or twenty years old; he may live only a few months, or a few minutes. The average length of life, according to Duvilard's tables, is twenty-eight years. At present it is thirty-three. One fourth of mankind die before their seventh year, and one half do not outlive their seventeenth. Those who survive this time enjoy a privilege which is denied to the rest of the human race.*

What is so short an interval, compared to the general duration of time, to the age of the earth and of the worlds? It is one minute in eternity. Our brief life is not, cannot be

* Rambosson. "The Laws of Life." *Paris,* 1871. P. 121.

anything but an accident, a rapid and passing phenomenon, which hardly counts for anything in the history of nature.

On the other hand, the physical conditions of terrestrial life are detestable. Man is a martyr, exposed to every sort of suffering : owing partly to the defective organization of his body, incessantly menaced with danger from external causes, dreading the extremes of heat and cold ; weak and ailing, coming into the world naked, and without any natural defence against the influence of climate. If, in one portion of Europe, and in America, the progress of civilization has secured comfort for the rich, what are the sufferings of the poor in those very same countries ? Life is perpetual suffering to the greater number of the men who inhabit the insalubrious regions of Asia, Africa, and Oceania. And then, before there was any civilization at all, during the period of Primitive Man, a period so immense that it stretches back to a hundred thousand years before our epoch, what was the fate of humanity ? It was a perpetual succession of suffering, danger, and pain.

The conditions of human existence are as evil from the moral as from the physical point of view. It is granted that here below happiness is impossible. The Holy Scriptures, when they tell us that the earth is a valley of tears, do but render an incontestable truth in a poetic form. Yes, man has no destiny here but suffering. He suffers in his affections, and in his unfulfilled desires, in the aspirations and impulses of his soul, continually thrust back, baffled, beaten down by insurmountable obstacles and resistance. Happiness is a forbidden condition. The few agreeable sensations which we experience, now and then, are expiated by the bitterest grief. We have affections, that we may lose and mourn their dearest objects; we have fathers, mothers, children, that we may see them die.

It is impossible that a state so abnormal can be a definitive condition. Order, harmony, equilibrium reign throughout the physical world, and it must be that the same are to be found again in the moral world. If, on looking around us, we are forced to acknowledge that suffering is the common and constant rule, that injustice and violence dominate, that force triumphs, that victims tremble and die under the iron hand of cruelty and oppression; then it must be that this is only a temporary order of things. It cannot be otherwise than a moment of transition, an intermediary period which Providence condemns us to pass through rapidly, on our way to a better state.

But, what is this new condition, what is this second existence which is to succeed to our terrestrial life? In other words, what becomes of the human soul after death has broken the bonds which held it to the body? This is what we have to investigate.

That being, superior to man in the scale of the living creatures which people the universe, has no name in any language. The *angel* acknowledged by the Christian religion, and honoured by an especial *cultus*, is the only approach we have to a realization of the idea. Thus Jean Reynaud calls the superior creature, who is, he believes, to succeed to man after his death, an *angel*.   But we will put aside the word altogether, and call the perfected creature who, in our belief, comes after man in the ascending series of nature, the *superhuman being.*

CHAPTER THE THIRD.

WHERE DOES THE SUPERHUMAN BEING DWELL?

E have seen that of the three elements which compose the *human aggregate,* one only, the soul, resists destruction. After the dissolution of the body, after the extinction of the life, the soul, detached from the material bonds which chained it to the earth, goes away, to feel, to love, to conceive, to be free, in a new body, endowed with more powerful faculties than those allotted to humanity. It goes away to compose that which we call the superhuman being. But where does this new creature dwell?

All students of nature know that life is spread over our globe in prodigious proportions. We cannot take a step, our eyes cannot glance around us, without everywhere encountering myriads of living beings. The earth is nothing but a vast reservoir of life. Examine a blade of grass in a field, and you will find it covered with insects, or inferior animals. But your eyes will not suffice for this examination; you must have recourse to the microscope. With the aid of the magnifying glass, you will discover that this blade of grass is the refuge of an active population, which are born, multiply, and die with prodigious rapidity on their almost imperceptible domain.

From this blade of grass you may draw inferences and conclusions respecting the vegetation of the entire globe.

The fresh waters which flow upon the surface of the earth are also the receptacle of a prodigious quantity of organic existence. Without mentioning the plants, and the animals which live in the waters of the rivers and streams, and are visible to the naked eye, if you take a drop of water from a pool, and place it under the microscope, you will see that it is filled with living beings, who, though so small that they escape our unassisted vision, are none the less active, and all hold their appointed place in the economy of nature. We know how thickly peopled with inhabitants is the great drop; but, without speaking of beings visible to all, the fishes, the crustacea, and the zoophytes, or of the marine plants, creatures, invisible except under microscopical examination, abound to such an extent in sea water, that one single drop of it, so examined, displays innumerable quantities of these microscopic animals and plants.

From this drop of water you may draw inferences and conclusions respecting the entire mass of waters which occupy the basins of the seas, and form three-fourths of the surface of our globe.

In order that some conception may be reached of the enormous numbers of the living beings contained in the seas now, and formerly, we may fitly recall in this place a fact well known to geologists. It is, that all building stone, all the

2

calcareous earth of which chalk hills and banks are formed,
are entirely composed of the pulverized and agglomerated
remains of the shells of mollusca, visible or microscopic,
which, in the most remote ages of the existence of the globe,
peopled the basin of the seas. The whole of this formation is composed of the accumulation of shells. If life has
been lavished with such profusion in the waters during the
geological periods, it must be equally lavished now, in almost
similar ways, because the actual conditions of nature do not
differ from what they were in the primitive ages of the
globe.

The air which surrounds us is, like the earth and the seas,
a vast receptacle of living creatures. We see only a few
animals cleaving the aërial space, but the *savant,* who looks
beyond the simple appearance of things, discovers myriads of
existences in the air.

The air seems to us very pure, very transparent, but only
because it is not sufficiently illumined by light to enable us
to perceive the particles, or foreign bodies, which are floating
about in it. When we allow one ray of daylight to penetrate
into a closed room, one thread of solar light, we can discern a
luminous streak flung across the chamber, while the remaining
portion is still in darkness. We all know that, thanks to the
powerful light, and its contrast with the surrounding obscurity,
the luminous streak is seen to be filled with light, slender
floating bodies, rising, descending, fluttering with the motion
of the air. That which is perceptible in the atmosphere of a
brightly-lighted room is necessarily existent in the entire

atmosphere surrounding our globe, so that the air is everywhere filled with these specks of dust.

Of what are these specks of dust formed? Almost entirely of living creatures, of the germs of microscopic plants
(cryptogamia), or of the eggs of inferior animals (zoophytes).
So-called spontaneous generation, so largely discussed of late
in France and other countries, is merely due to these organic
germs which fill the atmosphere, and which, falling into the
water, or into the infusions of plants, give birth to forms of
vegetation, which have been imputed to spontaneous generation; that is to say, to a creation without a germ, a generation
without a cause, which is an error. Every living thing has
parents, which are always discoverable by science and attention.

Those animals and plants which are called parasites furnish another example of the extraordinary profusion with
which life is distributed over the earth. Animals and plants
which live on other animals or on other plants, and which
feed on the substance of their involuntary entertainers, are
called *parasites*. Each of the mammals has its parasites,
such as fleas, lice, &c., and man has the flea, the louse, and
the bug. So each vegetable has its parasite. The oak gives
shelter and food to lichens and various cryptogamia, and even
on its roots we find particular kinds of cryptogamia, such as
the truffle. Thus we see that life plants itself, grafts itself
upon life.

But, more than this, these parasites in their turn have
their smaller parasites, so minute as only to be microscopically

discerned. Take a lichen off an oak and examine it with a magnifying glass, and also examine a flea, or a nit, and you will behold the curious spectacle of a parasite attached to another parasitical creature, and living upon its substance. From the great vegetable the alimentary substance passes to the visible parasite, and from that to the invisible. In this little space life is superposed and concentrated. Such a fact proves with what prodigious abundance life is spread over our globe.

Thus, then, we see that the surface of the globe, the fresh waters, and the salt seas, and, finally, the atmosphere, are inhabited by immense numbers of living beings. Life abounds on the earth, in the waters, and in the air. Our globe is like an immense vase, in which life is accumulated, pressed down, and running over.

But, the earth, the air, and the waters are not the only places at the command of nature. Above the atmosphere there extends another region, with which astronomers and physicists are acquainted, and which they call *ether* or *planetary ether*. The atmosphere which surrounds our globe, and is drawn with it in its course through space, as it is drawn with it in its rotation upon its own axis, is not very high. It does not extend beyond thirty or forty leagues, and it diminishes in substance in proportion to its elevation above the earth. At three or four leagues in height the air is so rarefied that it becomes impossible for men or animals to breathe it. In aërostatic ascents it is impossible to go beyond seven or eight kilometres, because at that height the air loses so much density, is so highly rarefied, that it no longer serves for purposes of respiration, nor counterbalances the effect of the interior pressure of the body on the exterior. After that height, the density of the air decreases more and more, until there is absolutely no air. At that point begins the fluid which astronomers and physicists call *ether*.

This ether is a true fluid, a gas, analogous to the air we breathe, but infinitely more rarefied and lighter than air. The existence of the planetary ether cannot be disputed, since astronomers take account of its resistance in calculating the speed of heavenly bodies, just as they take account of the resistance of the air in calculating the motions of bodies traversing our atmosphere.

Ether is, then, the fluid which succeeds to atmospheric air. It is spread, not only around the earth, but around the other planets. More than this, it exists throughout all space, it occupies the intervals between the planets. It is, in fact, in ether that the planets, which, with their satellites, compose our solar world, revolve. The comets, too, in their immense journeys through space pass through ether.

The uneducated mind is disposed to believe that above the air which surrounds the terrestrial globe, there is nothing more, that all is void. But no void exists anywhere in nature. Space is always occupied by something, whether it be by earth, by water, by atmospheric air, or, finally, by *planetary ether*.

It has just been said that life abounds upon the globe, swarms upon the earth, clusters in the air and in the waters.

Is the ethereal fluid which succeeds to our atmosphere, and which fills space, equally inhabited by living beings? This is a question which no *savant* has ever yet asked himself. In our opinion, it would be very surprising that life, which we may say overflows in the waters and in the air, should be absolutely wanting in the fluid which is contiguous to the air. Everything, then, indicates that the ether is inhabited. But who are the beings who dwell in the planetary ether? We believe that they are those *superhuman beings,* whom we consider to be resuscitated men, endowed with every kind of moral perfection.

The chemical composition of planetary ether is not known. Astronomical phenomena have taught us its existence, but not its components. We believe it may safely be asserted that the ether does not contain oxygen. In fact, oxygen is the fundamental element of atmospheric air; and as, in proportion as they ascend into that air, the respiration of men and animals becomes more and more difficult, it is, in our opinion, presumable, that this difficulty is caused by the approach of a description of gas impossible to breathe; and which, therefore, excludes human life from the superior regions of the air. A man, rising in a balloon towards the ether, is like a fish half drawn out of the water, half exposed to the air. The fish is breathless and palpitating in a place which is fatal to him; thus it is with man, when he rises by degrees through our nether atmosphere, and draws near to the ether. It seems to us that we may, at once, conclude, from this, that there is no oxygen in planetary ether.

It seems not unlikely that the planetary ether may be composed of hydrogen gas, excessively rarefied, that is to say, of an extremely light gas, still further rarefied, and rendered infinitely more subtle by the absence of all pressure. We are induced to conclude that the ether in which the planets revolve is hydrogen, because, from observations made of late years during the solar total eclipses, it has been ascertained that the sun is surrounded by burning hydrogen gas.

In the language of every nation, the space which lies beyond our atmosphere is called by the same name, that of *heaven*. It is, then, in the universally recognized *heaven* that we place our superhuman beings. In this we are in accord with popular belief and prejudice, and we recognize this argument with satisfaction. These prejudices, these presentiments are frequently the outcome of the wisdom and the observation of an infinite number of generations of men. A tradition which has a uniform and universal existence, has all the weight of scientific testimony.

In accordance with this phrase, and the immemorial tradition, the most widely-spread modern religions, Christianity, Buddhism, and Mahometanism, assign *heaven* as the sojourn of the elect of God.

Thus, we find science, tradition, and religion at one on this point; and that it was a scientific truth which found utterance by the lips of the priest who said to the martyred king upon the scaffold: "Son of Saint Louis, ascend to heaven."

CHAPTER THE FOURTH.

DO ALL MEN, WITHOUT DISTINCTION, PASS, AFTER DEATH, INTO
THE CONDITION OF THE SUPERHUMAN BEING ?—RE-INCARNA-
TION OF IMPENITENT SOULS.—RE-INCARNATION OF CHILDREN
WHO HAVE DIED IN INFANCY.

DEATH is not a termination, it is a change. We
do not die; we experience a metamorphosis.
The fall of the curtain of death is not the
catastrophe, it is only a deeply moving scene
in the drama of human destiny. The agony is not the pre-
lude to annihilation, it is only the obligatory suffering which,
throughout all nature, accompanies every change. Every one
knows that the insect world, the cold and motionless chry-
salis, rends itself asunder that the brilliant butterfly may
come forth. If you examine the butterfly a moment after it
has left its temporary tomb, you will find it trembling and
panting with the pain of bursting through the trammels which
had held it. It needs to rest, to calm itself, and to collect
its strength before it soars away into the air which it is
destined to traverse. This is a symbol of our death agony.
In order that we may cast aside the material covering which
we leave behind us here below, and rise to the unknown

spheres which await us beyond the tomb, we must suffer. We suffer, in the body, from physical pain, and in the soul, from the anguish with which we contemplate our approaching destiny, wrapped, as it is, in the most appalling darkness.

But here a difficulty presents itself. Do all men, without distinction, pass into the condition of the superhuman being? An infinite range of qualities and of moral perversion is an attribute of humanity. To it belong good and evil, the honest man and the criminal. Let us inhabit whatsoever spot of earth we may, let the culture of our minds be what it may, whether we be savages or civilized men, learned or ignorant, whether we contemplate contemporary generations or those of far distant times, there exists one universal morality, one law of absolute equity. Everywhere, in all times, it has been a bad action to kill one's neighbour, to take another's goods, to ill-treat one's children, to be ungrateful to parents, to live on bad terms with one's wife, to conspire against the liberty of others, to lie, and to commit suicide. From one end of the earth to the other, these actions have been esteemed evil.

There exists, therefore, in the sphere of nature, and in the absolute meaning of the words, good souls and perverse souls. Must we believe that both the good and the wicked are called, without distinction, to undergo the change of nature which elevates us to the condition of superhuman beings? Are both classes admitted, upon the same footing, to the felicity of the new life, which is reserved for us beyond the tomb? Our conscience, that exquisitely accurate sentiment which dwells within us, and which never deceives, tells us that this could not be.

But how is the separation of the good grain from the tares to be effected by natural forces only? How is the process of sorting, in itself extremely difficult to explain, when one takes into account the complication of the natural question by the mingling of moral and physical influences, to be carried out? We can only state our individual sentiment, not in the dogmatic sense of imposing it on any one, but simply as a testimony to be registered.

It seems to us that the human soul, in order to rise to the ethereal spaces, needs to have acquired that last degree of perfection which sets it free from every besetting weight; that it must be subtle, light, purified, beautiful, and that only under such conditions can it quit the earth and soar towards the heavens. To our fancy, the human soul is like a celestial aërostat, who flies towards the sublimest heights with swift strength, because it is free from all impurity. But the soul of a perverse, wicked, vile, gross, base, cowardly man has not been purified, perfected, or lightened. It is weighed down by evil passions and gross appetites, which he has not sought to repress, but has, on the contrary, cultivated. It cannot rise to the celestial heights, it is constrained to dwell upon our melancholy and miserable earth.

We believe that the wicked and impenitent man is not called to the immediate enjoyment of the blessed life of the ethereal regions. His soul remains here below, to re-commence life a second time. Let us remark, at once, that he re-commences this life without preserving any recollection of his previous existence.

It will be objected to this, that to be born again without retaining any remembrance of a past life, would be to fall into the nothingness to which we are condemned by the materialists. In fact, it is identity which constitutes the resurrection; and without memory there is no identity. The individual, therefore, as an individual, would fall into nothingness if he were born again without memory.

This remark is just. If, after our resurrection to the state of superhuman beings, we were to lose, absolutely and irreparably, all remembrance of our former life, we should be, indeed, the prey of nothingness. But, let us hasten to add, that this loss of memory is of but short duration. Oblivion of our past life is only a temporary condition of our new existence, a sort of punishment. The remembrance of his first terrestrial life will return to each individual, when, by perfecting processes meet for the needs of his soul, he shall have merited the attainment of the condition of a superhuman being. Then he shall recall the evil actions of his first existence, or of his numerous existences, if it has been his lot to have several probations, and the thought of those evil deeds will still be his chastisement, even in the blissful abode to which he shall at length have attained.

To such persons as refuse assent to these views, we would remark that the question of rewards and punishments after death is the rock upon which all religions and all philosophers have split. The explanation of the punishment of the

wicked which we offer, is at least preferable to the hell of the
Christian creed.   A return to a second terrestrial life is a less
cruel, a more reasonable, and a more just punishment than
condemnation to eternal torment.   In the one case the penalty
is in proportion to the sin.   It is equitable and indulgent,
like the chastisement of a father.   It is not eternal punishment for a sin of short duration, it is a merciful form of
justice, which places beside the penalty the means of freedom
from the sin.   It does not shut out all return to good by a
condemnation without appeal to all eternity, it leaves to man
the possibility of retracing the road to happiness from which
his passions have led him astray, and of recovering, by de-
serving them, the blessings which he has forfeited.

Thus, in our opinion, if the human soul, during its sojourn
here below, instead of perfecting, purifying, and ennobling
itself, has lost its strength, and its primitive qualities,—if, in
other words, it has been misused by a perverse, gross, uncultivated, mean, and wicked individual,—then, in that case, it
will not quit the earth.   After the death of that individual,
the soul will tenant a new human body, losing all recollection
of its previous existence.   In this second incarnation the imperfect and earth-laden soul, deprived of all noble faculties
and bereft of memory, will have to re-commence its moral
education.   This man, born again as an infant, will recommence his existence with the same uncultivated and feeble
soul which he possessed at the moment of his death.

These *re-incarnations* in a human body may be numerous.
They must repeat themselves until the faculties of the soul

are sufficiently developed, or until its instincts are sufficiently ameliorated and perfected for the man to be raised above the general level of our species. Then only the soul, purified and lightened of all its imperfections, can quit the earth, and after the death of the flesh soar into space, and pass into the new organism which succeeds that of man in the hierarchy of nature.

We must add, here, that the fate of children who die young, either while at the breast or only a few months old, before the soul has undergone any development, is analogous. Their souls pass into the bodies of other children, and re-commence a novel existence.

CHAPTER THE FIFTH.

WHAT ARE THE ATTRIBUTES OF THE SUPERHUMAN BEING?—
THE PHYSICAL FORM, SENSES, DEGREE OF INTELLIGENCE,
AND FACULTIES OF THE SUPERHUMAN BEING.

NOTWITHSTANDING the daring of such an attempt, let us now endeavour to form some idea of the radiant creatures which float in the mysterious and sublime regions of that empyrean which hides them from our view. Let us try to discern the attributes, form, and qualities of the superhuman being.

Like the human, the superhuman being possesses the three elements of the aggregate, the body, the soul, and the life. In order to gain some idea of him, we must examine each of these three elements separately.

The Body of the Superhuman Being.—We might perhaps conceive a superhuman being without a body; we might imagine that the soul, purely spiritual, constitutes the blessed dweller in ethereal space. But it is not thus that we do conceive him. Absolute immateriality appears to us to apply only to a being much more elevated in the moral hierarchy than the superhuman one—a being of whom we shall speak hereafter. We believe that the inhabitant of the ethereal spaces has a body; that the soul, leaving its terrestrial dwelling, incarnates itself in a body, as it did here below. But this body must be provided with qualities infinitely superior to those which belong to the human body. First, let us inquire what the form of this body may be. The painters of the Renaissance, whom modern artists follow in this respect, give to the angel the form of a young and handsome man, furnished with white wings, which bear him through the air on his celestial missions. This image is both coarse and poetic. It is poetic because it responds to the idea which we have of the radiant creature who dwells in ethereal space; and it is coarse, because it gives to a being far superior to man the physical attributes of man, which is inadmissible.

Painters who, like Raphael, represent the angel by the head of a child, with wings, give a far more profound expression to the same thought. By suppressing the larger portion of the body, and reducing the seraphic being to the head, the seat of intelligence, they indicate that in the angel of the Christian belief the spiritual dominates, in immense proportion, over the material part.

We shall not be expected to delineate the form of the dwellers in the realms of ether. We can only say, that, as ether is an excessively subtle and rarefied fluid, it necessarily follows that the superhuman being who is to float and fly in its light masses, must be wonderfully light, must be composed of extraordinary subtle substances. A slight material tissue, animated by life, a vaporous, diaphanous drapery of living matter, such do we represent the superhuman being to our fancy.

How is this body supported? Does it need food for its maintenance, like the bodies of men and of animals? We may reply with confidence that food—that tyrannous obligation of the human and the animal species—is spared to the inhabitants of the planetary ether. Their bodies must be supported and refreshed by mere respiration of the fluid in which they exist.

Let us consider the immense space occupied in the lives of animals by their need of alimentation. Many animals, especially those which live in the water, have an incessant need of food. They must eat always, without intermission, or they die of inanition. Among superior animals, the necessity for eating and drinking is less imperious, because the respiratory function comes to their aid, bringing into the body, by the absorption of oxygen and a small proportion of azote, a certain amount of reparative element, as a supplement to alimentary substances. Man profits largely by this advantage. Our respiration is a function of the highest importance, and it bears a great share in the reparation of all our organs. The oxygen which our blood borrows from the air in breathing, contributes largely to our nutrition. The respiratory function in birds is very active, and the organs which exercise it are largely developed, and in their nutrition also oxygen counts largely, and takes the place of a certain quantity of food.

It is our belief that the respiration of the ether in which he lives, suffices for the support of the material body of the superhuman being, and that the necessity for eating and drinking has no place in his existence.

I do not know whether my reader forms an exact conception of the consequences which would result from the theory, that the superhuman beings whom we are contemplating are exempted from all need of food. Those consequences will be most readily comprehended, if we consider that it is the pressing obligation of procuring food which renders the lives of animals so miserable. Forced incessantly to seek their subsistence, animals are entirely given up to this grovelling occupation; thence come their passions, their quarrels, and their sufferings. It is much the same in the case of man, though in a less degree. The necessity for providing for the aliment of every day, the obligation of earning his daily bread—as the popular phrase has it—is the great cause of the labours and the sufferings of the human species. Supposing that man could live, develop himself, and sustain his life without eating—that the mere respiration of air would supply the waste of his organs—what a revolution would be effected in human society. Hateful passions, wars, and rivalries would disappear from the earth. The golden age, dreamed of by the poets, would be the certain consequence of such an organic disposition.

This blessing of nature, refused to man, assuredly belongs to the superhuman being. We may conclude also that the evil passions, which are a sad attribute of our species, would be unknown in the home of these privileged creatures. Released from the toil of seeking their food, living and repairing their functions by the mere effect of respiration—an involuntary and unconscious act (as the circulation of the blood and

absorption are unconscious acts in men and animals)—the inhabitants of the ethereal spaces must be able to abandon
themselves exclusively to impressions of unmixed happiness
and serenity.

The forces of our body become rapidly exhausted; we cannot exercise our functions for a certain time without experi-
encing fatigue. In order to transport ourselves from one
place to another, to carry burthens, to go up or down any
height, to walk, we are obliged to expend these forces, and
lassitude immediately ensues. We cannot exercise the
faculty of thought for more than a certain time. At the end
of a short period attention fails, and thought is suspended.
In short, our corporeal machine, beautifully ordered, is subject to a thousand derangements, which we call diseases.

From the sense of fatigue, from the continual menace of
illness by organic derangement, the dwellers in the ether are
free. Rest is not for them, as for us, a necessity ensuing on
exercise. The body of the superhuman being, inaccessible to
fatigue, does not need repose. Unembarrassed by the mechanism of a complicated machine, it subsists and sustains
itself by the unaided force of the life which animates it. Its
sole physiological function, probably, is the inhalation of
ether, a function which, it is easy to conceive, may be exercised without the aid of numerous organs, if we see a whole
class of animals—the Batrachian—for whose respiration the
bare and simple skin suffices.

If we admit, that the only function which the superhuman
being has to exercise is that of respiration, the extreme sim-

plicity of his body will be easily understood. The numerous
and complicated organs and apparatus which exist in the
bodies of men and animals, have for their object the exercise
of the functions of nutrition and reproduction. These functions being suppressed in the creature whom we are considering, his body must be proportionably lightened. Everything
is reduced to respiration, and the preservation and maintenance of the faculties of the soul; all is in harmony with
those ends. We admire, with good reason, the wise mechanism of the bodies of men and animals; but, if human anatomy
reveals prodigies in our structure, marvellous provision in
securing the preservation of the individual and his reproduction, what infinitely greater marvels would, if we were but
permitted to study it, be revealed by the organization of the
body of the superhuman being, in which everything is calculated to secure the maintenance and the perfection of the soul.
With what astonishment should we learn the use and the
purpose of the different parts of that glorious body, discover
the relations of resemblance or of origin between the living
economy of the human, and the living economy of the superhuman, being, and divine the relations which might exist between the organs of the superhuman being and those which
he should assume in another life, still superior, in which he
should be the same being, again resuscitated in new glory and
fuller perfection!

The special organization of the being whom we are describing would give him the power of transporting himself in a
very short space of time from one place to another, and of

traversing great distances with extraordinary rapidity. We are but simple human beings, and yet by thought we devour space, and travel, in a twinkling, from one end of the globe to another; may we not therefore believe that the bodies of superhuman beings, in whom the spiritual principle is dominant, are endowed with the privilege of passing from one point in space to another, with a rapidity which the speed of electricity enables us to measure?

The superhuman being, who does not require to eat or drink, or rest, who is always active, and incessantly sensible, has no need of sleep. Sleep is no more necessary for the reparation of his forces, than food for their creation. We know that man is deprived of one third of his existence, by the imperious necessity for sleep. A man who dies at thirty years of age, has in reality lived for twenty only; he has slept all the rest of the time! What a poor notion this conveys of the condition of man! Whence arises this need of sleep? It arises from the fact that our forces, impaired by their exercise, require inaction and motionlessness for their repair—this is attained in the kind of temporary death produced by the suspension of the greater portion of the vital action, in sleep. During sleep, man prepares and stores up the forces which he will require to expend during the ensuing period. He devotes the night to this physical reparation, as much in obedience to what he observes in all the other portions of creation, as in obedience to the customs of civilization. But it is probable that all the forces of the superhuman being are inexhaustible, and that they do not require sleep, which is one of the hardest

conditions of human existence. Everything leads us to believe that perpetual wakefulness is the permanent state of
the superhuman being, and that the word "sleep" would
have no meaning for him.

Darkness must be equally unknown to all those beings
who float in the ethereal spaces. Our night and day are
produced alternatively by the rotation of the earth upon her
axis, a rotation which hides the sun from her view during
one half of her revolution. This rotatory motion draws our
atmosphere with it, but its influence extends no further, the
ether which surmounts our atmosphere is not subject to it.
That fluid mass remains motionless, while the earth and its
atmosphere turn upon their axis. The superhuman beings,
who, according to our ideas, inhabit the planetary ether, are
not drawn into this motion. They behold the earth revolving beneath them, but, being placed outside its movements,
they never lose sight of the radiant sun-star.

Night, we repeat, is an accidental phenomenon, which belongs to the planets only, because they have a hemisphere
now illumined, and then not illumined by the sun; but
night is unknown to the remainder of the universe. The
superhuman beings, who people the regions far above the
planets, never lose sight of the sun, and their happy days
pass in the midst of an ocean of light.

Let us pass on to the consideration of the senses
which these superhuman beings probably possess, pre-
mising:

1. That the superhuman being must be endowed with the

same senses which we possess, but that those senses are infinitely more acute and exquisite than ours.

2. That he must possess special senses, unknown to us.

What are the new senses enjoyed by the superhuman being? It would be impossible to return a satisfactory reply to this question. We have no knowledge of any other senses than those with which we ourselves are endowed, and no amount of genius could enable any man to divine the object of a sense denied to him by nature. Try to give a man born blind an idea of the colour, red; and he will answer: " Yes, I understand! It is piercing, like the sound of a trumpet!" Try to give a man born deaf an idea of the sound of the harp, and he will answer: "Yes! It is gentle and tender, like the green grass of the fields!" Let us renounce, once for all, any attempt to define the senses with which nature endows the beings who people the ethereal plains; these senses belong to objects and ideas the mere notion of which is forbidden to us.

There is a well-known story of a man born blind, upon whom the famous surgeon Childesen operated. Having recovered his sight, the patient was a long time learning the use of his eyes; he was obliged to educate those organs, step by step, and by slow degrees to form his intelligence. Equally well known is Condillac's beautiful fiction, in which he imagines a man born into the world without the senses of sight, speech, and hearing, and who is, therefore, destitute of ideas. By degrees, he is endowed with each of these senses, and the philosopher thus composes, bit by bit, a soul which feels, and a mind which thinks. This philosophical idea has been greatly admired. Like the man-statue of Condillac, we are only, while here below, imperfect statues, endowed with but a small number of senses. When, however, we shall have reached the superior regions destined to our ennobled condition, we shall be put in possession of new senses, such as our reason dimly perceives, and our hearts long for.

We cannot, as we have previously said, divine what the new senses which shall be granted to the superhuman being are to be, because they belong to objects and ideas of which we are ignorant, and to forms which are exclusively proper to worlds at present hidden from our eyes. The kingdom of the planetary ether has its geography, its powers, its passions, and its laws; and the new senses of men, resuscitated to that glorious existence, will be exercised upon those objects.

The only thing which we can safely prognosticate is that all the senses which we now possess will then exist in their full perfection—sight, hearing, touch, taste, and smell. It is allowable to deduce this process of future perfection by reasoning from the extraordinary development of certain senses in the case of animals.

The sense of smell is developed in the hunting dog to a degree which surpasses our imagination. How can we understand this quite ordinary fact, that the dog perceives the scent which has emanated from a hare or a partridge which has passed by the place at which he is smelling many hours previously, and is now several leagues away! The perfection of sight in the eagle and other birds of prey astonishes us equally. These birds, floating at an immense height, see their prey upon the earth, creatures much smaller than themselves, and descend upon them without deviating from the perpendicular line of their flight. The bat, accidentally deprived of sight, supplies this deficiency so well by the sense of touch, by means of his membranous wings, that he guides himself through the air, and finds his way to the interior of human dwellings, as unerringly as if he had the full use of his eyesight. To such a degree of exquisite sensibility has the sense of hearing attained among native Indian tribes, that a man, laying his ear against the earth, will detect the tread of an enemy at the distance of a league. Among musicians, also, how must the sense of hearing be cultivated by a man, who, partly by a natural gift, and partly by practice, comes to be able to detect the most minute difference in the tone of one instrument among fifty different kinds, all played at once, in an orchestra. Supposing that the senses of the superhuman being should have acquired the degree of extraordinary activity which is common to animals, and, in certain cases, to man, we can form some estimate of the power and extent of such a sensorial system.

We can also arrive at some idea of the perfection of the senses attained by resuscitated man, by considering the accession of power which our own senses may receive by the assistance of science and art. Before the invention of the microscope, no one ever imagined that the eye could penetrate the mysteries of that world in miniature well named the *Infinitely Little*, until then absolutely unknown; no one had ever divined, for instance, that in one drop of water might be seen myriads of living beings. These beings have existed throughout all time, but man has been able to contemplate them for only two centuries. Our visual power over microscopic beings was until then unknown. The least enlightened, the most careless student of this day, regards with indifference things which Aristotle, Hippocrates, Pliny, Galienus, Albertus Magnus, and Roger Bacon could not have contemplated, or even suspected to exist. The discovery of the telescope, in the days of Kepler and Galileo, hurled back the boundaries of the human intellect and threw open to its investigation a domain hitherto sealed from its sight. There, where Hipparchus and Ptolemy had seen nothing, Galileo, Huyghens, Kepler, made, in a few nights, by the aid of the telescope, discoveries of hitherto unsuspected celestial splendour. The satellites of Jupiter and Saturn, a multitude of new stars, the phases of Venus, and, at a later period, the discovery of new planets only to be seen by the telescope, the observation of spots on the sun, and the revolution of the nebulæ into collections of stars, were the almost immediate consequences of the invention of the telescope. Thus we learned that, by the aid of art, the human eye can penetrate the most distant regions of heaven.

Let us now suppose all the powers of the telescope and all those of the microscope concentrated in the sense of vision ; that is to say, that in addition to all objects placed at ordinary distances, it can discern all microscopic objects, and at the same time all the celestial bodies invisible to the naked eye, and you will have an idea of what the sense of sight is, in the superhuman being.

There is no occasion to dwell upon the extraordinary proportions which our accumulated knowledge would assume, if our sight could enjoy those extraordinary powers of extension, if it could perform simultaneously the functions of the telescope and the microscope. Science would march forward with the tread of a giant. What enormous progress would be made by chemistry if our eyes could penetrate into the interior of all bodies, beholding their molecules, estimating their relative volume, their arrangement, and the form and colour of their atoms. A glance would reveal to us secrets of chemical solutions such as the genius of a Lavoisier could not penetrate. Physics would contain no further mysteries for us, for we should know, by simply using our eyes, everything which we are now painfully striving to divine by reason, and by the aid of difficult and uncertain experiments. We should *see* why and how bodies are warmed and acquire electricity. We should have the explanation of the mathematical laws in obedience to which the physical forces, light, heat, and magnetism are exercised. Our eyes would suffice for the solution of those physical and mechanical problems before which the genius of such men as Newton, Malus, Ampère, and Gay-Lussac stands still.

We do not doubt that the superhuman being is endowed with sight thus marvellously perfect.

We might carry this argument out in detail, applying it to all the other senses, but enough has been said to illustrate the exaltation and perfecting of those senses which man possesses only in their rudiments, in the favoured dwellers in a superior sphere. We will only add, that the result of such a degree of perfection of the senses is, that the superhuman being can move with a rapidity, of which light and electricity only can give us some notion, that is to say, that these perfected senses can be used at great distances, and with great promptitude. If the entire body of the superhuman being can transport itself with wonderful rapidity from one place to another, as we have already admitted, his senses can also act from, and at great distances. We do not think we can err in comparing the actions of the dwellers in the invisible world which we presume to investigate, with the phenomena of light and electricity.

Does sex exist in the superhuman being? Assuredly not. The Christian religion defines its absence in the angel. The angel of the Christian creeds has the features of either man or woman, the mild face of a youth, or the pathetic beauty of a girl. Sex is suppressed, the individual is androgynous. Thus, too, it must be in the case of the superhuman being. The reciprocal affection which reigns among the blessed dwellers in the ether does not require diversity of sex.

The affections undergo a purifying process, according as they are elevated, from those of the animals to those of man. The animals have but little of the sentiment of friendship. Love, with its material impulses, is almost all they know. The sentiments of affection possessed by animals, apart from their carnal instincts, reduce themselves to those of maternity,

which are strong and sincere, but of short duration. Their
young are the objects of attentive care and caresses while
their helplessness demands such aid, but as soon as they can
live on their own resources they are abandoned by the
mothers, who no longer even recognize them. There is no
constant, lasting affection in animals, except the sentiment of
love, which is caused by their sexual necessities. The sentiments of affection entertained by man are numerous, and frequently noble and pure. We love our mothers and our sons
as long as our hearts beat in our breasts. We love our
brothers, our sisters, and our relations with a sentiment in
which there is nothing carnal, and which is deeply rooted in
the soul. If love is often inseparably attached to physical
desires, it can, nevertheless, shake itself free from them, and
a disinterested friendship frequently survives the extinction
of sensual feeling. In this respect we are far superior to the
animals. Let us go a step further, even to the supernatural
being, the next link in the chain to ourselves, and we shall
find the sentiment of affection entirely detached from the consideration of sex. In that sublime and blessed realm which
they inhabit, superhuman beings are all of the same organic
type. They need not, in order to love one another, to belong
to two opposite sexes, or different groups of organization : their
tenderness is the **result** of the serenity of the infinite purity
of souls, of the sympathy evoked by common perfections.

On the other hand, the ethereal region which awaits us is
the scene of the reunion of those who have loved one another
in this world. There the father will find the son, and the

mother will rejoin the daughter, torn from each by death, there husbands and wives will meet, and the separation of friends come to an end. But, under their new form, in the perfected body wherein their regenerated souls shall dwell, there is no more sex, and love is for all an ideal, noble, and exquisitely pure sentiment.

How blind and self-interested is love here below! How narrow and egotistical a sentiment is friendship. It cannot enlarge itself without pain and difficulty, to embrace the totality of the human kind. Why is it so hard for it to lift itself up to the sublime Creator of the worlds? Why do we not love God as we love our neighbours? In the upper world it will be far otherwise. Our faculty of loving, limited here by fleshly bonds, will be set free there, from every sensual restraint. Man, resuscitated to glory, will love his wife as he loves his children, his friends, and his brethren. His affections will never more be degraded by his senses. The happiness which this purified sentiment, constantly received from ever living sources, will afford him, will suffice to fill and satisfy his soul. His power of loving will be extended to all nature, it will be spread abroad over the most elevated spheres; his soul will be exalted by the sublime sensations of this universal love, this wide sympathy with the whole creation. True charity, comprehending the entire universe, will burn in all hearts. The love of God will rule over all these multiplied affections, from the height of His infinite power, and the fervour of our sentiments of love for our kind will be crowned by our sublime adoration of the Creator of all.

But, it will be said, if superhuman beings are of no sex,
how are they to be reproduced, how is the species to be kept
up, and multiplied ?   There will be no need of reproduction,
the species of the superhuman being will not require to be
maintained, or multiplied.   The reproduction, the preservation of his species is the business of the inhabitants of the
inferior worlds, of the earth and the planets.   Such is their
lot, such the task imposed upon them by nature.   But reproduction is unknown and unnecessary to the fortunate beings
who dwell in the planetary ether.   From the earth and the
other planets fresh and ever fresh phalanxes are despatched
to them.   The battalions of the elect are recruited by arrivals
from the lower worlds.   Below is the multiplication of individuals ; above is the sojourn of blessed beings, who have no
need of maintaining their species, because the laws of their
destiny differ from those which rule the lot of terrestrial man.
Reproduction is the task of inferior worlds, permanence is the
inheritance of the world above.

The Soul of the Superhuman Being.   In an excellent volume
of popular science, the *Universe*, by Dr. Pouchet, director of
the Museum of Natural History at Rouen, we find a striking
definition.   Dr. Pouchet informs us that a German naturalist,
Bremser, lays down, as a principle, that, in man, matter and
spirit exist in almost equal parts ; that is, to say, that man is
half spirit and half matter.   Bremser, in advancing this proposition, takes his stand upon the fact that, in man, it is
sometimes spirit which governs and subdues matter, and

sometimes matter which dictates laws to spirit, with equal power and success on the side of each.*

Admitting, with the German philosopher, that this relation is true, we would say, that, while in man the proportion of the soul is fifty in one hundred, this proportion, in the super-human being, is undoubtedly from eighty to eighty-five in one hundred. Of course we only employ this valuation to make our idea comprehensible, and give these figures only to prove that facts in the intellectual order may be submitted

---

* " We must consider," says Bremser, " that man is not a spirit, but only a spirit limited, in different ways, by matter. In a word, man is not a god, but, notwithstanding the captivity of his spirit in his corporality, it retains sufficient freedom to enable him to perceive that he is governed by a spirit more exalted than his own, that is to say, by a God.

"It is to be presumed, in the supposition that there will be a new creation, that beings far more perfect than those produced by preceding creations will see the light. In the composition of man, spirit holds to matter the proportion of fifty to fifty, with slight occasional differences, because it is now matter, and again spirit which predominates. In a subsequent creation, should that which has formed man not prove to be the last, there will apparently be organizations in which spirit will act more freely, and be in the proportion of seventy-five to twenty-five.

"It results from this consideration that man, as such, was formed at the most passive epoch of the existence of our earth. Man is a wretched intermediary between animal and angel, he aspires to elevated knowledge, and he cannot attain to it; though our modern philosophers sometimes think so, it is really impossible. Man wishes to make out the primary cause of all that exists, but he cannot get at it. With less intellectual faculty, he would not have had the presumption even to desire to know these causes; and, if he were more richly endowed, they would have been clear to him."—*L'Univers*, pp. 760-761.

to weight, measure, and comparison, all which the world supposes to be impossible.

The soul has a preponderating share in the superhuman being. That is what we need to know, and to remember. Let us now endeavour to analyze the soul of the superhuman being, as we have analyzed his senses.

If the senses of the superhuman being are numerous and exquisitely acute, the faculties of his soul, which are intimately allied to the exercise of the senses, and depend on their perfection, must also be singularly active and powerful. We know that in men the faculties of the soul are feeble and limited. We have so short a time to pass upon the earth, that very powerful faculties would be of no use to us; they would not have time to be developed, or efficaciously employed. But everything is magnified and elevated in the superior world which awaits us; consequently the faculties of the thinking creature who inhabits the realms on high must be numerous and of vast extent.

We must repeat, concerning the faculties of the soul of the superhuman being, what we have just said concerning his senses. The superhuman being must be provided with new faculties, and also those faculties which he has brought with him from the earth must be singularly perfected. To determine the nature and the object of the new faculties bestowed upon the superhuman being would be impossible, because those faculties belong to the superior world which is unknown to us; they respond to moral wants of which we have no conception. Let us, therefore, renounce all idea of discover-

ing the nature of those new faculties, and content ourselves
with examining the degree of perfection which may be attained by those faculties of the soul which actually belong to
man.

Attention, thought, reason, will, and judgment, all which
render us what we are, must acquire special force and sure-
ness in the superhuman being. La Bruyère has said that there
is nothing more rare in this world than the *spirit of discernment;* which means that judgment and good sense are excessively rare. When we have lived for a while among men,
we recognize how thoroughly well founded the saying is. We
may safely assert, without being over-misanthropical, that
among a hundred men there will be not more than one or two
possessed of sound judgment. In the majority of instances,
ignorance, prejudices, and passion contend with judgment, so
that, as La Bruyère says, good sense is much more rare than
pearls and diamonds. This great and precious faculty of
judgment, in which the majority of human beings are de-
ficient, cannot be wanting in the inhabitants of the other
world; there it must be the universal rule, here it is the
exception.

The most precious of all faculties, enabling us to form large
and lofty ideas and comparisons, whose outcome is knowledge, is memory. But how imperfect, changeable, weak,
and, one may say, sickly, is our memory! It is absolutely
mute respecting the whole period which preceded our birth,
and during which, nevertheless, we existed. It is also as
silent respecting all that concerns the early portion of our

life. We retain no recollection of the care which was lavished upon our childhood. A child who loses its mother in infancy has never known a mother; for it, the mother has never ᵣxisted. If those who saw us in the cradle did not recount our actions during that period, we should be entirely ignorant of them. We have to witness the successive stages of infancy, the sucking child, the long clothes, the staggering steps, the little go-cart, in order to realize that we too have been like that infant, have gone through those stages of being. Memory, which is not developed at all in man until he is a year old, and which becomes extinct in old men, is subject, even when it is at its highest point of activity, to innumerable weaknesses, caused by illness or the want of exercise, so that in fact our hold of this faculty is always precarious. We cannot doubt that in the other life it will have the power, the certainty, and scope which it lacks here below.

At the same time, our memory will be enriched by a number of new subjects. The soul, beholding and understanding the worlds which surround it, will be able to fix the geography of all those different places in its memory. It will know the physical revolutions, the populations, and the legislation of these thousand countries. The superhuman being will know what exists in such planets and their satellites as come within his reach, or as he shall visit. Just as, in order to gain information, we visit America or Australia, so the superhuman being visits Mars or Venus, and furnishes his memory with millions of facts, which it retains and reproduces at will. What immense power must memory, always supplied and always ready at call, bestow on the mind and reason !

Languages are only the expression and the assembling of ideas. Condorcet has said that a science always reduces itself to a well-constructed language. The mathematical sciences employ a language which is perfect, because the science of mathematics is perfect. The language spoken in the planetary spaces must be perfect, because it expresses all the knowledge of superhuman beings, and this knowledge is immense. The more the mind knows, the better it expresses :—the superhuman being, who is highly informed, will have a very expressive language, which will also be universal.

The language of mathematics is understood by the peoples of both hemispheres. Algebra can be read by a Frenchman or a German, as well as by an Australian or a Chinese, on account of the simplicity and perfection of the conventional signs which it uses. The language of mathematics, which is truly universal, makes us infer that the language spoken in the planetary space must be also universal, and common, without distinction, to all the inhabitants of the ethereal worlds.

Owing to the immense scope of their faculties, and to the perfection of their language, in itself a certain means of increasing and exalting their knowledge, superhuman beings have a power of reasoning, and a clearness of judgment, which, added to the immense number of facts stored in their memory, place them in possession of absolute science. Arduous questions, before which the mind of man humbly con-

fesses its powerlessness, or which drive him mad if he persists
in the effort to solve them, such as the thought of the Infinite,
the idea of the First Cause of the Universe, the Essence of
Divinity, all these problems, forbidden to us, are easily accessible to those mighty thinkers. He who is regarded by
mankind as a genius of the first order, an Aristotle, a Keppler,
a Newton, a Raphael, a Shakespeare, a Molière, a Mozart, a
Lavoisier, a Laplace, a Cuvier, a Victor Hugo, would be
among them a babbling child. No science, no moral idea
is above their conception. Beneath their feet rolls the earth,
with the splendid train of the planets, its sisters; they behold the planets of our solar system gravitating in harmonious
order round the great central star, which deluges them with
its light. From the height of their sublime abode they witness the infinitely various spectacles furnished by the ele-
mental strife of our poor globe, and those which resemble it;
and, happier than terrestrial humanity, they admire the works
of God, while knowing the secret of their mechanism. In
the moral order they have penetrated the great *Wherefore !*
They know why man exists, and why they themselves exist.
They know whence they come, and whither they are going;
and we, alas ! know neither. Where, to our eyes, there is
only confusion, they perceive harmony and order. The designs of God are distinctly apparent to them, and also the
events of the lives of nations and individuals, which often
seem to us cruel, unjust, and bad on the part of God; but
they understand that these events are just and useful, and
worthy of our heartfelt gratitude.

We also think, that in the ethereal spaces time is an element which does not count. We believe this, because time does not exist for God, and all superhuman beings approach, by their perfections, the entirely spiritual nature, and consequently approach God. We are confirmed in this belief by the fact, that very profound grief resists time, that there is no limit in duration to the great blows struck at the human soul, that the loss of a beloved being is felt as keenly after a long interval as when he was taken away.

Thus, time, which is everything to man, which is not only, according to the English adage, "money," but is also the instrument of our wisdom, our studies, and our attainments—far otherwise precious than money—time does not count in the life of the superhuman being. He awaits, without impatience and without suffering, the arrival of the beings whom he has loved and left upon the earth at his peaceful abode ; and when their re-union takes place, he and they enjoy happiness which no inquietude concerning the future can ever trouble. Enabled to despise, to put aside the idea of time, the superhuman being looks on with unutterable serenity, tranquillity, and majesty, at the majestic spectacle, always new and always marvellous, of the revolutions of the stars, and the great movements of the universe.

The Life of the Superhuman Being.—In completion of our speculation upon the attributes of the superhuman being, we shall consider the life which animates him and gives his body its active qualities.

We have said that, in our belief, the superhuman being

proceeds from the soul of a man which has domiciled itself afresh, in a new body, in the bosom of the world of ether. Is this body destined, at the end of a more or less prolonged period to perish, to be dissolved, to restore its elements to matter, as they are restored by the human body ? Shall life be withdrawn from the body of the superhuman being, and shall the soul take flight thence ?

We believe that it will be so. Life everywhere implies death, and is its necessary term. We do not cast anchor in the current of the waters of life. If the soul of the superhuman being resides in a living body, this body must die, and its material elements must return to the common reservoir of nature. The torch of life is extinguished in the spaces, as it is extinguished upon earth.

We believe the superhuman being to be mortal. After an interval, whose duration we shall not attempt to fix, he dies ; and the soul which dwelt within him escapes, like a sweet perfume from a broken vase. What becomes of the soul which has torn itself away from the body, cold in death ? We shall seek after the answer to this question in our next chapter.

CHAPTER THE SIXTH.

WHAT BECOMES OF THE SUPERHUMAN BEING AFTER DEATH?—
DEATHS, RESURRECTIONS, AND NEW INCARNATIONS IN THE
ETHEREAL SPACES.

IN the living nature which surrounds us, there is a continually ascending scale of gradual perfection, from the plant to man. Taking mosses and algæ, which represent the rudimentary condition of vegetable organization, as our point of departure, we pass on through the whole series of the perfecting processes of the vegetable kingdom, and we reach the inferior animals, zoophytes and mollusca. From thence we ascend to the superior animals by insensible degrees, and thus fully attain to man. Each step of this ladder is almost imperceptible, so finely arranged are the transitions and the shades; so that there is a really infinite chain of intermediate beings, at one end of which are the algæ, and at the other ourselves. And yet we think it possible that between us and God there should be no kind of intermediate being! that in this scale of continual progress, there should be an immense void between man and the Creator! We think it possible that all nature, from the lowest vegetable to mankind, should be arranged in successive and innumerable degrees, and that be-

tween man and God there should exist only a desert, an immeasurable *hiatus.* Evidently, this is impossible, and that
such an error should ever have been countenanced by religion
and philosophy is only to be explained by ignorance of natural
phenomena. It is impossible to doubt that between man
and God, as between the plant and the animal, the animal and man, there exist a great number of intermediate
creations, which establish the transition of humanity into
the divinity which governs it, in infinite power and majesty.

That these intermediate beings exist, we are certain. They
are invisible to us, but, if we refused to admit the existence
of everything which we cannot see, we should be very easily
refuted. Let a naturalist take a drop of water from a pond,
and, shewing it to an ignorant person, tell him, " this drop of
water, in which you do not see anything, is filled with little
animals, and with miniature plants, which live, are born and
die, like the animals and plants, which inhabit our farms."
The ignorant person would probably shrug up his shoulders,
and consider the speaker crazy. But if he were induced to
apply his eye to the magnifier of a microscope, in order to examine the contents of the drop of water, he must acknowledge
that the truth had been told him; because, in this drop of
water, in which he could at first see nothing, his eye, when
assisted by science, would discern whole worlds.

A great number of living beings can therefore exist where
we see nothing, and it is feasible to science to open the eyes
of the multitude in this respect.

We desire to assume the position of the naturalist of whom we have spoken. Between man and God, the ignorant crowd and a blind philosophy perceive nothing; but, when we replace the eyes of the body by those of the spirit, that is to say, when we make use of reason, analogy, and education, these mysterious beings come to light.

We have already, in studying the superhuman being, described one of those intermediate creations between man and the divinity, and defined the existence of one of those landmarks placed by nature on the high-road of infinite space. But the ladder does not break off at its first step, and we are convinced that numerous living hierarchies intervene between the superhuman being and the radiant throne of the Almighty. We have said elsewhere, that, in our belief, superhuman beings are mortal. What becomes of them after their death? Let us now take up the thread of our deductions.

We believe that—the superhuman being having died at the end of a term whose duration we have no means of knowing—his soul, perfected by the exercise of the new faculties which it has received, and the new senses with which it has been endowed, enters into a new body, provided with senses still more numerous and more exquisite, and endowed with faculties of still greater power, and thus commences a fresh existence.

We call the being who succeeds to man *angel*, or superhuman; we may call his succession in the ethereal realm, *arch-angel*, or *arch-human*.

The actual moment of the passage from one life to another,

must be, as it is in the case of man, a time of moral and physical pain. The supreme periods at which a metamorphosis takes place in a sensible being are crises full of anguish and torment.

We will not endeavour to penetrate the secrets of the organization of the new being whose existence we thus trace, and who is superior to the superhuman being in the natural hierarchy ; because our means of investigation fail us at this point. We have ventured to form some conjecture respecting the body, the soul, and the life of the superhuman being, because in that case, however adventurous our excursion into unknown spheres, we had a point of comparison and induction in the human species. But all induction respecting the arch-human being who succeeds the superhuman, is wanting, for we could only perceive the latter by means of conjectures and analogies which we must not carry farther.

We will, therefore, abstain from pursuing this kind of investigation, permitting the reader to exercise his own imagination upon the form of the body, the number and perfection of the senses, and the extent of the faculties of the happy creature who succeeds to the superhuman being, and who dwells, like him, in the immensity of ethereal space. We will only add that we do not think a second, a third, or a fourth incarnation arrests the succession of the chain of sublime creations, which float in the infinitude of the heavens, and which proceed from a primitive human soul, which has grown in perfection and in moral power. It surpasses our faculty to define, by the unassisted light of our reason and our knowledge, the number of these beings who go on succeeding one another in ever-increasing perfection. We can only say that we believe the creatures, which compose this ladder of perfections in succession, must be very numerous.

At every stage of his promotion in the hierarchy of nature the celestial being beholds the growth of those wings which symbolize his marvellous power to us. Each time his organs become more numerous, more flexible, have greater scope. He acquires new and exquisite senses. He acquires more and more power of extending his beneficent empire, of exercising his faculty of loving his fellows and all nature, and, above all, of comprehending and reading the designs of God. Deeper and deeper affections engage his soul, for the tenderness and the happiness engendered in its pure satisfaction, are granted to him to console him for the sufferings of death, to which he is always condemned. It is thus that the happiness of the elect is augmented. It is thus that the beings who inhabit the boundless plains of the invisible world employ each of their lives in preparing for the life which is to follow, in securing by a wise exercise of their freedom, industrious culture of their faculties, strict observance of morality, and continuous beneficence, a more noble, more animated, and happier destiny in the new spaces which await them, in the development of their sublime destiny.*

Nevertheless, as everything comes to an end in this world,

* On this subject see the book of Dupont de Nemours, " *Philosophie de l'Univers*," quoted by M. Pezzani in his " *Pluralité des existences de l'âme*," pp. 216-218.

so must everything have an end in the surrounding spheres. After having traversed the successive stages and rested in the successive stations of their journey through the skies, the beings whom we are considering must finally reach a defined place. What is this place, the ultimate term of their immense cycle across the spaces? In our belief, it is the sun.

CHAPTER THE SEVENTH.

ACCORDING to our system of thought the sun is the central place in which souls which come from the ethereal spaces are finally gathered together. After having undergone the successive incarnations which we have described, souls, primitively human, finish by reaching the sun, by dwelling within the borders of the star-king.

This, then, is a fitting place for a description of the sun from the physical and astronomical point of view. Such a description will at once reveal the entirely sovereign part played by that globe which has no fellow. The astonishing attributes which belong to it, the unimaginable power which it wields, will sufficiently explain the place at the summit of the ascending scale of nature, which we assign to the sun.

In the first place, the sun is totally different from the other stars of our world. He resembles nothing, and nothing can be compared with him. Neither planets, satellites, asteroids, nor comets can give us any idea of him. His immense volume, his physical constitution, his exceptional properties place him in a totally separate rank, and afford full

justification to those who claim for him a separate and sovereign place.

The enormous mass of the sun at once proclaims his
supremacy. The sun is sufficiently vast to receive everything
which could come to him from all the other planets. He
surpasses in volume the united size of all the celestial bodies
which revolve around him. He is six hundred times larger
than the entire assemblage of the planets with their satellites,
of the asteroids and the comets which compose what is called
the solar world; that is to say, the world of which we form
a part. The proportion in which the sun exceeds the earth
in volume is, then, necessarily enormous; since he is larger
than all the other stars put together. He is *one million three
hundred thousand* times larger than our globe.

It is only by drawing that we can give an exact idea of
the comparative sizes of the sun and the other planets. The
reader will find in the accompanying illustration (Fig. 1) a
figure which exactly represents the comparative dimensions
of the sun, and the largest planets of our world. The earth,
represented by a dot, gives an idea of what Mars, Mercury,
and Venus, which are smaller than the earth, must be.

It takes three years to circumnavigate the earth. To circumnavigate the solar globe, under similar conditions, would
take three hundred years. If human life be not more prolonged in the sun than on the earth, an existence would not
suffice to enable a traveller to become acquainted with the
surface of the globe he inhabits.

Weight is thirty times more intense on the surface of the

Fig. 1.— Comparative Dimensions of the Sun and the Planets

sun than on the earth. We know that a body which falls
upon the earth traverses, in the first second of its fall, a space
of four metres, nine centimetres. In the sun a falling body
traverses 144 metres in the first second of its fall. It follows
from this, that a human body, if transported to the sun,
would weigh about 2000 kilogrammes, the weight of an elephant. The body of a dog or of a horse would weigh twenty-
eight times as much as upon our earth, so that these animals
would remain fixed to the surface. The conditions of nature
must therefore be entirely different in the sun from what they
are in the group of planets to which the earth belongs.

The sun sheds rays from perpetual fire, a characteristic that
appertains to him alone among all the stars of our world. Of
himself he burns, and sheds abroad light and heat. The
other stars are neither warm nor luminous, and if the sun
did not exist, they would be plunged into eternal darkness
and eternal cold. This privilege alone ought to make us
comprehend the immense importance of the central star.

The light and heat which emanate from the sun are constant; they are never interrupted, and they never lose their
force. Thus, a second characteristic—constancy of illumination—separates the sun from all the other celestial bodies of
our world.

The intensity of the real heat of the sun has been measured by the physicists. This result was attained in an
endeavour to determine by experience the quantity of heat
which accumulates in a given time, upon a certain portion
of the earth's surface, exposed to the sun's rays, and adding

5

to that element the quantities of heat which would be absorbed by the atmospheric air, the ethereal spaces, and the soil.

Pouillet, the French physicist, who undertook this critical
investigation, arrived at certain results, which he states as
follows:

"If the total quantity of heat emitted by the sun was exclusively employed to melt a layer of ice applied to the solar
globe, and covering it completely in all its parts, that quantity
of heat would be able to melt, in one minute, a layer of eleven
metres, eighty centimetres, and in one day a layer of seven-
teen kilometres in thickness."

"'This same quantity of heat,' says Professor Tyndall,
'would boil 2900 milliards of cubical kilometres of water, at
the temperature of ice.'"

The astronomer Herschel found, that, in order to extinguish
the sun, to prevent his "giving out caloric," according to the
scientific phrase, it would be necessary to dash a stream of
iced water, or a cylindrical column of ice, eighteen leagues in
diameter, against its surface, at a rate of speed of 70,000 leagues
per second.   A comparison adopted by Professor Tyndall gives
us an amazing view of the intensity of the calorific force of
the sun.   "Imagine," says he, "that the sun is surrounded
by a layer of peat, seven leagues in thickness, the heat produced by its combustion would be the same as that produced
by the sun in one year."   The physicists have measured the
intensity of the sun's light with exactitude, as they had previously measured his heat.

It is known that the solar light is 300,000 times stronger

than that of the full moon, and 765,000,000 stronger than that of Sirius, the most brilliant of the stars.

Bouguer discovered, by experiments made in 1725, that the sun, at a height of 31° above the horizon, gives a light equal to that of 11,664 candles, placed within 43 centimetres of the object to be lighted, and equal to 62,177 candles placed within one metre.

According to this result, if we take account of atmospheric absorption, and of the law of the variation of the intensity of light, which decreases in inverse ratio to the square of distance, the light given by the sun at its zenith would be 75,200 times greater than that of a single candle, placed within one metre. Wollaston had arrived at a similar conclusion. By means of experiments of another kind, made during the months of May and June, 1799, Wollaston found that 59,882 candles, at one metre, give as much light as the sun. Supposing the sun to be in the zenith, the lightening power of that great star would be equivalent to 68,009 candles.

There is but little difference between this valuation and that of Bouguer, who states the result at 75,200 candles.

Whatever may be the intensity of the light of the sun, we now possess other sources of light which approach to it. Such is the oxhydric light, produced by burning hydrogen gas by means of a current of oxygen gas, or air, a method of lighting which has recently been employed in Paris and in London. This light is equal in power to more than 200 candles. A thread of magnesium burning in the air, develops a prodigious

5—2

quantity of light, which may be taken as equivalent to that
of 500 candles. The electric light produced by a voltaic
battery of from 60 to 80 coils, produces a luminous arc equal
to the light of 800 or 1000 candles. In the latter instance the
voltaic arc, according to Bouguer and Wollaston, would give
75 times less light than the sun, supposing the luminous electric point to be placed at a distance of one metre.

With very powerful batteries, it has been possible to go
further, and produce a light not much inferior to that of the
sun. Messieurs Fizeau and Foucault, by comparing the light
of a voltaic arc, produced by the action of three series of
Bunsen's coils, of forty-six couples each, with the light of the
sun in a clear sky in April, have established that the light-
giving power of the sun is not more than twice and a half
that of the electric light.

The preceding numbers represent the light-giving power of
the sun upon our globe, taking into account atmospheric absorption. Arago, on endeavouring to determine the intrinsic
light-giving power of the sun, found that the intensity of the
solar light is 52,000 times greater than that of a candle placed
at one metre. But, according to more recent researches for
which we are indebted to Mr. Edmond Becquerel, the result
obtained by Arago is greatly inferior to the truth, and the
light of the central star is 180,000 times greater than that of
a candle placed at one metre.

All the planets, attended by their satellites, and all the
comets which accidentally manifest themselves to us, turn
round the sun. The sun remains motionless in the midst

of this imposing procession of stars, which circulate around him, like so many courtiers paying him homage.

Thus, the sun is the heart of our planetary system ; everything is drawn, everything converges towards him.

Half-informed persons will exclaim, " What can be more simple ! The sun being six hundred times the size of all the other stars put together, the phenomenon of the condition of all those stars around the sun is explained by the law of attraction, which prescribes that bodies shall attract in proportion to their mass. If the sun attracts the stars of our world to itself, it is because his mass is greater than that of all the other stars collectively." But such an answer would be erroneous, involving the common error of taking a word for a thing, an hypothesis for an explanation, of putting a term of language in the place of a logical consideration. When Newton conceived the hypothesis (and the phrase) of *reciprocal attraction of matter,* he was careful to state that he only proposed to characterise by a name a phenomenon which in itself is entirely inexplicable, and of which we know nothing but the exterior mode of its manifestation, that is to say, the mathematical law. We know that bodies go towards each other in the ratio of their masses, and in the inverse ratio of the square of their distances ; but why do they go towards each other? This is what we do not know, and what we probably never shall know. If, for the word *attraction* we were to substitute the word *electrization,* or, as Keppler did, the words *affection, sympathy, obedience,* &c., we should have a new hypothesis, with a new name, but the mathematical law would remain the same, the hypothesis only would be changed. The real cause which makes small bodies rush towards large ones, and the stars of lesser magnitude revolve round the stars of greater magnitude, is an impenetrable mystery to mankind.

Whatever may be the hypothesis by which we seek to explain the fact, it is certain that the sun holds the planets with their satellites, the asteroids and the comets, suspended above the abysses of space, and that they journey through the heavens in unintermitting obedience to his guiding influence. The sun draws with him all the stars which follow and surround him, like flatterers of his power, like humble slaves of his universal preponderance. Like the father of a family in the midst of his progeny, the sun peacefully governs the numerous children of sidereal creation. Obedient to the irresistible impulsion which emanates from the central star, the earth and the other planets circulate, roll, gravitate, around him, receiving light, heat and electricity from his beneficent rays, which are the first agents of life. The sun marks out for the planets their path through the heavens, and distributes to them their day and night, their seasons and their climate.

The sun is, then, the hand which holds the stars above the unfathomable abysses of infinite space, the centre from which they obtain heat, the torch which gives them light, and the source whence they derive the principle of life.

From all time the immense and unique task fulfilled by the sun in the economy of nature has been understood. But this great truth has only been deeply studied in our days. Science has gone far beyond all the imagination the poets had conceived relative to the preponderance of the sun in our world. By means of numerous experiments and abstruse calculations, modern physicists have proved that the sun is the first cause of almost all the phenomena which take place on our globe, and that, without the sun, the earth and no doubt all the other planets would be nothing but immense wastes, gigantic corpses, rolling about, frozen and useless, in the deserts of infinite space.

Professor Tyndall, who has added largely to the discoveries of physics and mechanics, has brought out this truth very strongly, and the results to which he has been led may be said to form the most brilliant page of contemporary physical science.

We shall now endeavour to explain how it is that everything on the earth, and no doubt on all the other planets also, is derived from the sun, so entirely, that we may affirm that vegetables, animals, man, in short, all living beings, are but the productions, the children of the sun ; that they are, so to speak, woven out of solar rays.

In the first place, the sun is the primary cause of all those movements which we observe, in the air, in the water, or in the ground under our feet, and which keep up life, feeling, and activity on the surface of our globe.

Let us consider the winds, which have such important relations with all the physical phenomena of our globe. Whence proceed the winds ? From the action of the sun. The sun

heats the different portions of the earth very unequally, be-
stowing much more warmth on the tropical and equatorial
regions than on the other latitudes, which he leaves exposed
to cold.   On each point of the earth which is struck by the
rays of the sun, the layers of air near the ground are dilated
and raised, and immediately replaced by colder layers from
the temperate regions.   Thus the periodical winds are produced.   Across the hemispheres two great aërial currents are
perpetually blowing, going from the equator to each of the
poles; one, the upper current, towards the north-east in the
northern hemisphere, and towards the south-east in the
southern hemisphere; the other, the lower current, in a contrary direction.

The movement of the earth gives rise to other regular
winds.   The action of heat and of evaporation, added to the
unequal distribution of the continents and the seas, produce
others, which are irregular.   Thus, for example, in the great
valleys of the Alps, as in those of the Cordilleras, the warmth
of the air regulates the afflux of the cold air of the mountains,
and brings on tumultuous winds, and, in fact, hurricanes.

The sea breezes arise from the difference in the temperature of the shore during the day and the night.   By day,
the sun has warmed the shore and produced a considerable
dilatation of the air.   When the sun quits the horizon, this
hot air is replaced by cool currents from the inland.   The
same phenomenon is reversed in the morning, when the sun
returns; the shore is warmed, the hot air rises, and is replaced by the colder air of the sea, which then goes inland.

Thus, the evening breeze comes from landward, and the morning breeze from seaward.

We see, therefore, that the great atmospheric movements which we call the winds, are due to the successive appearances and disappearances of the sun, as are also the lesser movements which we call breezes. The position of the sun, constantly varying according to the period of the year, and the hour of the day, explains the inequality and the continuous existence of the aërial current.

The general cause of the winds which preserve the homogeneity of the air in all the terrestrial regions, is the heat of the sun dilating the atmospheric air; its absence, on the other hand, causes that gaseous mass to contract.

The *watering of the globe,* that is to say the rain, an element indispensable to the exercise of life, is another consequence of solar heat. The waters of the seas, the rivers, and the lakes, those which steep the soil, or are exhaled from vegetable matter, are gradually transformed into vapour by the action of the sun's heat, and form clouds and invisible vapour. When the sun has quitted the horizon, these vapours grow cold in the bosom of the atmosphere in which they floated, and fall down upon the earth again in the form of dew, of fog, and of rain.

When the cooling of the watery vapour in the bosom of the atmosphere is more intense, instead of rain we have snow, that is to say, a fall of congealed water. It is chiefly on the summit of mountains that snow falls and accumulates, because the temperature of elevated places is always cold. In very great altitudes the snow, remaining for long periods on the tops of the mountains, passes into an intermediate condition, between snow and pure ice, and ends by forming those great expanses of congealed water which are called glaciers. During the hot seasons the glaciers melt by degrees; the water resulting from this melting process, flows down the slopes of the mountains into the valleys, and gives rise to springs, rivers, and streams. These streams and rivers run into the ocean, from which they are again evaporated by the action of solar heat, and reconstitute clouds and invisible vapour.

Thus is established and maintained that incessant circulation of the waters which lie on the surface of the earth, their continual exchange with the aërial masses, whose effect is to water the globe, a phenomenon necessary to the exercise of the functions of organized beings.

The regular currents which furrow the waters of the ocean are also the result of the action of solar heat. From the poles to the equator the waters of the sea are unequally heated, and this absence of equilibrium in the temperature of the sea occasions a regular furrow, or line from the poles to the equator, resulting from the displacement of the waters, the cold waves rushing in to replace the hot. The unequal evaporation caused by the unequal distribution of heat at the equator and the poles, concurs to produce a similar result, by augmenting the degree of saltness at the equator, without augmenting it at the poles, occasioning a certain difference in density, and finally displacement for want of equilibrium. The currents of the sea are thus entirely produced by the action of the sun.

We see, therefore, that the winds, the watering of the globe, and the currents of the sea are the consequence of solar heat.

The movement of the magnet is another physical result of the action of the sun, if it be true, as Ampère says, that the magnetic currents which traverse the terrestrial globe are nothing but *thermo-electric* currents engendered by the unequal distribution of heat on the surface of the globe.

In addition to being the agent of powerful physical forces, the sun is a valuable agent of chemical forces,—indeed, this is the greatest part which he plays in the phenomena of nature. The light and heat of the sun produce the most important chemical actions on the earth's surface ; those on which the exercise of vegetable and animal functions depend. If the sun did not exist, life would be banished from the terrestrial globe. Life is the child of the sun, as I shall endeavour to prove to you.

The operations of photography serve to make us understand how it is that the sun presides over chemical action in the vegetable world. What is photography ? What does that curious phenomenon which fixes a drawing formed by light upon a sheet of paper, consist of ? A paper steeped in chloride or iodide of silver is placed in the focus of the lens of a dark camera, and the image formed by the lens is made to fall upon paper sprinkled with water. The portions of the picture not exposed to light produce no effect upon the salt of silver, which is incorporated with the paper, but the portions exposed to light decompose the salt of silver, and turn it black, or dark violet colour. On withdrawing this paper from the apparatus, where the operations have been carried on in darkness, we have a drawing which reproduces, in black, the luminous image formed by the lens. By certain means this image, solely produced by the chemical action of light, is rendered fixed and unalterable.

All the salts of silver thus exposed to light undergo an analogous decomposition. Nor are they the only salts which light modifies. Compounds of gold, platinum, and cobalt, properly prepared, may also be altered under the influence of direct or indirect rays, when exposed to the sun, or to his diffused light.

The light of the sun possesses the power of bringing about the combination of several other bodies. This is the case with hydrogen and chloric gas. If you mix equal parts of chloric gas and hydrogen in a bottle, and expose the mixture to the sun, an immediate combination will take place between the two gases, and chlorohydric acid gas will be formed. The combination will take place with so much force that it will be attended by a considerable escape of heat. If you throw the bottle containing the mixture up into the air, towards a space where the sun is shining, the bottle will break before it falls, with a violent explosion, at the moment of its contact with the light.

We might multiply examples of the chemical action produced by light only on substances belonging to the mineral kingdom, but it is sufficient for our purpose to say that the chemical action of light is still more powerful and more general in the vegetable than in the inorganic realm. This is a phenomenon of such importance that it is impossible to believe it otherwise than a premeditated design of nature.

One of the most fruitful discoveries of modern science is the recognition of the fact, that the respiration of plants depends upon the presence and the direct action of light, that is to say, that the decomposition of the carbonic acid which circulates in the tissue of vegetables, and which has been breathed up from the soil by the roots, takes place only when the plants are exposed to the sun. The labours of Priestley, Charles Bonnet, Ingenhouz and Senuebier, have taught us that the decomposition of carbonic acid into carbon, which remains fixed in the tissue of the plant, and into oxygen, which disengages itself from it, can take place only under the direct or indirect influence of the sun's rays. Our readers may easily convince themselves of this fact. Place a handful of green leaves in a glass full of water, and expose the glass to the sun. At the close of the day the upper portion of the glass will be filled with gas, which is nothing but pure oxygen, the result of the breathing of the leaves.

All the importance, all the value of such a phenomenon will be evident, if we reflect that it takes place over the whole extent of the globe, and that the respiration, which means the life of all the vegetable masses which cover the earth, depends solely upon the light of the sun. It is by means of the respiration of the plants, which restores oxygen to the atmospheric air, that nature makes up for the withdrawal of oxygen by the respiration of animals, by the continual absorption of that gas by numerous mineral substances, and by the frequent combustions, natural and artificial, which occur in the world. The result of these combustions would be the disappearance of the greater portion of the oxygen contained in the air, if there did not exist a permanent machinery for the restitution of that oxygen. This permanent machinery is the respiration of plants, produced by solar light. So absolute is the dependence of plants for their respiration on the action of the sun's light, that if it be intercepted by clouds, the escape of oxygen from them suffers a marked diminution. If the light of the sun be suddenly stopped, which occurs during a total solar eclipse, the escape of oxygen ceases, and the plants transpire carbonic acid only, as they always do during the night.

It is for this reason that a plant kept in complete darkness loses its colour, and becomes white. It does not respire, it emits carbonic acid gas without retaining carbon, it becomes etiolated, according to the scientific phrase, which means that the plant no longer lives at the cost of the external air, or of gas furnished by the soil, but consumes its own substance. The whitened salads which we prefer are not green only because they are grown in darkness, and the mushrooms brought to table are white only because they are reared in cellars.

M. Boussingault, who has studied vegetation in darkness, finds that the leaves of a vegetable which has never had any light at all, in its first appearance and development, never exhales oxygen, its respiration furnishes carbonic acid gas only. The plant, therefore, breathes just as an animal does. We must observe in this case that the substance of the seed only supplies this product. The plant borrows nothing from without, consumes nothing but the elements which were contained in the seeds, and dies when those nutritive elements are exhausted. The duration of its existence depends entirely on the weight of the seed whence it has sprung. If a well-developed plant be kept in darkness, the same fact may be observed. The plant gives out nothing but carbonic acid, and, as it borrows nothing from without, it perishes when it has thus devoured its own substance. M. Sachs says, in his *Physiologie Végétale*, that the movements proper to the leaves of many vegetables cannot take place if the plant is kept in darkness. Plants so kept remain always in the condition which Linnæus defined as *sleep*. Flowers contained in natural coverings, which in a great measure debar them from the light of the sun, do indeed produce colours, but those flowers are formed inside their natural coverings, at the expense of substances contained in their leaves, which could not be produced except under the influence of light. The same truth applies to fruits.

Leaves, flowers, fruits, are then, as the German physiologist, Moleschott, has said, "beings woven of air by light." The same author adds : "When we contemplate the brilliant colours of the flowers, and when their delicious perfume gives serene satisfaction to that poetic faculty which exists, though it may slumber deeply, in the soul of every man it is still the light which is the mother of colour and of perfume."

The influence of the sun on vegetation is of fundamental importance. Without the sun no plant would grow upon our globe. In those regions which are permanently deprived of the powerful and beneficent torch of nature, towards the extreme north, all vegetation is stunted, and higher still, it does not exist. Absence of light, and cold, are the causes of the complete disappearance of the natural adornment, and the useful tribute, which elsewhere vegetation furnishes to the earth. In the hot regions, vegetation is vigorous and extensive, in proportion to the abundance of sunshine poured upon them. There is nothing to be compared to the luxuriant vegetation of the tropical countries in both hemispheres. The vegetation of Brazil, of equatorial Africa, and the intertropical regions of India, is renowned for its abundance and variety.

Agriculture, enlightened by modern chemistry, has brought to light the special importance of the sun in promoting the activity of vegetation, and producing combinations of substances not to be attained by any action except that of the sun. M. Georges Ville, a professor at the Museum of Natural History in Paris, states, as the result of numerous experiments, that the activity imparted to vegetable production by the sun is truly miraculous. No chemical fact, no theory, according to the learned professor, can explain the mystery of solar influence, and its prodigious power over the development and produce of vegetables.

Let us remark, before we leave this subject, that by a providential circumstance the present generations of mankind are profiting by the chemical force of the sun which nature has stored in her great vegetable *depôts* for thousands of centuries. For instance, what is coal, which feeds all our industries, supplies our steam machines, ships, engines, and locomotives? It is the residue of those gigantic forests which covered the earth during the geological periods. The substance of the trees of the forests of the ancient world was at first changed into peat, which, becoming more and more compact by the action of ages, was finally pressed into the hard and heavy body which we call coal. But what was the cause, what was the first agent, which produced the trees of those forests, in the antediluvian times? It was the chemical force of the sun. This force, or, if the term be preferred, the products of the chemical force of the sun, have been accumulated and preserved in the wood, and then in the coal which that wood has become. We find it thus, and we use it, to our present profit.

Thus, the glowing sunshine which lighted and warmed the ancient world, is not lost to us. Contemporary generations inherit those very rays, and that same chemical force. The power of the sun, which has slumbered in the coal for millions of years, arouses itself for us, comes forth into the day, and transforms itself in our hands into a mechanical agent.

The light and heat of the sun, which play so great a part in the vegetable kingdom, exercise influence of a similar kind over the animal kingdom. If we reflect that plants are indis-

6

pensable to the food of the majority of animals, that the
creation of vegetables necessarily preceded that of terrestrial
animals (since vegetables constitute their food), and that
animals must inevitably disappear from the earth if plants
ceased to exist; we shall be led to acknowledge that animals
originate as certainly, though indirectly, from the force of the
sun as the plants themselves.

Besides, it can be proved that the action of the sun is
directly indispensable to the maintenance of animal life.
In the first place, is it not the fact that solar light and heat
exercise an immense influence on the health of animals and
of man? To convince ourselves of that, we need only compare men who pass the greater part of their lives in the air
and sunshine, with men who live in dark houses, in the
narrow streets and lanes of great cities. Not only are these
dwellings unwholesome because they are damp, but they are
fatal to health because they are not enlivened by the presence
of the sun.

Light, altogether indispensable to the exercise of respiration in plants, is not indispensable in the same degree
to the respiration of animals. It is, however, certain that
the products of the respiration of man and animals are less
abundant by night than by day. Moleschott has found that
the quantity of carbonic acid gas exhaled by an animal is
augmented by the intensity of the light of day, and is at its
minimum in complete darkness; "which amounts to this,'
adds that author, "that the light of the sun accelerates
molecular action in animals."

Thus, the rays of the sun are a primary condition of the existence of animals, because they produce the formation of plants, the essential basis of the alimentation of animals and of man, and because they preside over the fulfilment of many of their physiological functions. We find views of precisely the same order as those we have endeavoured to express, eloquently put forward in Professor Tyndall's work on " Heat :"

" And as surely as the force which moves a clock's hands is derived from the arm which winds up the clock, so surely is all terrestrial power drawn from the sun. Leaving out of account the eruptions of volcanoes and the ebb and flow of the tides, every mechanical action on the earth's surface, every manifestation of power, organic and inorganic, vital and physical, is produced by the sun. His warmth keeps the sea liquid, and the atmosphere a gas, and all the storms which agitate both are blown by the mechanical force of the sun. He lifts the rivers and the glaciers up the mountains ; and thus the cataract and the avalanche shoot with an energy derived immediately from him. Thunder and lightning are also his transmuted strength. Every fire that burns and every flame that glows dispenses light and heat which originally belonged to the sun. In these days, unhappily, the news of battle is familiar to us, but every shock and every change, is only an application or misapplication of the mechanical force of the sun. * * * * The sun comes to us as heat ; he quits us as heat ; and between his entrance and departure the multiform powers of our globe appear. They are all special forms of solar power ; the moulds into which his strength is temporarily poured, in passing from its source through infinitude."—p. 431.

G—2

The mechanical force which the heat of the sun represents has been calculated, and the numbers thus ascertained are curious. In order to understand how a heat agent can be expressed by figures of mechanical force, we must have a general idea of that theory which constitutes the most valuable creation of natural philosophy in our day ; we allude to *the mechanical theory of heat*, or the doctrine of the *mutual transformation of physical forces.*

Experience has proved that heat changes, under our eyes, into a mechanical force. See how, by the action of the steam engine, watery vapour becomes cold, and the dispersed heat immediately produces a mechanical force, and you will understand how it is that we maintain that heat tranforms itself into force. This being admitted, it is easily explicable that one of those elements may be represented by the others, or that at least we may represent the value of both force and heat by a common unit. This common unit is called a *caloric*, and expresses the quantity of heat requisite to raise the temperature of a kilogram of water one degree. On the other hand, the term *kilogrammeter* is used to express the quantity of force requisite to raise a kilogram to the height of one yard (*métre*) in a second.

Physicists have succeeded in solving the difficult problem, which consists of ascertaining how many kilogrammeters may be produced by a *calorie*, transformed into mechanical labour. The works of Mayer, Joule, Helmholtz, Hirn, Regnault, &c., establish that a calorie is equivalent to 425 kilogrammeters, that is to say that the quantity of heat requisite to raise the temperature of a kilogram of water to 1 degree centigrade produces a mechanical action represented by the elevation of a weight of 425 kilograms 1 yard (*mètre*) in height in the space of a sound. 425 kilograms are called the *mechanical equivalent of heat.*

With this information at our service, we are enabled to calculate in units of mechanical force the work done by solar heat, by transforming itself into mechanical force. And, if we calculate the total heat of the sun diffused over the earth, during a given time, we can calculate the sum of the forces which all this distributed heat would develop on the surface of the earth, if it were all employed in mechanical labour. In one year every square yard of the surface of the earth receives 2,318,157 calories, that is to say, more than 23,000,000,000,000 of calories to each space of 2 acres, 1 rood, 35 perches.*

To understand the intensity of this force, we must conceive a steam engine, which, instead of working at 200 or 300 horse-power, like the engines of our larger steamers, should work at 4,163 horse-power. And this, we must bear in mind, refers only to the small space above mentioned. If we calculate the entire surface of the earth, we arrive at the astounding total of 217,316,000,000,000 horse-power. In order to conceive such a force, we must picture to ourselves 543,000,000,000,000 steam engines each working without relaxation day and night, at 400 horse-power. That is the

* Represented by the French word *hectare.*

amount of work which the heat of the sun does for our globe alone.

The physical and mechanical actions which take place on our planet, vegetation, the phenomena of animal life, industrial and agricultural operations absorb only a very small quantity of this enormous mass of forces. Professor Tyndall says on this subject, in the book we have already quoted :—

"Look at the integrated energy of our world—the stored power of our coal-fields; our winds and rivers; our fleets, armies, and guns. What are they? they are all generated by a portion of the sun's energy which does not amount to $\frac{1}{2300000000}$th of the whole. This, in fact, is the entire fraction of the sun's force intercepted by the earth, and in reality we convert but a small fraction of this fraction into mechanical energy. Multiplying all our powers by millions of millions, we do not reach the sun's expenditure."—p. 433.

In this chapter we have analyzed the different physical and vital effects produced upon our globe by the light and heat given out by the sun. We have considered its action upon animate and inanimate nature. We have seen that the sun is really the great cause of physical action on our globe, and that he is also the first principle of both vegetable and animal life. Without the sun life would be banished from the terrestrial globe ; as we have already said, life is the offspring of the sun.

We know that in speech, heat and life are almost synonymous words. In every language we find it said that persons are *frozen by death*, in *the icy sleep of death*, that *cold is deathlike*, &c. This image is an exact expression of the reality.

An animal or a plant, when deprived of life is necessarily cold. A shiver is the precursor of every malady, and the sure forerunner of death. Every dead body is a cold body. It may be said that in the animal form cold takes the place of life, as in inanimate bodies cold succeeds to heat. Let us now consider the following facts. It is solely by the prolonged action of heat that plants can germinate, grow, and develop themselves; in order to come to perfection, every plant requires an ascertained number of degrees of heat, and botanists and agriculturists know quite accurately the total number of degrees of heat requisite to ripen their cereals, and make their fruit-trees bear. A prolonged and undisturbed accumulation of heat is indispensable to produce life in the impregnated egg of a bird, so that by employing caloric in a hatching machine, the process of hatching may be artificially perfected. The eggs of viviparous animals are sustained by the heat of the mother's body, and besides, as Hervey says, everything that has life proceeds from an egg (omne vivum ex ovo). If we recall to mind that, after the development of the germ in mammiferous animals, the unvarying maternal heat is indispensable to the formation of the organs of the fœtus, we shall be led to inquire whether heat does not directly produce life, whether heat does not transform itself into vital force. Modern philosophers who have propounded the *Mechanical Theory of Heat*, that is to say the profound and admirable doctrine of the mutual conversion of forces, the professors who have proved by mathematical evidence that heat converts itself into mechanical force, and the converse, might perhaps complete their brilliant synthesis by adding that heat, which converts itself into mechanical force, can also transform itself into life, or into vital force, and that the splendid theory of the transformation of forces does not apply to inanimate bodies only, but finds an astonishing confirmation in animate bodies.

Thus heat and life would be the manifestation of one and the same power, and the cause of life would be found to dwell, like the cause of mechanical force, in the sun.

CHAPTER THE EIGHTH.

THE fundamental importance of the sun in the general economy of our world being finally established, our readers will not be surprised to hear that we assign that radiant and sublime abode to the human souls released from the earth, and successively purified and perfected by the long series of their multiplied incarnations in the bosom of the interplanetary spaces. Some philosophers have perceived this truth. The astronomer Bode placed the most elevated intelligences in the sun. "The happy creatures which inhabit this privileged abode," he says, "have no need of the alternate succession of day and night; a pure and unextinguishable light illumines it for ever. In the centre of the light of the sun, they enjoy perfect security, under the shelter of the wings of the Almighty."* Under what form may we picture to our fancy the inhabitants of the sun? We cannot answer this question

* Quoted by Flammarion in his "*Pluralité des mondes habités.*"

without being acquainted with the *geography of the sun*, or as astronomers call it, his *physical constitution*, which differs essentially from that of the planets, of their satellites, and of the comets. He is unique in his position and office in the planetary system,—he must therefore be specially constituted. What is this special constitution? What is the geography of the sun?

Would that it were in our power to reply to this question with precision; would that we could describe the configuration of the sun. Unhappily, science has not yet reached that point. The problem of the sun's true nature is full of uncertainty. Astronomers are divided between two opposite theories, and that which seems to be the best supported, is too recent to be set forth in a dogmatic fashion. We can only summarize the actual condition of our knowledge on this question, explain the theory which seems conformable to ascertained facts, and applying it to the subject on which we are engaged, endeavour to deduce the physical condition, which, in our opinion, would belong to the inhabitants of the king-star.

Until the great epoch of the discovery of the telescope, at the beginning of the seventeenth century, in the time of Keppler and Galileo, only vague and arbitrary ideas respecting the sun prevailed. The educated, as well as the vulgar, beheld in it merely a globe of fire; the most learned declared that they found in it *pure fire, elementary fire, the principle of light, and of fire.* But as no means existed of examining the surface of the sun, and as his real distance from the earth was either unknown, or very imperfectly understood, a prudent reserve was maintained on this question. The discovery of the telescope immediately placed the astronomers in possession of the celestial realm; it enabled them to sound the depths of space, and to study the apparent configuration of the stars, including the sun himself. A few hours' observation with the astronomical spy-glass, and more was learned of the nature of the sun, than in the two thousand years of more or less philosophical reverie which preceded the discovery of the telescope.

With a glass which magnified the apparent diameter of the sun only twenty-sixfold, Galileo, repeating the observations of Fabricius, discovered the spots on the sun. Although Galileo did not use the smoked glasses which have since been found so useful, and although he limited his observations to the horizon, watching the great star at its rising and its setting, or when it was veiled by slight clouds, he studied its spots carefully, and described them faithfully.

We may observe that this discovery astonished the philosophers of that period, who were entirely submissive to the authority of Aristotle. The *incorruptibility of the sun* was held in the schools as a sacred principle, according to Aristotle, and these unfortunate spots perplexed the philosophers. The peripatetics vied with each other in proving to the Florentine astronomer that the purity of the sun was an unassailable principle, and that the spots which he had perceived existed only on his eyes, or on the lens of his glasses.

But Galileo had seen correctly, and soon every one could convince himself of the reality of the phenomenon he had proclaimed. Not only do spots exist upon the disc of the sun, but they furnish the only means which we possess of becoming acquainted with the physical and astronomical peculiarities and properties of the great star. The examination of these spots led to the discovery that the sun revolves like the other planets, and that he accomplishes the entire revolution upon his axis in a period of twenty-five days. The sun's days are therefore twenty-five times as long as ours. Here, however, we must remark upon the word *day*. To us, the *day* signifies the periodical return of the earth to the same point, after a complete revolution upon its axis, with an alternation of light and darkness. It is quite otherwise in the case of the sun, which, being self-luminous in all his parts, can never have any night.

We have said that the examination of the sun's spots established his rotation upon his axis. In fact, if we patiently observe the motion of a spot, or of a group of spots, we remark that it advances slowly from one edge of the solar disc to the other; for instance, if the point of departure be the eastern edge, the spot or group will advance with uniform speed towards the western edge, taking fourteen days to accomplish the distance. If we wait fourteen days more, we shall again perceive the same spot making its appearance on the eastern edge of the disc, the interval having been consumed in passing over the opposite and, of course, invisible side of the sun. The spot has therefore taken twenty-eight days to reappear, which twenty-eight days do not, however, represent the exact duration of the revolution of the sun himself. It must not be forgotten that the earth has not remained motionless during this long observation ; she, too, has gone round in the sun, as the spots have done. This sort of advance, which causes us to see the same spot for a longer time than we should have seen it, if the earth remained motionless, is of three days' extent, the deduction of which from the twenty-eight given days, allows twenty-five days for the real duration of the sun's rotation upon his axis.

In the sun seasons are unknown as well as days. Time seems to have no existence for the beings who occupy that radiant dwelling-place. The changes, and the succession of things for us which constitute time, are unknown to their sublime essence. Duration has no measure in that blessed world.

The dweller in the sun must behold the revolution of the planets around him, performed according to the same laws, but with different rates of speed. The phases of the planets and their satellites, the phases of Mars and Venus, or those of the moon, which we perceive from the earth, are unknown to them ; they see only the hemisphere of those globes which is illumined by their own immense country. They behold, in larger dimensions, the globes of Mercury and Venus, and in lesser dimensions the Earth and Mars. The distant planets, Jupiter, Saturn, and Uranus, must seem very small to them. Neptune they probably cannot see at all. The comets must be for a long time invisible to the inhabitants of the sun, who behold their flaming mass rushing towards them in ever-increasing size. They also see some comets sinking away into space, and others falling on the surface of the sun himself, to be lost and absorbed in his substance.

Thus, the spots on the sun have revealed to us an important peculiarity of his astronomical character, his revolution upon his axis. They have also given us the only exact ideas which we possess of the physical constitution of the sun.

The accompanying plate conveys an idea of what the spots on the sun consist of. Figures 2 and 3 represent the general aspect of these appearances. In the centre is a black space perfectly marked. To this succeeds a space in grey tinting, whose outlines melt by degrees into the rest of the luminous mass. The first region is called the Umbra; the second, the Penumbra.

These words must be distinctly understood. The part indicated by the term *Umbra* is only dark relatively to the illumined portion. This Umbra is very luminous, its brilliancy is two thousand times that of the full moon. We are merely dealing with comparisons here. The solar spots are often of very considerable dimensions. They have been found 30,000 leagues in breadth, and could swallow up the earth, which is only one-tenth of that magnitude. They are not permanent, sometimes they remain for months, or even years, but the greater number increase and decrease rapidly, and disappear in a few weeks. They are incessantly changing in form and in extent, and they grow and diminish. It is evident

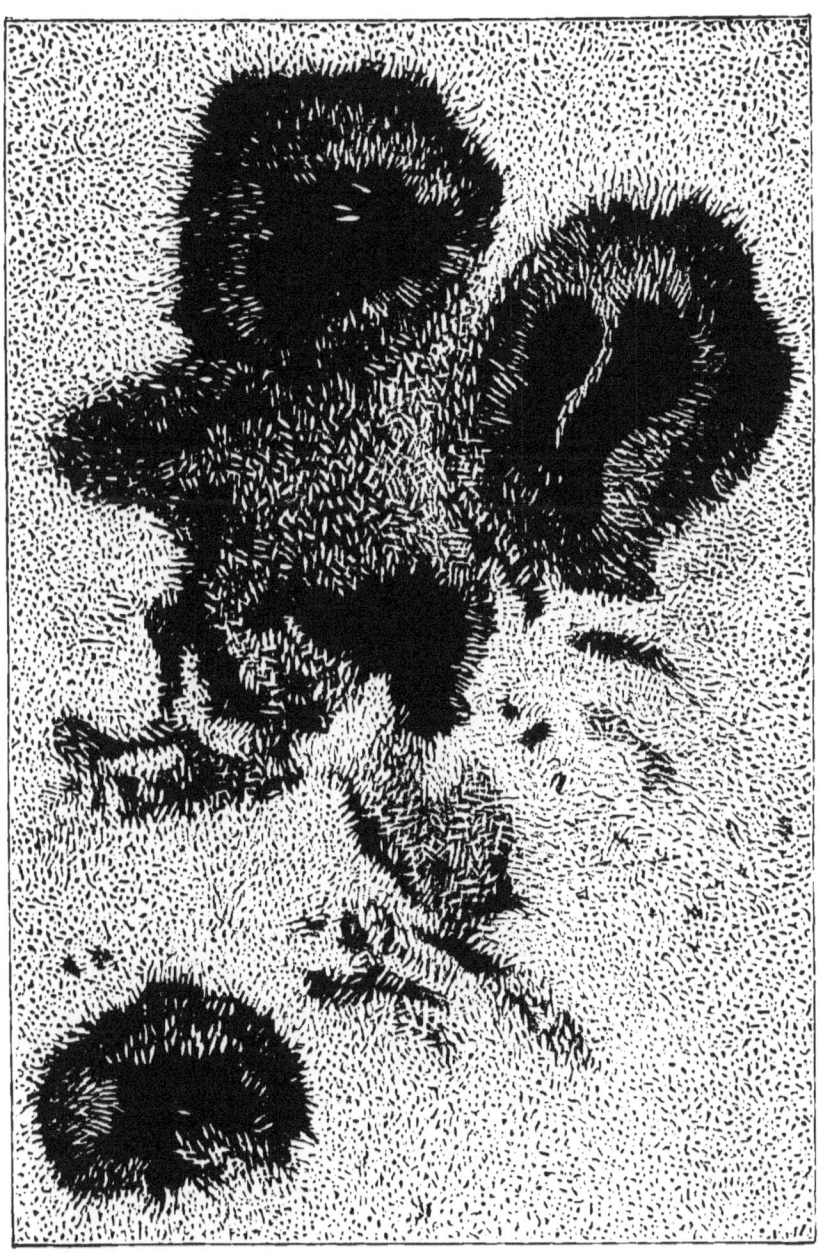

Fig. 2.—Group of Solar Spots observed in 1861 by Nasmith.

that they are regulated by a violent interior movement, and that they are the seat of tumultuous motion. Something like whirlwinds are seen to sweep across the regions occupied

Fig. 3.—Another Solar Spot observed by Nasmyth.

by the spots, and to carry them away, like the waves of a furious sea, or the flames of a conflagration. Gigantic bridges of apparently burning matter have been observed, thrown

7

from one edge to the other of adjacent spots, uniting them by
a shining band, and then this same band has stretched itself
out and caught hold of other spots. Of a sudden the whole
edifice has been seen to be swept away by fresh whirlwinds.
Signs of a prodigious commotion, of gigantic perturbation, are
always evident. These hurricanes, these tempests of flame,
are of a widely different grandeur from the hurricanes and the
tempests of our atmosphere, because the atmosphere of the
sun is several thousands of yards in height, and covers an
extent of surface 1,300,000 times greater than ours.

We have just said that the sun has an atmosphere. Such
is the conclusion to which the careful examination of the
great star has led.

From the earliest times at which the sun was observed,
a theory of its constitution was formulated, which was
perpetuated down to the present age, without receiving
authoritative contradiction. In the eighteenth century the
astronomers Herschel and Wilson developed this theory,
which was popularized in our time by the writings of Humboldt and Arago.

According to this theory, the sun is composed of a dark
nucleus, and a burning atmosphere, which is the only source
of the light proper to this star. Arago and Humboldt called
the incandescent atmosphere of the sun, the *photosphere.* Heat
and light would not, therefore, come to us from the nucleus,
but only from the photosphere.

The spots are explained, according to this theory, by admitting that they are openings accidentally formed in the sun's

atmosphere by gases discharged from volcanic craters, or in some other way. Through these openings the dark nucleus of the sun is seen. The *penumbra* of the spots are formed by the lower parts of the atmosphere of the sun, which is either hot or luminous. This lower portion of the atmosphere, reflecting the light emitted by the upper portion or photosphere, is slightly warm, and only partially illumined.

This theory of the constitution of the sun, and of the solar spots, seemed for a long time satisfactory. A similar explanation, that is to say, by partial eruptions of gas from volcanic craters, was assigned to the kind of black dotted appearance observed on the surface of the solar disc, and which is exactly reproduced in the two figures here given.

The brilliant spots scattered over the surface of the sun, which touched here and there with points of intense luminosity, are called *faculæ*. These brilliant points are said to proceed from local accidents, which cause an escape of light and heat from certain parts of the solar atmosphere.

Thus, according to this theory, the sun would be a solid body, opaque and dark like the planets, surrounded by an atmospheric layer, which would prevent any heat in the nucleus. Outside that layer would be a second atmosphere, the *photosphere*, which only would be luminous, and capable of emitting light and heat. Dark nucleus, dark atmosphere, luminous photosphere, such would be the constituent elements of the sun, according to Wilson, William Herschel, Humboldt, and Arago. To any who hold this theory, it is

7—2

not impossible to believe that the sun may be inhabited by beings who differ but slightly to man, or who are endowed with an organization similar to that of the inhabitants of the earth. If the body of the sun be preserved by the interposition of a cold, and but slightly conducting atmosphere from the rays of the photosphere which burns at an immense distance, we can believe that creatures organized almost like ourselves could live within it. The heat of the burning photosphere can reach it through the thickness of the lower atmosphere with only the degree of heat necessary to maintain life. The light thus filtered is brilliant, but not dazzling, and admits of the existence of beings of organization similar to those who live on the earth.

To this conclusion Arago came :

"If I were asked," said the astronomer, "is the sun inhabited? I must reply that I do not know. But, if I were asked whether the sun can be inhabited by beings of organization similar to that of dwellers upon our globe, I should not hesitate to reply in the affirmative."

At the present day Arago would hesitate, for science has made a great advance in the question of the physical constitution of the sun. The new method invented by MM. Kirchhoff and Bunsen, and known as analysis of the luminous spectrum, being applied to the solar rays, has given rise to an entirely new conception of the nature of the sun. We have returned to the opinion of the physicists of the middle ages, who regarded the sun as a globe of fire, a sort of gigantic torch.

It would be impossihle to enter into the details of the optical experiments which rendered accurate analysis of the solar rays possible, and enabled us to deduce a new theory of the constitution of the sun from their properties. We shall confine ourselves to explaining this theory, as it evolves itself from the experiments of M. Kirchhoff.

According to the German philosopher, the sun is not, as it has hitherto been supposed, a cold, dark, and solid body, surrounded by a burning atmosphere; it is a globe, a sphere, probably liquid, which burns throughout its whole mass, and in all its parts. This incandescent globe is surrounded by a very heavy atmosphere, formed of the vapours which proceed from the incandescent globe, and which are themselves kept burning in consequence of the high temperature of all those masses of fire.

How are the spots on the sun to be explained according to this theory? M. Kirchhoff admits that, owing to unknown causes, a cooling process may take place in the vaporous atmosphere which surrounds the body of the sun. This cooling process would form at certain points condensations of vapour analagous to the condensation of the vapour of water, which on our globe produces clouds and rain. These agglomerations of condensed vapours would form a species of cloud in the atmosphere of the sun, and those clouds, which would intercept the light of the solar disc from us, would produce the effect of a spot on this disc. The cloud, once formed, cools portions of the neighbouring vapours, and, by provoking a partial condensation, gives rise to the *penumbra* which sur-

round the *umbra.* Thus, according to M. Kirchhoff, the
solar spots are clouds suspended in the sun's atmosphere.
Galileo had previously propounded an analogous hypothesis.
Without abandoning M. Kirchhoff's theory we may mention
another explanation of the spots. A German physicist considers the spots, not as clouds in the sun's atmosphere, but as
partial solidifications of the liquid matter which forms the
body of the sun ; a kind of scoria, analogous to those which
may be observed in crucibles containing matters in a state of
fusion, and which come from particles of metal not yet melted,
or which are beginning to solidify. The penumbra of the
spots would be the half molten, and consequently, half-trans-
parent pollicule which always surrounds the edges of metallic
scoria with a semi-liquid ring.

M. Faye, a French astronomer, has propounded a theory,
which somewhat modifies that of M. Kirchhoff. He thinks
that the nucleus of the sun is neither solid nor liquid, but
entirely gaseous. The solar spot, he, like M. Kirchhoff, takes
to be an opening made accidentally in the sun's atmosphere
by the condensation of vapours on certain points of that
atmosphere. According to M. Faye, the spots are due to vertical currents of vapour ascending and descending, and the
interception of the light of the sun's atmosphere by the
predominant intensity of the ascending current.*

The new theory, the result of the optical experiments of the
German physicists, appears to explain all the facts which have
been observed, and it has therefore been generally accepted.

* See "*Le Soleil,*" by M. A. Guillemin, pp. 194—208.

Some divergences exist on questions of detail, but astronomers are nowadays almost unanimous in regarding the sun as a great body, incandescent in all its parts, as a globe in a state of fusion, surrounded by a burning atmosphere, or, as M. Faye states it, a simple agglomeration of incandescent gases.

CHAPTER THE NINTH.

THE INHABITANTS OF THE SUN ARE PURELY SPIRITUAL BEINGS.
—THE SOLAR RAYS ARE EMANATIONS FROM THE SPIRITUAL
BEINGS WHO LIVE IN THE SUN.—THESE BEINGS THUS PRODUCE
ANIMAL AND VEGETABLE LIFE UPON THE EARTH.—THE CON-
TINUITY OF SOLAR RADIATION, INEXPLICABLE BY PHYSICISTS,
EXPLAINED BY THE EMANATION FROM THE SOULS OF THE IN-
HABITANTS OF THE SUN.—THE WORSHIP OF FIRE, AND THE
ADORATION OF THE SUN AMONG DIFFERENT PEOPLES, ANCIENT
AND MODERN.

FROM the discussion of physical astronomy contained in the preceding chapters, we have con-
cluded, with MM. Kirchhoff and Faye, that the
sun is a mass of burning gases. But, our
readers will ask, if this be so—if the sun is a gaseous incandescent mass, or a globe of matter in a state of fusion, surrounded by an atmosphere of burning gas, where do you place
its inhabitants, and under what form do you picture them?

We have already said, that at each step of their promotion
in the hierarchy, the creatures who live in the planetary
spaces and have succeeded to the superhuman being, grow
in perfection, their senses are multiplied, their intellectual
power is considerably extended. In proportion as the creature, who in the beginning was human, is raised by successive

deaths and resurrections in the scale of inter-planetary being, the material substance, which, united to its spiritual principle, formed its radiant individuality, is diminished. In further exposition of our system, we must state our belief that this superior being, when he has been sufficiently perfected and exalted, by his different incarnations, by the multiplied stages in the immensity of the heavens, finally becomes pure spirit. When he attains the sun, he is free from all material substance, from all carnal alloy. He is a flame, a breath; all is intelligence, sentiment, thought, in him; nothing impure is mingled with his perfect essence. He is an absolute soul, a soul without a body. The gaseous and burning mass of which the sun is composed is, therefore, appropriate to receive these quintessential beings. A throne of fire is a fitting throne for souls.

We might even go further, and maintain that not only is the sun the asylum and receptacle of souls which have finished the course of their peregrinations in this world, but that it is nothing else than a collection of those souls which have come to it from the other planets, after having passed through the intermediate states which we have described. The sun may be only an aggregation of souls.

Since the sun is the first cause of life on our globe, since he is, as we have proved, the origin of life, feeling, and thought, since he is the determining cause of the existence of everything possessing organization upon the earth, why may we not hold that the rays which the sun pours upon the earth and the other planets are nothing else than the emanations

from these souls ? that they are emissions from the pure spirits
dwelling in the central star, directed towards us, and the
other planets, under the visible form of rays ?

If this hypothesis were accepted, what magnificent, what
sublime relations existing between the sun and the globes
which gravitate around him, would be revealed to us ! A continual exchange would be established between the sun and
the surrounding planets, an unbroken circle, an inexhaustible
communion, radiant emanations which should generate and
maintain activity and motion, thought and sentiment, which
should keep the flame of life burning everywhere ! Let us
think of the emanations from souls dwelling in the sun descending upon the earth in solar rays. Light gives existence
to plants, and produces vegetable life, accompanied by sensibility. Plants, having received this sensible germ from the
sun, communicate it, aided by heat likewise emanating from
the sun, to animals. Let us think of the germs of souls, placed
in the breasts of animals, developing themselves, becoming
perfected by degrees, from one animal to another, and finish-
ing by becoming incarnate in a human body. Let us think,
then, of the superhuman being succeeding to man, springing
up into the vast plains of ether, and beginning the series of
numerous transmigrations which, from one step to another,
will lead him to the summit of the scale of spiritual perfection,
from which every material substance has been eliminated, and
where the soul, thus exalted to the purest degree of its essence,
penetrates into the supreme abode of happiness, and of intellectual and moral power—the sun.

Such may be this endless circle, such this unbroken chain, binding together all beings in nature, and passing from the visible to the invisible world.

To those persons who may declaim with severity against the system which we have ventured to put forward, we shall put a question which cannot fail to embarrass them, for science has never been able to solve it. We shall ask them how the light of the sun, and the heat which results from it, are maintained? It is evident that the enormous quantities of heat and light which the sun sends out in torrents into space, must come from a source which cannot be inexhaustible, which has need of renewal, otherwise the sun would become extinct. As there is no effect without a cause, it is plain that the inconceivable quantity of forces which the sun distributes by his burning rays, must be derived from some place. M. Guillemin, in his work on the sun, passes in review the different theories which have been adopted, up to the present day, to explain solar radiation. The following is an analysis of a chapter of M. Guillemin's work on the " Maintenance of Solar Radiation."

Pouillet has calculated that if the sun were not supplied with something to make up for the losses he sustains, he must cool at the rate of one degree in a century. But this calculation falls short of the truth. Pouillet supposed that the specific heat of the sun is the greatest which can be conceived. The specific heat of the sun is, it is true, unknown, but instead of placing it at the maximum power, which it is not proved to be, we might suppose it, by an allowable hypothesis, to be equal to that of water, which is well known. Now if we grant to the sun the specific heat of water, we rectify Pouillet's calculation, and we arrive at the conclusion that the sun, if not furnished with any resources from which to repair his losses, would be entirely extinct at the end of 10,000 years. Professor Tyndall, whose experiments are more recent than those of Pouillet, and inspire greater confidence, says : "If the sun were a block of coal, and it were supplied with sufficient oxygen to enable it to burn at the degree of heat proper to that star, it would be entirely consumed at the end of 5000 years." Now the sun has existed for millions of years, for the transition periods of our globe, in which the first living beings were manifested, are traced back to millions of years. And yet his heat has not sensibly diminished since those distant ages. The proof that it has not diminished, is that the climates of the globe at the present time are the same as they were in the tertiary or quaternary epoch. In the tertiary or quaternary strata the same plants and the same animals which exist at present are found. Speaking of times nearer to our own, we may observe that the productions of the soil remain unchanged during the 2000 or 3000 years, whose traditions and historical archives we possess.

The sun has lost none of his heat during millions of years. Where has he gotten this heat from ? Where does he get it from now ? By what means is that unquenched fire kept up.

To this question neither **astronomy** nor physics has ever

furnished a satisfactory reply. Treatises, whether astronomical or physical, give us nothing but hypotheses, which we cannot accept.

At first it was said that the sun, turning on his axis in twenty-five days, produced by this movement a perpetual friction of his surface against the element in which he moves, in other words, against the ether. But if that were the case, this friction ought to engender a similar heat on the surface of the planets, whose rotatory motion, and especially the motion of translation in their orbit, is much more rapid than that of the sun turning on his axis. Besides, if we calculate the elevation of the temperature which would result from the friction of the sun against the ether, we shall find that the heat would hardly suffice to maintain the radiation of the solar star during one century. This hypothesis is therefore untenable.

Another theory, better supported, has been put forward by the physicists Mayer, Watterston, and Thompson; it explains the maintenance of the solar heat by a constant fall of meteors on the surface of the solar star.

A multitude of corpuscles gravitate round the sun, and approach him with sufficient nearness to be attracted by his surface, and fall upon it. These are *asteroids*, which turn in whirling swarms around the sun. A shower of corpuscles, of meteorolites, may be always falling on his surface. Their fall would cause a great development of caloric, in consequence of the transformation of their enormous speed into heat, and this caloric would suffice, according to the authors of this theory, for the maintenance of solar radiation.   Let us quote Professor Tyndall on this point :

" It is easy to calculate both the maximum and the minimum velocity imparted by the sun's attraction to an asteroid circulating round him.   The maximum is generated when the body approaches from an infinite distance, the *entire pull* of the sun being then exerted upon it.   The minimum is that velocity which would barely enable the body to revolve round the sun close to its surface.   The final velocity of the former, just before striking the sun, would be 390 miles a second, that of the latter 276 miles a second.   The asteroid, on striking the sun with the former velocity, would develop more than 9000 times the heat generated by the combustion of an equal asteroid of solid coal ; while the shock, in the latter case, would generate heat equal to that of the combustion of upwards of 4000 such asteroids.   It matters not therefore whether the substances falling into the sun be combustible or not ; their being combustible would not add sensibly to the tremendous heat produced by their mechanical collision. Here then we have an agency competent to restore his lost energy to the sun, and to maintain a temperature at his surface which transcends all terrestrial combustion.

" The very quality of the solar rays—their incomparably penetrative power—enables us to infer that the temperature of their origin must be enormous ; but in the fall of asteroids we find the means of producing such a temperature."—P. 423.

The fall of these asteroids on the surface of the sun would be followed by an increase in the bulk of that star, and there has been no such increase since the earliest period of its observation.   Also, the augmentation of the sun's bulk by these foreign bodies, would have produced an accelerant motion in the orbits of all the stars, which, however slight, would be distinctly perceptible; whereas, for the 2000 years of celestial observation, whose records we possess, unbroken and perfect regularity in the progression of the stars of our solar world is registered.

There is another objection to this hypothesis. It is that it presupposes a solid and resistant medium in the sun. This medium does not exist, according to the new solar theory, which considers this star to be formed of vapour and of gas, or, at most, of a liquid sphere. Another proof that this resistant medium does not exist, is to be found in the fact that several comets, among others those of 1680, and of 1843, have passed so close to the sun at their perihelion, that their movements must have been greatly disturbed by the resistance of a dense medium. The movements of these comets, were, however, quite unaffected by this cause; they were observed to reappear at the moment indicated by the regular curve of their orbit.

The absence of a resistant medium in the sun has been regarded as so grave an objection by one of the authors of this theory, Mr. Thompson, that he has abandoned it, as incompatible with facts.

Another hypothesis has been proposed, for explaining the maintenance of solar heat. The substances which now form the sun have not always been collected together in their present state of aggregation. At first, his molecules were, relatively, extremely distant from one another, and formed a *chaotic*, or confused mass. Under the influence of attraction, they drew together by degrees, and agglomerated themselves into a nucleus, which has become the centre of attraction of the whole mass. This simply amounts to saying that the sun began by being in the state of nebulosity, and passed at a later period into the condition of adherent and continuous matter.

"The molecules of solar nebulosity," says Balfour Stewart, "precipitating themselves upon one another, produced heat ; as, when a stone is thrown with force from the top of a precipice, heat is also the ultimate form into which the potential energy of the stone is converted."

This system of explanation of the primary origin of the planets is in general favour. Having drawn themselves together to form a continuous whole, the elements of the sun would have changed their physical condition, and the result of this change would have been an enormous escape of heat, sufficient to explain the origin of the solar focus. We know, in fact, that condensation of matter always accompanies an escape of heat ; and it has been calculated that a dimunition of only a thousandth part from the actual bulk of the sun would suffice to maintain the solar heat for 20,000 years.

M. Helmholtz, the author of this ingenious theory, has also calculated that "the mechanical force equivalent to the mutual gravitation of the particles of the nebulous mass would have been originally equal to 454 times the quantity of mechanical force actually disposable in our system," $\frac{453}{454}$ of the force coming from the conatus to the gravitation would therefore have been already expended. The author adds that the $\frac{1}{454}$ which remains of this original heat, would suffice to raise the temperature of a mass of water equal to the combined birth of the sun and the planets, to 28,000,000 of degrees centigrade ; this is a quantity of heat equal to 2500 times that which would be engendered by the combustion of the entire solar system, supposing it to be turned into a mass of coal.

These calculations are, doubtless, most interesting, but their defect is that they rest upon the conception of the sun's nebulosity, an hypothesis which requires closer examination before it ought to be accepted as the basis of so important a deduction. Besides, if the sun were warmed by a physical cause not in action at the present time, his heat, however great it may be estimated to be, must necessarily have been diminishing as long as the sun has been in existence. Now, we repeat that it does not appear that the heat of the sun has ever suffered any diminution. The theory of nebulosity is therefore no more securely founded in principle than the other hypotheses which have preceded it.

Thus, we find that neither astronomy nor physical science offers us any satisfactory explanation of the constant maintenance of solar radiation. Common sense tells us that this furnace, constantly in activity, must be as unceasingly fed, but science is as yet unable to discover the nature and source of its aliment.

There, where science places nothing, we venture to place something. In our belief solar radiation is maintained by the continuous, unbroken succession of souls, in the sun.

8

These pure and burning spirits are perpetually replacing the emanations perpetually sent through space by the sun, to the globes which surround him. Thus we complete that uninterrupted circle of which we have previously spoken, which binds together all the creatures of nature by the links of a common chain, and attaches the visible to the invisible world. We may venture to put forward this explanation of the maintenance of solar radiation with some confidence, since science can give us no exact information upon the point, and philosophy in this case only fills up the void left by astronomy and physics.

In short, the sun, the centre of the planetary aggregation, the constant source of light and heat, which sends forth motion, sensation, and life upon the earth, is, in our belief, the final sojourn of purified perfected souls, which have attained their most exquisite subtlety. They are entirely devoid of material alloy, they are pure spirits who dwell in the midst of the blazing atmosphere and the burning masses which compose the sun. That star, whose size far surpasses the bulk of all the others put together, is sufficiently vast to contain them. From their throne of fire, these souls, all intelligence and activity, behold the marvellous spectacle of the march of all the planetary globes which compose the solar world, through space. Placed in the centre of this vast world, understanding the secrets of nature, and all the mysteries of the universe, they are in possession of perfect happiness, of absolute wisdom, and of illimitable knowledge.

The Genoese naturalist, Charles Bonnet, was the first to bring forward general ideas upon the philosophy of the universe, in the same order as those which we have just developed. In his *Palingénésie Philosophique*, published in 1771, he introduces the doctrine of divers existences for the human soul, outside that of the earth. In a chapter appended to that work, and entitled, "Conjectures on the blessings to come," he draws a picture of the perfect happiness which we shall enjoy in that abode, and dwells, in the following eloquent words, on the transcendent knowledge which we shall possess, which will unfold to our view all the secrets of the physical and moral worlds :—

"If the Supreme Intelligence," says Charles Bonnet, "has varied all His works here below, so that nothing created is identical with anything else, if harmonious progression reigns among all terrestrial beings ; and one common chain unites them ; is it not probable that this marvellous chain is prolonged throughout all the planetary worlds ; that it unites them all, and that they are only constituent and infinitesimal parts of the same series ?

"At present we can see only a few links of this great chain; we are not even certain that we observe them in their habitual order ; we can only follow this admirable progression very imperfectly, and through innumerable windings in which we meet with frequent interruptions, but we always know that the breaches are not in the chain, but in our knowledge.

"When it shall have been granted to us to contemplate this chain, as I have supposed the intelligences for whom our world was chiefly made to contemplate it ; when, like them, we shall be able to follow its coils in other worlds, then, and then only, we shall understand their reciprocal dependence, their secret relations, the exact meaning of every link, and we shall rise by a scale of relative perfection to the most transcendent and luminous truths.

"With what feelings shall our souls be filled, when, having studied to its depths the economy of a world, we shall fly to another, and compare the two! How perfect shall our cosmology be then! How wide the generalization and great the fecundity of our principles, the succession, the mass, the exactness of our knowledge! What light shall be shed from so many different objects upon the other branches of our studies; upon physics, geometry, astronomy, rational science, and especially upon that divine study whose object is the Supreme Being.

"All these truths are chained together, and the most distant are held to the nearest by hidden links, which it is the end of understanding to discover. Newton, no doubt, exulted in having discovered the secret relation between the fall of a stone and the motion of a planet; when he shall be one day transformed into a celestial intelligence, he will smile at this child's play, and his profound geometry will be to him only the first elements of another Infinite.

"Man's reason has already penetrated beyond all the planetary worlds; it has raised itself up to heaven, where God dwells; it contemplates the august throne of the Ancient of Days, it beholds all the spheres rolling beneath His feet, and obeying the impulse of His hand, it hears the acclamations of all the intelligences, and, mingling its adoration and its praise with the majestic song of the hierarchies, it cries with the deepest consciousness of its own nothingness: 'Holy, holy, holy, is He who is eternal, and the All Good; glory be to God in the highest, and good-will towards man!' Oh! the depth of the riches of the Divine Goodness, which is not

satisfied with manifesting itself to men on the earth by
countless means, but will bring him one day to the celestial
dwelling-places, and satisfy the thirst of his soul with the
fulness of delight.   There are many dwellings in our Father's
home; had it not been so, He whom He sent to us would have
told us, and He is gone thither to prepare a place for us.   He
will come back and take us with Him; that where He is we
may be also.   *Where He is,* not in the outer court, not in the
vestibule, but in the sanctuary of universal creation, in the
holy of holies.   Where He is, who is the King of angels and
of men, the Mediator of the new covenant, the Author and
Finisher of our Faith, who has made the new way for us which
leads to life, who has made us free to enter into the Holy
Place, who has brought us near to the city of the living God,
to the heavenly Jerusalem, to the innumerable multitude of
angels, to God Himself, who is the Judge of all. . . . . In
this eternal dwelling, in the bosom of light, of perfection and
happiness, we shall read the general and particular history of
Providence.   Initiated, to a certain extent, in the profound
mysteries of His government, His laws, His dispensations, we
shall admiringly recognize the secret reasons of the many
general and particular events which astonish us, confound us,
and throw us into a state of doubt which philosophy does not
always dissipate, but which religion never fails to allay.   We
shall ceaselessly meditate upon the great book of the destinies
of the worlds.   We shall dwell particularly on the pages
which concern this little planet; the cradle of our infancy,
and the first monument of the paternal goodness of the
Creator towards man.   We shall discover, with astonishment,
the numerous revolutions which this little globe has undergone before it assumed its actual form, and we shall follow
with our gaze those which it is destined to undergo in the
course of ages; but our admiration and our gratitude will be

chiefly excited by the wonders of that great redemption, in which there are so many things beyond our feeble reach, which have been the objects of the studious research and the profound meditation of the prophets, and which the angels have desired to look into. One line on this page will contain our own history, and will develop to our view the why and the how of those calamities, trials, and privations which in this world try the patience of the just man, purify his soul, and enhance his virtues, while they crush and destroy the weak. When we have reached so elevated a degree of knowledge, the origin of physical and moral evil will no longer embarrass us; we shall confront them distinctly at their source, and in their most distant effects, and we shall acknowledge, from the evidence before us, that all which God does is well done.

"In this world we see effects only; and we even observe them in a very superficial manner; all the causes are hidden from us : then we shall see effects in their causes, consequences in their principles, the history of the individual in that of the species, the history of the species in that of the globe, the history of the globe in that of the worlds, &c. Now we see things only confusedly, and in a glass darkly; but then we shall see face to face, and shall know in some sort as we have been known; in short, because we shall have an infinitely more complete and distinct knowledge of the work, we shall also acquire an incomparably deeper sense of the perfections of the workman. And this knowledge, the most sublime, the most vast, the most desirable of all, will be incessantly perfected by intimate intercourse with the eternal source of all perfection! I cannot express this sufficiently, I do but stammer over it; words are wanting; would that I could know the language of the angels. If it were possible to a finite intelligence ever to exhaust the universe, it would still find the treasures of truth from eternity to eternity in contemplation of its author ; and, after a thousand myriads of ages consumed in such meditation, it would only have touched the edges of that science of which it may be even the highest intelligences possess no more than the rudiments. There is no true reality except in Him who *is*, for all which is, is by Him, before being out of Him ; there is but one existence, because there is but one Being whose essence it is to exist ; and all which bears the inappropriate name of being had remained shut up in necessary existence as the consequence in the principal."*

Before concluding this chapter, let us remark that the deductions of science concerning the sovereign part played by the sun in the general economy of nature, are in perfect harmony with the religious conceptions of the most ancient peoples. The worship of fire has reigned from time immemorial in Asia, and especially in ancient Persia. From the Persian shores sailed the first peoples, the Aryas, or Aryans, who occupied and peopled Europe. Fire worship was the first religion of ancient Asia. M. Burnouf dwells on this fact in his *Etudes sur la Science des Religions*, from which we quote the following passages :

" The men of that time (the Aryas) perceived that all the movements of inanimate things which take place on the earth's surface proceed from heat, which manifests itself, either under the form of fire which burns, or under the form of thunder, or under the form of wind ; but the thunder is fire hidden in the cloud, and rises with it into the air ;

* "Palingénésie Philosophique," vol. ii. pp. 427 and following.

—fire which burns is, before it manifests itself, shut up in the vegetable matters which supply it with aliment ; wind is produced when the air is stirred by heat, which rarefies it or condenses it on its withdrawal.

"Vegetables, in their turn, derive their combustibility from the sun, which makes them grow, by storing up his heat in them, and the air is warmed by the rays of the sun, the same rays which reduced the terrestrial waters to invisible vapours, and then to thunder-bearing clouds. The clouds spread the rain, make the rivers, feed the sea which the agitated winds trouble. Thus all this mobility which animates nature around us is the work of heat, and heat proceeds from the sun, which is at the same time "the celestial traveller," and the universal motor.

"Life also seemed to them to be closely allied to the idea of fire. The grand phenomenon of the accumulation of solar heat in plants, a phenomenon which science has since eluci- dated, was early perceived by the ancients. It is frequently pointed out in the Veddas in expressive terms. When they lighted the wood on the hearth they knew that they only 'forced' it to give out the fire which it had received from the sun. When their attention was directed to animals, the close bond which exists between heat and life, struck them in all its force ; heat maintains life, they found no living animals in whom was life without heat ; on the contrary, they saw that vital energy displayed itself in the proportion in which the animals shared in heat, and diminished in the same propor- tion. Life exists and perpetuates itself on the earth on three conditions only, that fire should penetrate the body under its three forms, of which one resides in the sun's rays, one in the ignited aliments, and the third in respiration, which is air renewed by motion. Now these two latter proceed, each after its own fashion, from the sun (sûrya) ; his celestial force is the universal motor, and the father of life : that which he first engendered, is the fire here below (agni) born of his rays, and his second eternal co-operator is air put in motion, which is also called wind, or spirit (vâyu)."*

The worship of the sun still exists among all the negro tribes which inhabit the interior of Africa ; it may even be said that it is the only religion of the African tribes, and this religion has existed among them in all times.

The ancient inhabitants of the new world had no other worship than that of the sun. This fact is established by the historical archives of the Indian races which we possess; such as the Aztecs or ancient inhabitants of Mexico, and the *Incas* or ancient Peruvians. Manco Capac, who subjugated Peru, and imposed his own laws upon the country, passed for the son of the sun.

Did not all these primitive people, whose customs extend back to the origin of humanity, when they rendered religious homage to the sun, obey a mysterious intuition, a secret voice of nature? However that may be, it is very remarkable that the religious conceptions of the most ancient people should be in such complete harmony with the most recent and most authoritative duductions of modern science.

* "*Revue des Deux Mondes,*" 15th April, 1868.

CHAPTER THE TENTH.

WHAT ARE THE RELATIONS WHICH SUBSIST BETWEEN US, AND
SUPERHUMAN BEINGS?

HAVING drawn a picture of the transmigrations of souls which, having belonged to men, attain, according to our belief, to the sublime dwelling-place of the solar spaces, we will now return to the superhuman being, and endeavour to find out whether that being, who immediately succeeds to man, who is a resuscitated man, incarnate in a new body, and living in the plains of ether, can place himself in relation with the inhabitants of the earth, notwithstanding the immense space which divides them. We have already endeavoured (ch. iv.) to discern the attributes of the superhuman being. Considering the number and extent of the faculties with which we believe him to be endowed, we cannot hesitate to accord to this mighty creature the power of communicating with our earth, and of exerting a certain influence there.

But how and by what means can such a communication be established? What is the agency whose existence we must presuppose, in order that beings floating in the ethereal spaces can produce an impression here below? What transcendent system of electric telegraphy does the superhuman being employ? On this point we are absolutely ignorant, but the fact that communication does exist between these beings and our globe appears to us to be certain; a conviction which we base upon the following grounds.

First, let us address ourselves to the popular feeling. As we have already said, we are not afraid of invoking vulgar prejudices and opinions, because they are almost always the expression of some great moral truth. Observations repeated thousands of times, traditions transmitted from generation to generation, and which have resisted the control of time, without being either altered or destroyed, cannot deceive. Only, when the people amidst whom this tradition has been formulated and preserved, are unenlightened, they translate their observations into a coarse form.

Let us inquire into the origin of those ghosts in which many civilized people firmly believe! Take away the absurd white sheet, and the human form with which the simple superstition of the peasantry invest them, and you will find in ghosts the idea of communication between the souls of the dead and the living, you will find the thought which we are endeavouring to put before you in a scientific form.

This popular notion about ghosts has extended to persons who appear to be educated and enlightened, but who are, in reality, as ignorant in matters of philosophy as the simple peasants, and who are, in addition, addicted to mysticism, which obscures their reason. We allude to *spiritualists*.

The term *spiritualists* is applied to the partisans of a new superstition which sprung up in America and Europe in 1855, as a result of the moral malady of *table-turning.* These good people imagine that they can, by their will, and according to their fancy, cause the souls of the dead, of great men, or of their own relatives and friends, to descend to the earth. They evoke the soul of Socrates or Confucius, as easily as that of a defunct relative, and they are so simple as to imagine that these souls come at their call to converse with them. A person who is called a *medium* is the intermediary between the invoker and the soul invoked. The medium, under the influence of an unconscious and habitual hallucination, writes down on paper all the answers made by the spirit, or rather he writes down everything that comes into his own foolish head, imagining himself to be faithfully transmitting messages from the other world. The people who listen to him take these things, which are simply the thoughts of the ignorant medium, for revelations from beyond the tomb.

In spiritualism there exists only one true and rational idea; it is the possibility of man's placing himself in relation with the souls of the dead; but the coarse means resorted to by the partisans of this mystic doctrine, cause every enlightened and educated man to repudiate any fellowship with them. We merely mention spiritualism in this place as a vulgar and foolish phase of the popular belief in ghosts. It has higher pretensions, but science and reason alike forbid us to admit them.

The fact of communication between superhuman beings

and the dwellers upon the earth being, it seems to us, proved, we shall now consider how those superhuman beings and men who live on the earth or on the other planets may be brought into relation with each other. It appears to us that this communication is chiefly in action during sleep, and through the medium of dreams. Sleep, that curious and ill-explained state, is the condition of our being during which a portion of our physiological functions, those which establish our connection with the external world, are abolished, while the soul preserves a part of its activity. In this condition, the body being seized by a kind of death, the soul, on the contrary, continues to act, to feel, and to manifest itself by the phemonena of dreams. Now, in the superhuman being, the spiritual portion, the soul, dominates immensely over the material portion. The superhuman being is, so to speak, all intelligence. Man, when he is in the condition of sleep and dreaming, approaches nearer to the superhuman being than when he is in a waking state; there is, then, more resemblance, more natural affinity between them. Consequently communications can be more easily established between these two beings who are drawn together by analogy of condition.

There is a saying, the result of repeated observation, which is logical and true. It is, *the night brings counsel.* Is not this as much as to say that it is during the night we receive the secret communications and the solitary advice of those beloved invisible beings who watch over us, and inspire us with their supreme wisdom? It is certain that when we have to make a decision, to unravel a thought, it often happens that we fall asleep in the midst of perplexity and uncertainty, and that the next day we awake, having taken our decision, unravelled our thought, which explains the phrase, *the night brings counsel.* Ancient times, and the middle ages, accorded an extraordinary importance to dreams. They were considered to be sent by God, as His warnings, hence the importance attached to their interpretation. "During sleep," says Tertullian, "the honours which await men are revealed to us; during sleep, remedies are indicated, thefts revealed, treasures discovered."*

Visions played a great part among Christians in mediæval times. It was during sleep that saints, inspired persons, and devotees received communications of an extraordinary order. We are far from believing that it is during sleep and dreams only that we can feel the presence and the influence of superhuman beings. There are few persons who have not felt, while waking, an unaccountable influence of this kind. We feel a soft, gentle impression, a sort of vague, mysterious push, which excites a spontaneous resolution, a sudden inspiration, an unhoped-for suggestion.

We must observe that all men are not recipients of these mysterious impressions. The superhuman being cannot manifest himself except to those whom he loves, and who remember him; to those whom he wishes to protect against the dangers and difficulties of this terrestrial life. A father, or a mother, snatched away from filial love by death, comes to speak to the soul which remains and mourns here below. A

* "Liber de animâ," ch. xlvi

son, torn in the dawn of life from the tenderness of his
parents, comes to console them for his loss, to enlighten them
with his advice, to furnish them, by the inspiration of his
lofty wisdom, with the means of sustaining all the trials of
this lower life.   Two friends are united, despite the barrier
of the tomb.   Two lovers, whom death has sundered, are
again brought together.   An adored wife, taken by death
from her husband, reveals herself to his heart.   Then all
those sentiments of mutual affection which subsisted between
them spring up again; death, which has appeared to sever the
ties between these souls, does no more than veil them from
the eyes of strangers.   Death is conquered; the phantom is
laid low, and we may cry with the prophet in the Scripture,
" Oh, Death ! where is thy sting?   Oh, Grave, where is thy
victory ?"

In order to receive these communications, a man must possess a pure and noble mind, and he must have preserved the
cultus of those whom he has lost.   A mother who has been
indifferent to her child during his life, or has forgotten him
after his death, cannot expect to receive secret manifestations
from him for whom she has felt but little tenderness.   The
friend from whose heart the image of the friend removed by
death has been effaced, must renounce such priceless manifestations.   The man who is abandoned to low and vicious
instincts and perverse inclinations, must not flatter himself,
however faithfully he may have preserved the memory of the
dead, that these messages shall come to him.   A pure and noble
creature only can communicate with these privileged beings.

There exists in our hearts a moral force which no philosophy has been able to explain, which no science has been able to analyze, which is called *conscience.* Conscience is a sacred light burning within us, which nothing can obstruct, obscure, or extinguish, and which has the power of giving us sure and certain enlightenment on every occasion in our lives. Conscience is infallible. Nothwithstanding everything, in spite of our real or apparent interest, at all times, and in all places, speaking to the great and the small alike, to the powerful and to the weak, it always teaches to discern good from evil, the honest from the dishonest way. In our belief, conscience is the impression transmitted to us by a beloved being, snatched from us by death. It is a relative, a friend, who has left the earth, and who deigns to reveal himself to us, that he may guide us in our actions, trace out the path of safety for us, and labour for our good. Cowardly, perverse, base, and lying men exist, of whom we say that *they have no conscience.* They do not know how to distinguish good from evil; they are entirely wanting in moral sense. It is because they have never loved any one, and their souls, base and vile, are not worthy to be visited by any of those superior beings, who only manifest themselves to men who resemble them, or who have loved them. A man *without a conscience* is, then, one who is **rendered unworthy**, by the vicious essence of his soul, of the lofty counsels and the protection of those who are no more.

Our readers will have perceived that this idea of a supreme and invisible protector of man, who guides his heart, and enlightens his reason, has already been formulated by the Christian religion, which has derived it from Holy Scripture. It is the *Guardian Angel*, a mysterious and poetic type, a seraphic creature, whom God has charged to watch over the Christian, to guard him against snares, and constantly to direct him to the ways of sanctity and virtue. We observe this argument without having sought it. In short, we register our ideas as they deduce themselves logically from each other, without any bias. And when we find ourselves led into agreement with a dogma of the Christian religion, we note that concord with pleasure.

We would ask those persons who have read these pages to question themselves, to summon up their recollections, to reflect upon what has passed around them, and we are convinced that they will discover many facts in harmony with what we advance. The moral phenomenon of the impressions made by the dead on the mind of the living who have loved them, and who keep up the cultus of their memory, is one of those truths which every one holds by intuition, and whose entire verity he acknowledges when he finds it curtly formulated and put forward. We will not give our readers second-hand information by invoking facts of this kind which they may know; we can only recall a few which came under our observation, briefly, as follows :

One of our friends, an Italian Count, B——, lost his mother nearly forty years ago. He has assured us that he has been in communication with her every day since, without intermission. He adds that he owes the wise ordering of his life, his labours, his career, and the good fortune which has always accompanied his enterprizes, to the constant influence and secret counsels of his mother.

Dr. V——, a professed materialist, one who, according to the popular phrase, *believes in nothing*, believes, nevertheless, in his mother. Like Count B——, he lost her early, and has never ceased to feel her presence. He told us that he is more frequently with his dead mother, than he used to be when she was living. This professed apostle of medical materialism has, without being aware of it, conversations with an emancipated soul.

A celebrated journalist, M. R——, lost a son, twenty years of age, a charming, gentle youth, a writer, and a poet. Every day M. R—— has an intimate conversation with this son. A quarter of an hour of solitary recollection admits him to direct communication with the beloved being snatched away from his love.

M. L——, a barrister, maintains constant relations with a sister who, when living, possessed, according to him, every human perfection, and who never fails to guide her brother in every difficulty of his life, great or small.

Another consideration suggests itself in support of the idea which occupies us at present. It has been remarked that artists, writers, and thinkers, after the loss of one beloved, have found their faculties, talents, and inspirations increased. We might surmise that the intellectual faculties of those whom they have loved have been added to their own. I know a financier who is remarkable for his business capacities. When he finds himself in a difficulty, he stops, without troubling himself to seek for its solution. He waits, knowing that the missing idea will come to him spontaneously, and, sometimes after days, sometimes after hours, the idea comes, just as he has expected. This happy and successful man has experienced one of the deepest sorrows the heart can know ; he has lost an only son, aged eighteen years, and endowed with all the qualities of maturity, combined with the graces of youth. Our readers may draw the conclusion for themselves.

This last example may instruct us concerning a peculiarity of the superior manifestations which we are studying. We have just said that sometimes a certain time, some days for instance, are required for the production of the manifestations. The cause of this is that the superhuman being, to whom they are due, has much difficulty in putting himself in relation with the inhabitants of our globe. There are many beings on the earth whom he loves, and whom he would fain protect, and he cannot be in two different places at the same time. We may even suppose that the difficulties which human beings feel in putting themselves in relation with us, added to the spectacle of the sufferings and misfortunes which overwhelm their friends here below, are the causes of the only sorrows which trouble their existence, so marvellously happy in other respects. Absolute happiness exists nowhere in the world, and destiny has the power to let fall one drop of gall into the cup of happiness quaffed by the dwellers in ether, in their celestial abode.

Persons who receive communications from the dead have

remarked that these communications sometimes cease quite
suddenly. A celebrated actress, now retired from the stage,
had manifest communications with a person whom she had
lost by a tragical death. These communications abruptly
ceased. The soul of the dead friend whom she mourned
warned her that their intercourse was about to cease. The
assigned reason serves to explain why such relation cannot
be continuously maintained. The superhuman being who
was in relations with the terrestrial person had already risen
in rank in the celestial hierarchy, he had accomplished a new
metamorphosis, **and he** could no longer correspond with the
earth.

Among the French peasantry communication with the
dead is a general habit. In the country death does not involve the lugubrious ideas which accompany it among the
dwellers in cities. People love and cultivate the memory of
those whom they have loved, they hold as most happy those
whom the favour of Providence has early removed from the
misfortunes, the failures, the bitterness of terrestrial life, they
call on them, they confide in them, and the dead, grateful for
this pious memory of them, respond to the simple prayers of
these hearts. All the Orientals have that serene aspiration
towards death which in Europe exists exclusively among
country people. The Mussulmans love to invoke death, to
spread the idea of death everywhere. Every one knows the
melancholy proverb of the Arabs. "It is better to be seated
than standing; it is better to be lying down than seated; it is
better to be dead than living."

The preceding chapter terminated with a quotation from Charles Bonnet, the first of the naturalists who discerned the doctrine of the plurality of existences above the globe. We shall terminate this chapter with a quotation from another naturalist philosopher, a contemporary of Charles Bonnet, who defended that doctrine very cleverly. Dupont de Nemours, in his *Philosophie de l'Univers*, expresses himself thus, on the subject of the communications which may be established between us, and the superior beings, invisible inhabitants of other worlds, whom he calls *angels*, or *genii*.

" Why," said Dupont, " have we no evident knowledge of these beings, the necessity, convenience, and analogy of whom strike our reflective faculties which only can indicate them? of those beings who must surpass us in perfections, in faculties, in power, as much as we surpass the lower animals and the plants?—who must have a hierarchy as various, as finely graduated as that which we admire among the living and intelligent beings over which we dominate, and which are subordinate to us?—several others of whom may be our companions on earth, as we are of animals which, destitute of sight, hearing, and the sense of smell, of hands and of feet, do not know what we are even when we are doing them good, or harm?— some of whom are perhaps travelling from globe to globe, or, more excellent still, from one solar system to another, more easily than we go from Brest to Madagascar?

" It is because we have neither such organs or such senses as would be necessary to enable our intelligence to communicate with them.

" Thus do the worlds embrace the worlds, and thus are classified intelligent beings all composed of matter which God has more or less richly organized and vivified.

"Such is the probability, and, speaking to vigorous minds which do not shrink from novel suggestions, I will dare to say that such is the truth.

"Man is capable of calculating that it is frequently for his own interest to be useful to other species ; and, which is more valuable, more moral, and more amiable, he is capable of rendering them services for his own satisfaction, and without any other motive than the pleasure which it affords him to do so.

"That which we do for our lower brethren, we, whose intelligence is circumscribed, and whose goodness is very limited, the genii, the angels,—permit me to employ terms in general use to designate beings whom I only divine but do not know,— these beings who are so much more worthy than we, ought to do, and doubtless do, the same for us, with much more beneficence, frequency, and extent on all occasions which concern them.

"We know perfectly well that these intelligences exist, and it is of little importance to us whether they are, as some persons think, formed of a sort of matter, composed of mixed material, or not.   Their quota of intelligence is very brilliant, very remarkable, and evident ; in strong contrast with the properties of inanimate nature, which can be measured, weighed, calculated, and analyzed.

"In order to comprehend what is the action of superhuman intelligences, who can only be known to us by induction, reason, and comparison between what we ourselves are to even the most intelligent animals, which are efficiently served by us, but have not the smallest idea of us, we must pursue analogy farther.   These intelligences are above us, and out of the reach of our senses only because they are endowed with a greater number of senses, and with a more developed and more active life. These beings are more worthy than we are, they have many more organs and faculties, they must therefore, in employing their disposable faculties according to their will, just as we employ ours according to our will, be able to dispose, to work, to manœuvre all inanimate matter, and to do all this among themselves, and also with respect to intelligent beings who are their inferiors, with much more energy, rapidity, enlightenment, and wisdom than we possess, we who nevertheless do it for the beasts subordinate to us. It is, then, in harmony with the laws and the ways of nature that the superior intelligences should have power to render us, when it pleases them, most important services of which we are quite ignorant.

" These unknown protectors who observe us, unperceived, have not our imperfections, and must prize all that is good and beautiful in itself more highly than we can.

" We cannot, therefore, hope to please intelligences of a superior grade by actions which men themselves would condemn as odious. We cannot flatter ourselves with a hope of deceiving them, as we may deceive men, by exterior hypocrisy which only renders crime more despicable. They can behold our most secret actions, they can overhear our soliloquies, they can penetrate our unspoken thoughts. We know not in how many ways they can read what is passing in our hearts, we, whose coarseness, poverty, and unskilfulness limit our means of knowing to touch, sight, hearing, and sometimes analysis and conjecture.

" A celebrated Roman wished to have a house built, which should be open to the sight of the citizens. This house exists, and we inhabit it. Our neighbours are the chiefs and the magistrates of the great republic, who are invested with right and power to punish even our intentions, which are

no mystery to them. And those who most completely penetrate them in their smallest variations, in their lightest inflec-
tions, are the most powerful and the most wise.

"Let us then try, in so far as it depends on us, to keep
in accord with those in comparison with whom we are so
small, and, above all, let us understand our littleness. If it
be very important to us to admit to our complete friendship,
to our entire confidence, to our constant society, none but
men of the first rank of mind and character—if the sweet
competition of affection, zeal, goodness, and capacity which
is always going on between them and us, contributes to our
improvement every day, what shall we not gain by giving
them adjuncts, so to speak, higher and more perfect, who are
not subject, either to our ignoble interests, our passions, or our
errors, and before whom we cannot but blush. They do not
vary, they do not abandon us, they never go away, so soon
as we are alone we find them. They accompany us in travel,
in exile, in prison, in a dungeon; they are always floating
above the peaceful and reflecting brain.

"We can question them, and every time we do so, we may
be sure that they reply. Why should they not do so? Our
absent friends render us such service, but only those of their
number who inspire us with great respect. We can even
experience something of the kind with regard to an imaginary
personage, if he presents himself to our minds as uniting
several good and heroic qualities. How often, in difficult
circumstances and in the midst of the strife of different passages, I have asked myself,—In this case, what would Charles
Grandison have done? What would Quesnay have thought?
What would Turgot have approved of? What advice would
Lavoisier have given me? How shall I gain the approval of
the angels? What line of action will be most conformable
to the order, the laws and the beneficent views of the wise

and majestic King of the universe? For the homage, the
aspirations of a soul eager to do good, and careful to avoid
debasement, may also be raised to God, in salutary and pious
invocation." *

* Pezzani : " *Pluralité des Existences de l'âme,*" pp. 206-210.

CHAPTER THE ELEVENTH.

WHAT IS AN ANIMAL?—THE SOULS OF ANIMALS.—MIGRATIONS
OF SOULS THROUGH THE BODIES OF ANIMALS.

HITHERTO we have left animals out of our plan, although, owing to their immense number, and their influence upon the places which they inhabit, they play a highly important part in the world. It is now time to define the place in nature which our system assigns to them.

Have animals souls? Yes, in our belief, animals have souls; but among animals of all classes the soul is far from being endowed with an equal degree of activity. The activity of the soul is different in the crocodile and in the dog, in the eagle and in the grasshopper. In inferior animals, zoophytes and mollusca, the soul exists only in the condition of a germ. This germ develops itself, and becomes amplified according to the elevation of animals in the series of organic perfection. The sponge and the coral are zoophytes (animal plants). In these beings, the characteristics of animality, although they exist very positively, are obscure and hardly discernible. Voluntary motion, which is the distinctive characteristic formerly demanded for animals, is wanting in them; they are motionless, like the plants. Nevertheless, their nutrition is the same as that of animals, therefore they belong to the animal world. We cannot, however, grant to them a complete soul, but only the germ, the originating point of a soul. Among mollusca (such as marine and land shells, the oyster, the snail, &c.), the motions and the conduct of life are dictated by the will, and that suffices, in our belief, to reveal their possession of a soul, imperfect and very elementary, but certainly existent. Among articulated animals, the insects especially, will, sensibility, acts which denote reason, deliberation, and action resulting from deliberation, are numerous, and recurrent at every moment. They denote intelligence already active.

The smallness of the bodies of these animals is not an argument to be used against the fact of their intelligence. In nature nothing is great, and nothing is little; the monstrous whale and the invisible gnat are equal in the presence of its laws; both one and the other have received as their inheritance the degree of intelligence which is suitable to its need, and it is not by the scale of grandeur that we must measure the degrees of mind among living creatures. Every one is familiar with the prodigies of intelligence performed by associated bees, and by the ants, in their camps and hills. The habits of these two species of insects, which have been studied and expounded only in our age, fill us with wonder, almost with awe. But the bees and the ants do not constitute an exception among the insect class. It is very probable that in the entire class intelligence exists to the same degree as in bees and ants, for we do not see why two species of hymenopterous insects should exclusively possess this privilege, to the exclusion of other species of the same order, and all the other orders of the insect class. The fact is, that the bee has been studied profoundly, because that insect is an object of agricultural industry, and that, in consequence, it was for man's interest to understand its customs. This accounts for the successful surmounting of the difficulties attendant on the study of bees.

We may add, that the observer to whom our knowledge of bees is due, Pierre Huber, of Geneva, who published his fine works at the end of the last century, was blind, and that he was obliged to have recourse for all his observations to the eyes of an illiterate servant, François Burnens, which is a proof that this kind of study was not inordinately difficult.

The habits of other species of insects, still unknown to us, must, according to this, conceal marvels quite as great as those which the Hubers have revealed in the case of bees and ants.

Let us conclude that insects have souls, since intelligence is a faculty of the soul.

We may apply the same reasoning to fishes, reptiles, and birds. In these three classes of animals intelligence progresses towards perfection, the faculty of reason is manifest, and the degree of intelligence seems to march at a progressive rate from the fish to the reptile, and from the reptile to the bird.

In mammiferous animals we observe a degree of advance in intelligence upon the classes of animals we have just named. But, ought we to calculate the degree of intelligence of the different mammifers according to the order in which naturalists have classed these animals? Ought we to say that the strength of intelligence increases as we follow the zoological distribution of Cuvier, that is to say, that it rises from cetacea to carnivora, from carnivora to pachyderms, and from pachyderms to ruminants, &c. ? No, evidently not.

It would be absurd to apportion the intellect of animals to the place which they occupy in zoological classification. We do not possess any certain method by which to form such an appreciation in detail. We remain within the terms of a very acceptable philosophical thesis in advancing our belief, in a general manner, that the intellectual faculties of animals augment from the mollusk to the mammifer, following almost exactly the progressive scale of zoological classification, but to enter into the peculiarities of these orders would be to expose ourselves to certain contradiction. In zoophytes the soul exists as a germ; this germ develops itself and grows in mollusca, and then in articulated creatures and fishes. The soul acquires certain faculties, more or less obscure and dim, when it enters the body of a reptile, and these faculties are manifestly augmented in the body of a bird. The soul is provided with far more perfected faculties when it reaches the body of a mammifer. Such is the general outline of our system.

Let us now follow this system out to the end. In the first pages of this book, we have advanced our theory that the soul of man, at the close of its terrestrial existence, passes into the planetary ether, where it is lodged in the body of a new being, superior to man in intelligence and morality. If this theory be correct, if this migration of the soul of man into the body of the superhuman being be real, analogy obliges us to establish the same relation between the animals, and then between the animals and man.

We firmly believe that a transmigration, a transmission of souls, or of the germs of souls, throughout the entire series of the classes of animals takes place. The germ of a conscious soul which existed in the zoophyte and the mollusk passes, on the death of those beings, into the body of an articulated animal. In this first stage of its journey, the animate germ strengthens and ameliorates itself. The nascent soul acquires some rudimentary faculties. When this rudiment of a conscious soul passes out of the body of an articulated animal into that of a fish or a reptile, it undergoes a new degree of elaboration, and its power increases. When, escaping from the body of the reptile or the fish, it is lodged in the form of the bird it receives other impressions, which become the origin of new perfections. The bird transmits the spiritual element, already much modified and aggrandized, to the mammifer, and then, the soul, having again gained power, and the number of its faculties being augmented, passes into the body of man.

It is probable that in the case of the inferior animals many animate germs are united to form the superior being. For instance, the principal animators of a certain number of little zoophytes, of those beings who live in the waters by millions, may, probably, on quitting the bodies of those beings, be united in one in order to form the soul of a single individual of a superior order.

It would be impossible to specify from what particular mammifer the soul must escape, in order to penetrate a human organism. It would be impossible to decide whether, before reaching man the soul has successively traversed the bodies of several mammifers, of more or less complicated organism; if it has passed through the body of a cetacian, then of a carnivorous creature, then of a quadrumane, the last term of the animal series. A pretension to detail would be a stumbling block to such a system as ours.

To maintain, for instance, that our soul is transmitted to us by the quadrumane, would be incorrect. The intelligence of the quadrumane is inferior to that of many animals more highly placed than he in the zoological scale. Apes, which compose only one family in the very numerous order of quadrumana, are animals of middling intelligence. They are malicious, cunning and gross, and possess only a few features of the human face, and even these belong to but few species. All the other quadrumanes are bestial in the highest degree.

It is not, therefore, in the quadrumana that we must look for the soul to be transmitted to man. But there are animals endowed with intelligence which is both powerful and noble, who would have a title to be accredited with such an honour. Those animals would vary according to the inhabited parts of the earth. In Asia, it may be that the wise, grave, and noble elephant is the depositary of the spiritual principle which is to pass into man. In Africa, the lion, the rhino-ceros, the numerous ruminants which fill the forests may, perhaps, be the ancestors of the human race. In America, the horse, the wild ranger of the pampas, the dog, the faithful friend, the devoted companion of man, everywhere are, it may be, charged with the elaboration of the spiritual principle, which, transmitted to the child, is destined to develop itself, to increase in that child, and become the human soul. A writer in our time has called the dog a candidate for humanity. He little knew how true his definition is.

It will be urged, in objection, that man cannot have received the soul of an animal, because he has not the smallest remembrance of such a genealogy. To this we reply that the faculty of memory is wanting in the animal, or is so fugitive that we may consider it *nil*. The child can therefore receive from the animal only a soul unendowed with memory. And, in fact, the child itself is totally destitute of that faculty. At the moment of his birth he differs not at all from the animal as regards the faculties of his soul. It is not until twelve months have elapsed that the soul makes itself evident in him, and it is afterwards perfected by education. How, therefore, should the child remember an existence prior to his birth? Have we any memory of the time which we passed in our mother's womb?

Let us observe here that the progressive order which we have indicated for the migration of soul through the bodies of different animals, is precisely that which nature followed in the first creation of the organized beings which people our globe. It will be seen in ch. xiv., pp. 196—200, that plants zoophytes, mollusca, and articulated animals are the first living beings which appeared on our globe. After them came the fishes, and then the reptiles. After the reptiles birds, and at a later period mammifers appeared. Thus our system responds to the routine which nature has followed in the creation of plants and animals.

Such is the system which we have conceived as explanatory of the part assigned to animals on our globe. The basis of this system, as will be seen, is the intelligence accorded to animals. We entirely repel the generally held opinion, that beasts do not possess intelligence, and that it is replaced by an obscure faculty which is called instinct. But this theory gives no reason, it merely puts a word in the place of an explanation. By a simple phrase people imagine they resolve one of the great problems of nature. The timid and conventional philosophy of our time has hitherto accommodated itself to this method of eluding great difficulties, but the moment now appears to have come for a deeper study of the problems of nature, and for no longer remaining content with the substitution of words for things.

There was no hesitation in ancient times about according intelligence to animals. Aristotle and Plato expressed themselves quite clearly on this point : they admitted no doubt of the reasoning powers of beasts. The most celebrated modern philosophers, Leibnitz, Locke, and Montaigne ; the most eminent naturalists, Charles Bonnet, Georges Leroy, Dupont de Nemours, Swammerdam, Réaumur, &c., granted intelligence to animals. Charles Bonnet understood the language of many animals, and Dupont de Nemours has

10

given us a translation of the "*Chansons du Rossignol*" and the "*Dictionnaire de la Langue des Corbeaux.*" It is, therefore, difficult to understand how a contrary thesis became prevalent in this age, how Descartes and Buffon, the declared adversaries of animal intelligence, have succeeded in turning the scale in favour of their ideas.

Descartes regarded animals purely as machines, as automata provided with mechanical apparatus. It would be difficult to surpass our great philosopher in absurdity when he treats of these animal machines.* *Equidem bonus dormitat Descartes.* The systematic errors of Buffon on the same subject are well known.

The partizans of Descartes and of Buffon have popularized the idea of instinct put in the place of intelligence, of the word replacing the thing. But, in simple truth, what difference is there between intelligence and instinct? None. These two words only represent two different degrees of the same faculty. Instinct is simply a weaker degree of intelligence. If we read the writings of naturalists of this country who have studied the question, Frederick Cuvier (brother to George Cuvier), and Flourens,† who has but commented upon Frederick Cuvier's book on the more profound work of a learned contemporary writer, M. Fée of Strasbourg,‡ we shall easily find that no fundamental distinction between intelligence and

* This question is specially considered in Descartes' "*Discours sur la Méthode.*"

† "*De l'Instinct et de l'Intelligence des Animaux,*" Paris, 1861.

‡ "*Etudes Philosophiques sur l'Instinct et l'Intelligence des Animaux,*" Strasbourg, 1853.

instinct can be established, and that the whole secret of our philosophers and naturalists consists in calling the intelligence of animals, which is weaker than ours, *instinct.*

It is, then, the pride of mankind which has attempted to place a barrier, which in reality has no existence, between us and the animal. The intelligence of the animal is less de-veloped than that of the man, because his wants are fewer, his organs are less highly finished, and because the sphere of his activity is more limited, but that is all. And sometimes, even, we must not forget that the animal exceeds the man in intelligence. Look at the rude and brutal waggoner, beside his good and docile horse, which he mercilessly beats and abuses, while his faithful auxiliary fulfils his task with patient exactness, and say, is it not the master who is the brute, and the animal who is the intelligent being? In kindness—that sweet emanation of the soul—animals often excel men. Every one knows the horrid story of the man who carried his dog to a river to drown him, but who fell into the water himself, and was on the point of drowning. The faithful companion whom he had flung in to die was there; he swam to his master, and dragged him into safety. Then the dog's master, making his footing sure this time, seized the creature who had just rescued him, and drowned him.

According to our system, the human soul comes from an animal belonging to the superior orders. After having under-gone, in the body of this animal, a suitable degree of perfect-ing and elaboration, it incarnates itself in the body of a newly-born child of the human race.

We said, in a former chapter, "Death is not a termination, but a change; we do not die, we experience a metamorphosis." We must add to this, "Birth is not a beginning, it is a consequence. To be born is not to begin, it is to continue a prior existence."

There is not, therefore, properly speaking, either birth or death for the human species; there is only a continuous succession of existences, extending from the visible world through space, and connecting each with those worlds which are hidden from our view.

CHAPTER THE TWELFTH.

WHAT IS THE PLANT?—THE PLANT IS SENSIBLE.—HOW DIFFI-
CULT IT IS TO DISTINGUISH PLANTS FROM ANIMALS.—THE
GENERAL CHAIN OF LIVING BEINGS.

LINNÆUS has said, "The plant lives; the animal lives and feels; man lives, feels, and thinks."
This aphorism represented the state of science
in the times of Linnæus. But since the year
1778, that is to say, since the death of the great botanist,
Upsal, natural science has progressed, botany and zoology
have been enriched with innumerable facts and fundamental
discoveries, so that the Linnæan formula no longer represents the present condition of the sciences of organization.
We believe that the following proposition may be truthfully
substituted: "The plant lives and feels; the animal and
man live, feel, and think."

To accord sensibility to plants, is to transgress the classic
laws of natural history, so that the considerations and facts
which appear to us to justify this proposition ought to be
most carefully stated.

1. The plant feels the sensations of pleasure and pain.
Cold, for instance, impresses it painfully; it may be seen to
contract itself, as if shivering, under the influence of a sudden

or excessive fall of the temperature. An abnormal excess of temperature evidently causes it to suffer; when the heat is very great, leaves may be observed to hang down on the stems, curl up, and appear to wither; when the cool of the evening comes, the leaves rise up again, and the plant resumes it appearance of placid health. Drought also occasions manifest suffering to plants. Those who study nature with loving attention know that when, after a long period of drought, a plant is watered it exhibits signs of pleasure. On the other hand, a wounded plant, one from which a branch has been cut, appears to experience pain. A pathological liquid exudes from the wound, like the blood from a hurt animal; the plant is sick, and will die, if it do not receive the necessary succour. Thus persons who love plants will not cut flowers off their stems, they prefer to inhale their perfume, and contemplate their brilliant colours, on the stalk, without inflicting a painful mutilation upon the beautiful creatures which they admire.

The sensitive plant, if touched by the fingers, or even struck by a current of harsh air, folds up its leaves, and contracts itself. The botanist, Desfontaines, saw a sensitive plant, which he was bringing home in a carriage, contract its leaves while the vehicle was in motion, and expand them when it stopped, thus affording a proof that the movement distressed the plant. A drop of acid, or acrid liquid, placed on a leaf of a sensitive plant, will occasion a similar constriction. All vegetables present an analogous phenomenon. Their tissues contract when brought in contact with irritant substances. By rubbing the tips of a lettuce, the juice may be made to exude.

Vegetable sensibility exists by the same right as animal sensibility, since electricity kills plants as it kills animals, since narcotic poisons kill or stupefy plants as they kill and stupefy animals. One can narcotize a plant by watering it with opium dissolved in water, and MM. Gopport and Macaire have discovered that hydrocyanic acid kills plants as rapidly as animals.

2. Plants sleep at night. During the day they develop their vital activity, and when the night comes, or when they are in darkness, their leaves assume another position, that of repose; they fold themselves up. In the day-time, the upper surface of the leaf is turned to the sky, and the under surface towards the earth; this under surface, pierced with holes, or *stomata*, is the part through which absorption and exhalation take place, while the upper surface, in which there are no such openings, is only a sort of screen for the protection of the absorbing surface. It is therefore easy to understand that the horizontal attitude of the leaves is a position of vital activity, and that the refolding of those leaves during the night indicates a state of repose. It is precisely the same case with ourselves, when during the night we indulge our muscles, kept on the stretch during the day, with complete relaxation.

The *sleep of plants*, said to have been discovered by Linnæus, and which was certainly described for the first time in one of Upsal's *Thèses de Botanique*, and thoroughly elucidated

by Linnæus, is not a phenomenon limited to certain families
of plants.   There are very few vegetables which, during the
night, or in darkness, do not fold their leaves, and which do
not present a different appearance by day and by night.   The
Sensitive is the classic plant selected for its exhibition of this
phenomenon in all its intensity ; but this small leguminous
creature only presents us with an exaggeration of a fact
which exists in a lesser degree among almost all vegetables
with light leaves.   We may quote the following passage from
a former work on the subject of this phenomenon.

" The sleep of plants vaguely resembles that of animals. It
is a remarkable circumstance that the slumbering leaf appears
to wish to return to the epoch of its infancy.   It folds itself
almost as it was when in the bud, before it burst out, as it
was in the lethargic sleep of winter, sheltered beneath its
strong scales, or wrapped up in its warm down.   One would
think that the plant was trying every night to resume the
position which it occupied in its early time, just as the sleep-
ing animal gathers himself together, and folds his limbs as
they were folded in his mother's womb."*

Is it possible to deny the possession of sensibility to creatures which give us alternate sign of repose and of activity,
and who have the power of accommodating themselves to
various external impressions?   Fatigue cannot possibly be
anything but the consequence of the experience of an impression.

3. Numerous physiological functions are fulfilled by plants
as well as by animals ; and when we consider the number and

* " *Histoire des Plantes*," Paris, p. 111.

variety of these functions, it is difficult to understand how, if animals be, as the common consent of mankind declares them, possessed of sensibility, plants can be destitute of it. An ancient philosopher defined plants as *animals with roots*. We shall see, on examining the variety of functions performed by vegetables, whether this philosopher was not a far-seeing, wise man.

It would be difficult to name any function with which the animal is invested that the vegetable does not possess in a less degree. *Respiration*, for instance, is equally a property of plants and of animals. Among the latter, respiration consists in the absorption of the oxygen of the air and the emission of carbonic acid gas and watery vapour; among plants it consists in the emission of carbonic acid gas and watery vapour during the night, and during the day, under the influence of sunlight, of the emission of oxygen proceeding from the decomposition of carbonic acid. The function is evidently of the same nature in both the natural kingdoms.

Exhalation is a function common to vegetables and to animals. By the stomata of leaves, as by the pores of the skin of animals, watery vapour and various gases, according to the vital phenomena which take place in the interior of the tissues, are constantly being disengaged.

Absorption takes place in both kingdoms. If you pour water on the lower surface of a leaf, you will see that it will be absorbed with great rapidity. Sprinkle a bouquet of flowers with water, and the freshness of the withered blossoms will revive. Absorption is even more active in vegetable than in animal tissues.

The circulation of liquids in the interior of plants is accomplished by a complicated system of channels and vessels of every order and of every calibre, absorbent vessels, exhalant vessels.

Nothing is more varied than the disposition of these channels in the interior of plants, and their multiplicity indicates a circulatory function as complicated as that of animals.

It is then evident that vegetables have the same physiological functions as animals, but as yet we know those functions very imperfectly. It is very strange that while animal physiology is so far advanced in our day, vegetable physiology is almost in its infancy. We know very well how the digestion of food takes place in man and animals, we know how our blood circulates in a double system of vessels, called arteries and veins, and we know the central organ, the heart, through which the two liquids are carried by this double system. We see and we touch the organs of sensation and motion, that is to say, the nerves. More than this, we distinguish the nerves which produce sensation from those which rule motion. We know that the centre of nervous action in man and animals is double; that its seat is equally in the brain and in the spinal marrow.

Briefly, science has shed its brightest light on all the functions belonging to animal organization, while vegetable physiology remains in obscurity. Notwithstanding the labours of naturalists within the last two centuries, we cannot explain the life of plants with certainty. We cannot positively state how the sap, which is vegetable blood, circulates

in their channels. We do not even know with precision
whether a tree grows from the outside to the inside, or from
the inside to the outside. All the physiological functions in
the vegetable kingdom are hidden from us by a thick veil,
and it is only by lifting a corner of it with great difficulty
that we can catch a few gleams of light through the obscurity.
Nevertheless, all unexplained though they be as yet, physiological functions do exist in plants. Considering these
numerous functions, it appears entirely impossible that plants
should not have received the gift of sensibility. It is difficult
to believe, as Linnæus would have us believe, that they possess life, and nothing more.

We shall be told that vegetables have no nerves, and that
in the absence of every organ of sensation, we cannot accord
them the faculty of sensibility. But, we reply, that the imperfect state of vegetable anatomy and physiology forbids us
to come to any conclusion touching the existence or the
absence of nerves in plants. We are convinced that these
organs exist, but that botanists do not know how to discern
them, or have no means of distinguishing between them and
other organs.

4. The manner of multiplication and reproduction among
plants and animals is so analogous, that it seems impossible,
when we consider this extraordinary resemblance in the most
important functions, to refuse sensibility to plants, and accord
it to animals.

Let us consider the various modes of reproduction proper
to vegetables. Reproduction, or rather the fecundation which

precedes it, is executed in certain vegetables, by means of
an apparatus of the same typical form as that of the animal
kingdom. It is composed of a male organ, the stamen,
which contains the impregnating dust, pollen, and of a female
organ, the ovary, supported by a stalk, the pistil. The pollen
impregnates the ovula contained in the grains of pollen in the
ovary, as the seed of the male impregnates the ovula contained in the egg of the animal. In both cases the fruit of
the impregnation develops itself afterwards with the aid of
warmth and time. The vegetable egg grows and ripens, just
as the animal egg grows and ripens.

We may add that the analogy between the modes of reproduction, in the two kingdoms, animal and vegetable, does
not limit itself to these conditions of likeness; we may observe
resemblances in the specialities of the function. Particular
vitality, a turgid state of the tissues, accompanied by elevation of the local temperature, occur in the case of certain
plants at the moment of impregnation, especially in the
species of the family of Aroïdes. On placing a thermometer,
at that time, in the great floral covering of the Arums, an
excess of from 1° to 2° on the temperature of the surrounding
air will be denoted, an extraordinary fact in vegetable life,
for vegetables are always colder than the external air. How
can we believe that the plant in which this excitement takes
place has no feeling of its own condition? The plant, like
the animal, has its seasons of love, can it be that it has no
consciousness of them? Are we to believe that the plant
which becomes warm, in which life rises at the moment of

impregnation, has no more sensation than a stone? Such is not our opinion. We cannot understand life without sensibility—the one appears to us to be the indication of the other.

The analogy between the plant and the animal in their functions of reproduction is nowhere more evident or more curious than in a vegetable production which abounds in the waters of the Rhône, and has received the name of *Vallisneria spiralis.* In this plant the male and female organs are placed on different branches of the same plant. The female flowers are fixed to the ground by long, twisted, spiral stalks. But, when seeding time comes, the spirals of the stems unroll themselves, and the female flowers come up to the surface of the water and spread themselves out. The male flowers, not being placed like the female on elastic stems, cannot come up to the surface of the water. What do they do? They burst through their covering, and float around their females on the surface of the water. After that the current carries away the detached male flowers; and the female stem folds itself up again, and sinks to the bottom of the river, there to ripen its impregnated ovules.

The function of reproduction in plants is rich in conclusions in support of our thesis. The plants called phanerogamous are not reproduced only by impregnation by means of the visible sexual organs, the pistil and the stamen, they are also multiplied by grafts, buds, and cuttings. Cryptogamous plants, which have no sexual organs, are multiplied either by effects which detach themselves from the individual plant at a certain period of its vegetation as we see in the case of fungi, algæ, mushrooms, &c., or by fragments of the individual itself, which, being thrown into the ground, germinate and multiply themselves.

Animals, in their several classes, represent all these modes of reproduction ; there is not one which does not exist among them. Animals are not reproduced by eggs only, either interior or exterior, and by living young ones, they are equally multiplied, like vegetables, by offsets, by cuttings, and by ingraftment.

Multiplication by offsets may be observed in the fresh-water polype. Little buds which grow and lengthen come out of the body of this animal. While the bud is lengthening, he throws off other and smaller offsets, which throw off still smaller ones. All these are so many little polypes, which derive their nourishment from the principal polype. Having attained a certain size, these offsets separate themselves from the primitive individual, and constitute so many new polypes. Coral multiplies itself in the same manner. From the principal branch spring secondary branches which have originated in a bud or shoot, and these branches, inserting themselves into the chief stem, form new individuals. Thus the exterior aspect of the coral resembles a ramified tree rather than an animal.

Madrepores, another kind of zoophytes, resemble trees so closely, that for centuries they were supposed to be marine plants ; they too, like coral, are reproduced by offsets.

Multiplication by cuttings is seen in the fresh-water

polype. Take a fresh-water polype, and cut it into as many fragments as you choose. Each of these fragments, left to itself, will become a polype. These new individuals may be in their turn cut into pieces, which will produce as many new ones. This is multiplication by cuttings, exactly similar to the process in plants, so that the generation of fresh-water polypes does not differ from that of one of our fruit-trees. It is not only the entire polype which, thus cut to fragments, furnishes a new polype ; the skin of this animal can also produce one new individual or several. Is not this a vegetable ingraftment ?

A similar generation by ingraftment is to be observed in another instance, in the case of the fresh-water polype. Take different portions of the same polype, or those of different polypes, and join them at the ends, or lay them upon one another, and you will combine them so closely that they reciprocally nourish each other, and ultimately form only one individual. Here is vegetable ingraftment carried out in an animal.

5. Other points of resemblance exist between plants and animals. If they are not generally remarked, it is because the authors of the classics of natural history do not direct the attention of the reader to these facts. We are about to supplement their silence, and to bring the analogies between the two natural kingdoms into view.

Firstly, there exists in both a common and equally astonishing fecundity. Among plants, as among animals, one individual can give birth to thousands of individuals like him self.   Vegetables are even more fertile than the superior animals.   Trees produce every year, and sometimes for a century.   Mammiferous animals, birds, and reptiles produce infinitely less than trees; their pregnancy is less frequent, and takes place during a certain period in the life of the animal only.   The elm produces every year more than 300,000 seeds, and this may continue for a hundred years. Fish and insects approach most nearly to trees in fecundity. A tench spawns 10,000 eggs yearly, a carp 20,000.   Among insects, a female bee produces from 40,000 to 50,000 eggs. To these animals we may compare, among vegetables, the poppy, the fern, the mustard plant, which produce incalculable quantities of seeds.   We must not forget, besides, that vegetables multiply themselves in many ways, whereas each animal possesses but one mode of reproduction.

What we wish to establish, what is evident, is that among both animals and plants fecundity is equal, and equally prodigious.   From the point of view of this analogy, we may also quote the size of the species, which is extremely variable in both kingdoms, because both produce at the same time giant species and dwarf species.   Among animals, there are some of monstrous size, such as the whale, the cachalot, and the elephant, such as the gigantic reptiles of the ancient world, the ichthyosaurus, which was longer than the whale, the megalosaurus and the iguanadon, which were as large as the elephant.

To these colossi of the animal kingdom, we may oppose the colossi of the vegetable kingdom; the monstrous baobab gourd, which covers hundreds of square yards with its shade, the elm, whose trunk may grow to the size of a whale's girth, the *Eucalyptus globulus*, an Australian tree which is being acclimatized in Algeria and in the south of France, the *Sequioæa gigantea*, the giant of Californian forests.

If the two kingdoms of nature have their colossi, they have also their dwarfs, and their infinitely little. There are cryptogamic vegetables which are only to be seen with the microscope, and there are animalculæ equally invisible to the naked eye. If the animal kingdom can show, in its scale of size, the whale, and the microscopic *acarus*, the vegetable kingdom possesses a similar decreasing scale from the baobab to the lichens.

The same places are inhabited or resorted to by plants and animals. Both live on the same soil, as if for mutual aid. The two kingdoms combine at all points of the globe. We might name a number of places in which certain plants and certain animals thrive together. The chamois and the maple tree love the same mountains, the same high places; the truffle and the earth-worm dwell in the same underground region; the birch and the hare are found in the same place; the water-lily grows in the same fresh water with the aquatic worm; and the cod and the algæ prosper in the same submarine depths.

All vegetables and animals have an original country, but they can be acclimatized under other skies by human industry and skill. The chestnut-tree and the Indian cock, the

11

peach-tree and the turkey, transported to Europe, has each forgotten its native land.

Among both animals and plants there are amphibious creatures. The frog, and the other batrachians, live, like the reeds, on the earth and in the water. Both animals and plants can live as parasites. The animal world has the flea, the louse, the acarus; the vegetable world has its lichens, and its mushrooms.

Thus, equal fecundity, similar variety in the scale of size, analogy in habitation, which implies ideality of organization, possibility of transplantation and of acclimatization out of their original country, possibility of amphibious existence, parasitical life, all general conditions which suppose a great analogy of organization; we establish all these things in drawing the parallel between plants and animals. How, then, if we grant sensibility to one of these kingdoms, can we deny it to the other?

6. Plants, like animals, have their maladies. We do not now allude to maladies caused by parasites, like the sickness of the vine, due to the *oïdium Tuckeri*, the sickness of the petals, caused by other small mushrooms, that of the rose-tree, the olive-tree, of corn, &c., produced by parasitical cryptogams, which fix themselves on the plant, and change the normal course of its life; we speak of morbid affections, properly so called. The pathological condition and its consequences exist in the plant as in the animal. Stoppage, or febrile and abnormal acceleration of the sap in the vegetable, answer to stagnation of the blood, or its acceleration during fever, in the

animal; various excrescences of the bark, analogous to affections of the skin; the abortion of certain organs, and the capricious development of others; the secretion of pathological liquids which flow outside. This is a brief catalogue of the maladies to which trees, shrubs, and herbaceous vegetables are subject. A plant which passes too quickly and too often from intense cold to extreme heat, soon becomes ill, and necessarily perishes, like an animal exposed to those dangerous alterations. A shrub left in a current of cold air could no more live than an animal if kept in a similar place. In a word, the plant exhibits health or sickness, according to its conditions of existence. How can we admit that the being in which such changes take place, can be merely the passive subject of them, that it experiences neither pain nor pleasure in passing from health to sickness, or from sickness to health?

7. Sicknesses, or other causes, produce anomalies of form, or irregularities of structure in plants, as in animals. Just as in the animal kingdom *monstrosities* exist, there are monstrosities in the vegetable kingdom. The science which occupies itself with monstrosities in animals is called *teratology.* Geoffrey St. Hilaire has made some most interesting studies of the causes of the productions of monsters in the different classes of animals; but it has been perceived of late that an analogous science must be created, for the explanation of monstrosities proper to the vegetable kingdom, and Moquin Tandon has published a book upon *vegetable teratology.*

8. Old age and death are common to both plants and animals. Plants, after having survived the various mala-

dies which threaten them, do not escape a slow old age, and
death necessarily follows. With time, their vessels become
hardened, their size becomes reduced, they can no longer give
passage to the sap, or other liquids which ought to go through
them. Liquids are not aspired with the same regularity, they
no longer transude through the vegetable tissue with the
same precision; they remain stagnant in the vessels, become
corrupt there, and transfer their decomposition to the vessels
which enclose them. Thenceforth the vital functions cease
to be performed, and the plant dies. Things happen in a
like manner among animals. The thickening of the vessels,
the decrease of their power bring on the condition of old age,
in which the functions are disturbed and slackened; then
comes death, the inevitable end of all, in each kingdom of
nature.

Thus, when we compare animals and plants, and especially
when we consider the inferior beings in both kingdoms, it is
impossible to establish a precise line of demarcation between
them. The characteristics by which the old naturalists defined
the distinction between plants and animals, are now acknowledged to be without meaning, and this distinction becomes
more and more difficult in proportion as we make progress in
our knowledge of these creatures. Voluntary motion was regarded as the principal distinctive characteristic between the
two kingdoms of nature; but at the present day this characteristic can no longer be invoked. Elementary works on
botany now tell us about the fly-catching plant, which catches
the insect that crawls over its leaves, exactly as a spider

catches flies, and about the oscillating plant, whose leaves are endowed by voluntary motion, more distinct than that belonging to many animals.

Apart from these examples, drawn from classical works, we would ask what becomes of the argument for the immobility of plants, considered as a distinctive characteristic of the vegetable kingdom, when we see that zoophytes are fixed to the earth, and when, on the other hand, we see certain young plants, or their germs, such as the germs of algæ, mosses, and ferns, possessing the faculty of motion.

The *spores*, or reproductive organs of algæ, and the *impregnating corpuscles* of the mosses and ferns, possess the fundamental characteristics of animality, that is to say, they are provided with locomotive organs, and they execute movements which appear to be voluntary. Those singular creatures are seen to go and come in the interior of liquids, to endeavour to penetrate into cavities, to withdraw, return, and definitively introduce themselves with an apparent effort.

The German botanists regard these vegetable germs as belonging to the animal kingdom. Considering that only animals have the organs of motion, and that the spores of algæ and the impregnating corpuscles of mosses and ferns are provided with organs of motion, they do not hesitate to declare that in the commencement of their life, algæ, mosses, and ferns are in truth animals, which become plants when they fix themselves, and begin to germinate. French botanists have not yet ventured to adopt that view ; they are content to call the movable impregnating corpuscles of algæ, mosses, and ferns, *antherozoïdes,* but they do not dare to pronounce upon their animality. M. Pouchet says, in his work *L'Univers,* page 444 :

"Motion manifests itself spontaneously with extraordinary intensity in the *animalculæ* of several plants, which have spinal organs for this purpose, hairs by means of which they swim about in the liquid which contains them.

"Some of these, real animalcule plants, have the shape of eels, and move themselves by means of two long filaments attached to their heads ; others exactly resemble the tadpoles of frogs, and jump about in the cells of the mosses.

"Nevertheless, it is such creatures as these, whose locomotive organs are so plainly to be discerned, and which we can see, under the microscope, jumping about as nimbly as our acrobats, that certain botanists persist in considering, on theory alone, as motionless and insensible. Some philosophers certainly possess eyes, that they may not see !"

There are these germs of plants, and young plants which move, and on the other hand, almost all the adult zoophytes, sponges, corals, madrepores, sea-stars, byssus, &c., &c., to which we may add several mollusca (all those in shells), are fixed to the earth. In these cases we must take the plant for the animal, and the animal for the plant, if we positively hold by voluntary motion as an absolute distinction between animals and plants.

On the borders of the two kingdoms,—when we consider zoophytes in the animal, and cryptogams in the vegetable kingdom,—there is no longer, so to speak, either animal or plant ; the two seem to be confounded, and fused together.

If, before the discovery of the fresh-water polype, that

living creature had been presented to a naturalist, he would have felt puzzled how to class it. Seeing it multiplying itself by buds, by offshoots, by engraftment, he would doubtless have declared that this organized being was a plant. But if he had been made to remark that this same creature fed on living prey, which it seized and swallowed, that it had long and flexible arms, of which it formed a kind of net for the purpose of seizing this prey, which it conveyed into the interior of a digestive tube, our naturalist would have made haste to place the polype in the ranks of the animals. He would have been asked to observe that the polype may be turned inside out, like a glove, so that his interior skin becomes his exterior skin, and that, thus turned inside out, he lives, grows, and multiplies himself, precisely as he does before this curious reversal. Our naturalist, much embarrassed in the presence of so unheard of a fact, would doubtless immediately have begun to seek some intermediate kingdom between the animal and the vegetable, to which he might relegate this paradoxical being, which could not, with absolute certainty, be classed either with plants, or with animals.

The fact is, classifications are products of human science, nature knows nothing about them. We descend, by insensible degrees, from one kingdom to the other; we go from the man to the polype, and from the polype to the rose tree, by infinite gradations, and, on the confines of the two kingdoms, there is a whole series of creatures which it is very difficult to range under any system. For how long did naturalists hesitate before they regarded infusoria, coral, sponges, star-fish, gorgons, sea-anemones, and madrepores as animals? Even in the present day micrographers who study the microscopic beings proper to vegetable and animal infusions, such as the monads, polypoid worms, and numerous others, find the utmost difficulty in assigning these creatures to such or such a kingdom, and they sometimes decide rather arbitrarily upon placing them among animals or plants.

From all the considerations, all the facts which we have just advanced, we conclude that the sensibility of plants is not to be contested, since no one can think of denying that privilege to certain zoophytes which can with difficulty be distinguished from vegetables.

We see an imposing tree, a stately oak with sturdy branches, growing on the sea coast. Not far off, on the sand of the shore, lies a star-fish flung there by the waves. A few yards below, on the surface of the water, floats a sponge, a branch of coral, a madrepore. When the icy wind blows, when the hurricane lifts the angry waves, which is it, the animal or the plant that will manifest sensibility to the tempest? The sponge, the coral, the madrepore will remain as indifferent to the fury of the elements as the rock in which they are incrusted, or as the pebble on which the star-fish stretches out its four motionless arms. But, the majestic oak will shudder at every gust of the tempest; he will bend his branches and shut up his leaves to shelter himself from the icy blast or the furious storm; and a mere glance at his attitude will indicate to you that an abnormal perturbation reigns in the atmosphere. Would you seriously say, in that case, that the vegetable feels nothing, and that the animal is sensible? Would you not, on the contrary, be inclined to declare that the tree is the sentient being, and that the star-fish, the sponge, the madrepore, are the creatures which are destitute of feeling?

Pause beside still water and seek for the polype or fresh-water hydra which we have just mentioned. You will find it difficult to disentangle this zoophyte from the reeds and willows which surround it. You will find, at length, a kind of membranous tube, a few centimetres in length. Is that the polype you were looking for? Is it not rather the stubble of some reed or grass plant? This living twig, with nothing to distinguish it in appearance from a herbaceous plant, is constantly fixed in the same place, like an aquatic vegetable. It makes some faint movements, consisting simply of the open-ing and shutting of the orifice of the tube, which solely con-stitutes its being. Sometimes it lengthens, sometimes it con-tracts itself, by stretching out membranous arms, as fine as threads, by means of which it seizes and drags towards it the water insects which chance to pass near it. This is the one single characteristic of its animality. At this rate, an aërial plant, the *fly-catcher,* would be just as much an animal as our polype, since it catches the insects which venture to crawl upon its leaves.

At the bottom of the sea there is a very curious zoophyte, the *actinium,* or sea-anemone. For a long time this creature was confounded with the plants, and held to be an ocean

flower. Those who admire the beautiful, bright-coloured
actinia, in the Garden of Acclimatization, in Paris, who look
at them, waving on their flexible stem, shaking the coloured
appendages and fringes which adorn their heads, find it hard
to regard these charming queens of the waters otherwise than
as real flowers. And, in fact, for ages, the *sea-anemones* were
held to be marine plants.

In the last century, coral was held to be a marine
shrub, and it was even believed that the flowers of the coral
had been discovered. An academician of Paris, Count de
Marsigli, created a European reputation for himself by this
supposed discovery. Peyssonnel, a Provençal naturalist,
found the utmost difficulty in opposing this idea, and in
establishing the fact that these supposed flowers of the coral
were in reality young corals. He had the whole Academy of
Sciences against him; and his opposition to the ideas of the
Academy brought him into such disgrace, that he was obliged
to leave France and to go to the Antilles, where he died in
obscurity as a doctor of medicine. And all this because he
maintained that coral is not a plant, and does not produce
flowers !

The famous Genevese naturalist, Charles Bonnet, antici-
pating the knowledge of our day by more than a century,
has given a most interesting form to the parallel between
animals and plants, in his work entitled *Contemplation de la
Nature.* We cannot resist the pleasure of quoting the following
passage, in which Charles Bonnet shows in a striking manner
what are the difficulties in the way of distinguishing the

plant from the animal, and how those difficulties are disposed of by those who dispute the sensibility of plants:—

"Everything is graduated in nature," says Charles Bonnet, "and, in refusing to admit that plants are sentient, we force nature to make a jump without any assignable reason.

"We observe that feeling decreases by degrees from man to the nettle, and to the mussel, and we persuade ourselves that it stops there, because we regard these animals as the least perfect. But there are, perhaps, many degrees between the feeling of the mole and of the plant. There are, perhaps, still more between the most and the least sensible of the plants. The gradations, which we observe, ought to persuade us to this philosophy; the new beauty which it adds to the system of the world, and the pleasure to be derived from the multiplication of sentient creatures ought to contribute to induce us to admit it. I willingly admit that this philosophy is much to my taste. I love to think that those flowers which adorn our fields and our gardens with a brightness constantly renewed, those fruit trees which are so pleasant to our eyes and our palate; those majestic trees that compose the vast forests, which time seems to have respected, are so many sentient creatures partaking after their fashion in the sweetness of existence.

"Plants offer some facts to our observation which seem to indicate that they possess feeling, but we are not likely to perceive those facts, because of the strong persuasion that they are insensible, which has prevailed among us for so long. We ought to agree to consider the question *tabula rasa*, and to subject plants to a new, impartial, and unprejudiced examination. An inhabitant of the moon, possessed of intellectual faculties like ours, but without any preconceived ideas about the insensibility of plants, would be the philosopher whom we require. Let us imagine such an observer engaged

in studying the productions of our earth, and, after
having given his attention to the polypes and other insects
multiplied by the process of grafting, passing on to the contemplation of vegetables. He would, doubtless, take them
at the period of their birth. With this view, he would sow
seed of various species, and he would carefully watch their
germination. Let us suppose that some of those seeds have
been reversed in the sowing, the sprouting part turned downwards, the stem upwards; and the observer has the skill to
distinguish one end of the seed from the other, and knows
their functions. After some days, he will remark that the
seed has grown into this reversed position, that the stem is
turned upward, and the sprouting portion downward. He
will feel no surprise; he will attribute a circumstance which
is so hurtful to the life of the plant, to the mistake he has
made in sowing the seed. But, continuing to observe, he
will see the sprout and the stem each bending itself in the
opposite direction, and trying to attain the right position.
This change of direction will strike him as very remarkable,
and he will begin to suspect that the organized being which
he is studying is endowed with a certain amount of discernment. Too prudent, however, to pronounce upon these early
indications, he will suspend his judgment and pursue his in-
vestigations. The plants whose germination our physicist
has been observing, have been raised in the neighbourhood
of a hedge. Thus favoured, and carefully cultivated, they
have made great progress in a very short time. The soil
which surrounds them at some distance is of two opposite
qualities. That on the right of the plants is rich, damp,
and spongy; that on the left is dry, hard, and gravelly.
Our observer remarks that the roots, after having begun
by extending equally on both sides, have changed their
direction, and have spread out towards the rich and humid
soil; over which they are stretching, and thus threatening

to deprive the plants already there of their due share of nourishment. To prevent this inconvenience, he digs a ditch between the plants which he is observing and those they threaten to starve, and now he thinks he has provided against everything. But the plants, which he believes he has governed, disconcert all his precautions by extending their roots downwards, under the ditch, and gaining the other side.

"Surprised at this, he uncovers one of these roots, but without exposing it to heat, and holds a sponge steeped in water towards it. The root turns itself to the sponge, and when he changes its position, the root accommodates itself to each alteration.

"While our philosopher is meditating profoundly upon these facts, other facts equally remarkable present themselves almost simultaneously. He observes that all these plants have leaned away from the hedge, and are bending forward as though to present every portion of their bodies to the beneficent smiles of the sun. He sees that all the leaves are so turned that their upper surface is exposed to the sun, or to the fresh air, and that the lower surface is directed towards the hedge, or the ground. Former experience will have taught him that the upper surface of leaves serves chiefly as a defence for the lower surface, and that the latter is principally destined to pump up the moisture rising from the earth, and provide for the evacuation of what is superfluous. The direction of the leaves which he notices appears quite in harmony with his experiences. He studies this portion of the plant with increased attention.

"He remarks that the leaves of some species seem to follow the movements of the sun, so that in the morning they turn to the east, in the evening to the west. He sees that some leaves close themselves against the sun, others against the dew. He observes an analogous movement in certain flowers.

Afterwards, he observes that no matter what the direction of the plants relative to the horizon has been, the direction of the leaves is always that which he has at first noticed, he bethinks him of changing this direction, and of placing the leaves in a position exactly contrary to their natural one. He has already had recourse to similar means in order to assure himself of the instinct of animals, and to ascertain its bearings. With this view he bends perpendicular plants towards the horizon, and keeps them in that position. Thus, the direction of the leaves is absolutely changed ; the upper surface, which previously turned to the sun or to the fresh air, now looks towards the earth or the interior of the plant, and the lower surface, which formerly looked towards the earth or the interior of the plant, now turns to the sun, or the fresh air. But very soon all these leaves begin to move, they turn on their stem as on a pivot, and in an hour they will have resumed their former position. Our observer, wishing to assure himself whether leaves and branches when detached and plunged into water will preserve the inclinations which they manifest when upon the plant of which they formed a portion, subjects them to an experiment whose results leave him no doubt of the fact.

" He places wet sponges under the leaves, and he sees the leaves turn towards the sponges and endeavour to adhere to them by their lower surfaces. He also observes that certain plants, which he has shut up in his cabinet and in a cellar, have turned towards the window, or the grating respectively.

" Finally, the phenomena of the Sensitive Plant, its varied movements, the promptitude with which it contracts when touched, form the interesting subject which terminates his researches.

" Thus plentifully supplied with facts which all seem to tend to the support of belief in the sensibility of plants, which side will our philosopher take ? Will he surrender to these proofs? Will he suspend his judgment? I think he will take the first part."*

Charles Bonnet believes, in short, that the plant, as well as the animal, is endowed with sensibility.

According to the system which we have developed, the animal is possessed of a soul, which is still very imperfect, and endowed only with faculties corresponding to its needs. But, since the animal, in addition to the sensibility enjoyed by the plant, possesses intelligence also, we must conclude from thence that the plant has not a soul, properly so called, but only the rudiment, the commencement, in other words, the *germ* of a soul.

We know that the sun has the privilege of giving birth to organic life upon our globe, his rays have power to produce the formation of living tissues, plants or zoophytes, when they fall upon the earth or the waters, and we may draw this conclusion from all that has gone before, that the sun sends down upon the earth *animated germs* under the form of his rays, which emanate from the spiritualized creatures who dwell in the king-star.

Thus our system of nature completes itself; thus, thanks to solar radiation, the two ends of the immense chain of organized beings whose place and part in the vast theatre of the worlds we have attempted to define are united. Life begins in the waters, its first appearance is in plants and zoophytes; for these two classes of living creatures obey the same laws, and

---

* " *Contemplation de la Nature (Œuvres d'Histoire Naturelle de Charles Bonnet.*") Neuchâtel, 1781.

appear to have the same origin. The sun, by sending his vivifying rays upon theearth, produces the for mation of plants and zoophytes, which are the points of departure of organization. The *animated germ* deposited by the sun in plants and zoophytes grows, passes from the zoophyte to the mollusc, or articulated animal, and then undergoes a further development, by passing from the mollusc or articulated animal to the fish. This germ of a soul thus becomes a rudimentary soul, provided with certain faculties. In the zoophyte and the mollusc it had only sensibility; in the fish, and then in the reptile, and the bird, it has attention and judgment. The faculties are augmented in proportion as the animal mounts higher in the organic scale. Arrived at its summit, the human being, the soul is in possession of all its faculties, and especially of memory, which during the animal stages of the ascent is obscure and uncertain.

To accord sensibility to plants permits us to unite all the creatures of the living creation, and thus to complete our general system of terrestrial nature.

CHAPTER THE THIRTEENTH.

DOES MAN EXIST ELSEWHERE THAN ON THE EARTH ?—DESCRIP-
TION OF THE PLANETS.—PLURALITY OF INHABITED WORLDS.

THROUGHOUT the preceding chapters we have reasoned as if the earth were the whole universe. Indeed, almost all men believed that such was the case, from the first establishment of society until the last century. Great mathematical knowledge, profound study, and highly perfected optical instruments are requisite to rectify the false ideas, the errors, and the illusions which are the result of a simple view of the earth and the sky. Great efforts of the mind, and a very difficult struggle against the testimony of our senses are necessary to the recognition that the earth moves, and that the sun is motionless. In order to distinguish the place and the office of each of those softly beaming globes, in the midst of the uniformity of aspect presented by the stars which shine during the night, patient and severe observations, transmitted and repeated from age are indispensable, and, in addition, an excellent scientific method. Let us therefore not be surprised that men have taken so much time to comprehend the ordering of the universe, and that they had only the most childish con-

12

ception of them for thousands of years. The ancients, the
Greeks, the Romans, the Egyptians, knew nothing of the
universe, except the earth (nor did the Orientals, with the
exception of some truly learned men, who had divined the
general mechanism of the universe by methods unknown to
us, but they concealed their knowledge from the profane).
These ancients could speak of only a small portion of the
globe : of Europe, Asia, and the North of Africa. The remainder was a dead letter for the peoples of antiquity. After
them, and following their example, the first Christians reduced the universe to what they knew of it ; they believed
there was but one world, because they saw only one. The
earth was for them the universe. In the stars they saw only
brilliant spots, like silver nails in the celestial vault, to enhance the azure, and charm the eyes of men in the quiet of
the night. The moon was the natural beacon of the earth.
In the sky there was a shining track followed by the sun,
and the torch of day was no larger than the beacon of night.
The celestial region which spread itself above the sun and the
moon was the Empyrean of the ancients, the Paradise of the
Christians and the Mussulmans. It was at once the sojourn
of clouds and of light, the habitation of the elect of God, of
the saints and the just. Under the earth, and in its interior,
were immense abysses, gulfs, and cavities, the dark dwellings
of the damned.

This simple cosmogony, which merely translates what our
eyes show us, has been that believed by every people in their
infancy. Among the savage tribes of the two worlds, in

America and in Africa, as in the ancient East, among the Romans as among the Egyptians and the ancient Greeks, this coarse simplicity and absolute ignorance of the constitution of the world prevailed. On this profoundly false basis all the ancient religions were founded. The social customs of modern peoples are based upon the same errors. Language has consecrated them ; the earth is everywhere called the *world*, as the ancients called it (*mundus*, *κόσμος*) ; every one says the sun *travels*, or *goes*, from east to west, and that the stars *rise* and *set*.

Poetry has set its eternal seal on this vicious system, and has, so to speak, consecrated it, by clothing it with all the *prestige* of genius and imagination.

Modern astronomy has caused the false skies of antiquity to vanish away ; it has dispersed the pretensions of the celestial vault, sown with brilliant spots, and substituted a simple mass of coloured air. It has revealed the true office of each of those stars which we see by day or by night. It has fixed, in an indisputable manner, the real place of the earth in the universe, and, to say the truth, that place is singularly small.

We know now, that the earth, far from being herself the world, is only an imperceptible point of the world. If we only compare it with the sun, we know that our globe is one million three hundred thousand times smaller than the sun. This takes us far away from the idea of the ancient Greeks, who thought they ventured much in asserting that the sun was as big as the Peloponnesus.

In addition, the earth has been dispossessed of all privi-

leges.   It was believed formerly to be unique and unrivalled,
we now know that there are an infinity of other globes similar
to the earth, so that she is no more than one individual in a
group of other individuals who resemble her.   We know
that the earth figures among the planets, that she is only a
planet of our system.

What, then, is a planet? the reader will ask.   An attentive
gaze directed to the stars of night will make him understand
it.   Let him examine, on any fine evening, the star which is
pointed out to him as Mars or Jupiter, and to which a certain
position is assigned at a given hour.   Then, a few hours
later, let him come and look once more for Mars or Jupiter,
and he will perceive that the position of Mars or Jupiter,
with respect to the other stars, is changed.   Or he may do better
still.   Let him look at Mars or Jupiter through the telescope
of an observatory, or the glass of one of those open-air astronomers who are to be found in the public ways in Paris and
other great cities.   Thus he may see Mars or Jupiter change
his place under his own eyes.   While the other stars remain
motionless, Jupiter or Mars will pass away from the field of
the glass.

There are, then, fixed stars and movable stars.   The
movable stars are the planets (πλανήτης, from πλάνος, wandering).   The fixed stars are what we *call* stars.   It is not
difficult to distinguish the planets from the stars with the
naked eye.   The stars emit sparkling light, whence comes
their name, from the Latin *stellare*, to shine, and their light
twinkles.   The planets, on the contrary, shine with a steady,

mild, unvacillating light. The reason of this difference is, that the light shed by the stars is their own. The stars are so many suns resembling ours. They illumine worlds like our world, so prodigiously distant that we cannot even perceive them. The planets do not shine of themselves; they merely reflect, like gigantic mirrors, the light of the sun which illumines them, and renders them visible to us. Thus, the planets are stars which travel. They revolve around the sun. The earth, being a planet, is a travelling star, which revolves around the sun.

But the earth is not the only planet of our solar system. There are seven others, which do not differ essentially from the earth. The names of the eight planets which compose our solar system, are as follows, arranged according to their distance from the sun: Mercury, Venus, the Earth, Mars, Jupiter, Saturn, Uranus, and Neptune. Between Mars and Jupiter there is a collection of small bodies, which seem to be fragments of broken planets; they are called asteroïds. At present, in 1871, more than a hundred are known, and it is not yet fifty years since they were first sought for in the sky. These asteroïds may be collected together in our fancy, and formed into a separate group, which would be a ninth planet. Let us glance at the planets which compose our solar system.

Plates 4 and 5, which accompany these pages, will suffice to give an idea of the relative dimensions of the planets. In these two plates the planets are arranged according to the order of their distance from the sun. In plate 4, Mercury, Venus, the Earth, and Mars are represented; in plate 5, the asteroïds Jupiter, Saturn, Uranus, and Neptune. Mercury is the nearest planet to the sun, his distance from the central orb being only fourteen millions of leagues, which, in astronomy, is near neighbourhood. This planet revolves upon its axis with the same rapidity as the earth. The day, in Mercury, is only three minutes longer than ours (24h. 3ms.) Being closer to the sun than the earth is, Mercury turns more quickly round the sun, so that its year is only 88 days, whereas ours is 365 days.

We know that the sole cause of the inequality of the seasons, as well as of day and night in the planets, is the inclination of the star on its axis of rotation. If the planets, while revolving round the sun, retained the verticality of the axis which joins these north and south poles, there would be perfect equality in the distribution of the solar light and heat over the same latitudes ; along each parallel there would be a complete regularity in the lighting and warming of the planet ; the differences of heat and cold would not depend on anything but their greater or less distance from the sun. But this verticality only exists for two or three planets of our system. The others, and among them Mercury, Venus, the Earth, and Mars, are strongly inclined on their axis of rotation.

They revolve in a bent position, as if they had received a great blow on the shoulder, which had caused them to deviate from their primitive and regular situation. From this there results a very variable disposition of the duration of the light, and consequently of the heat, which these inclined planets receive from the horizontal rays of the solar star.

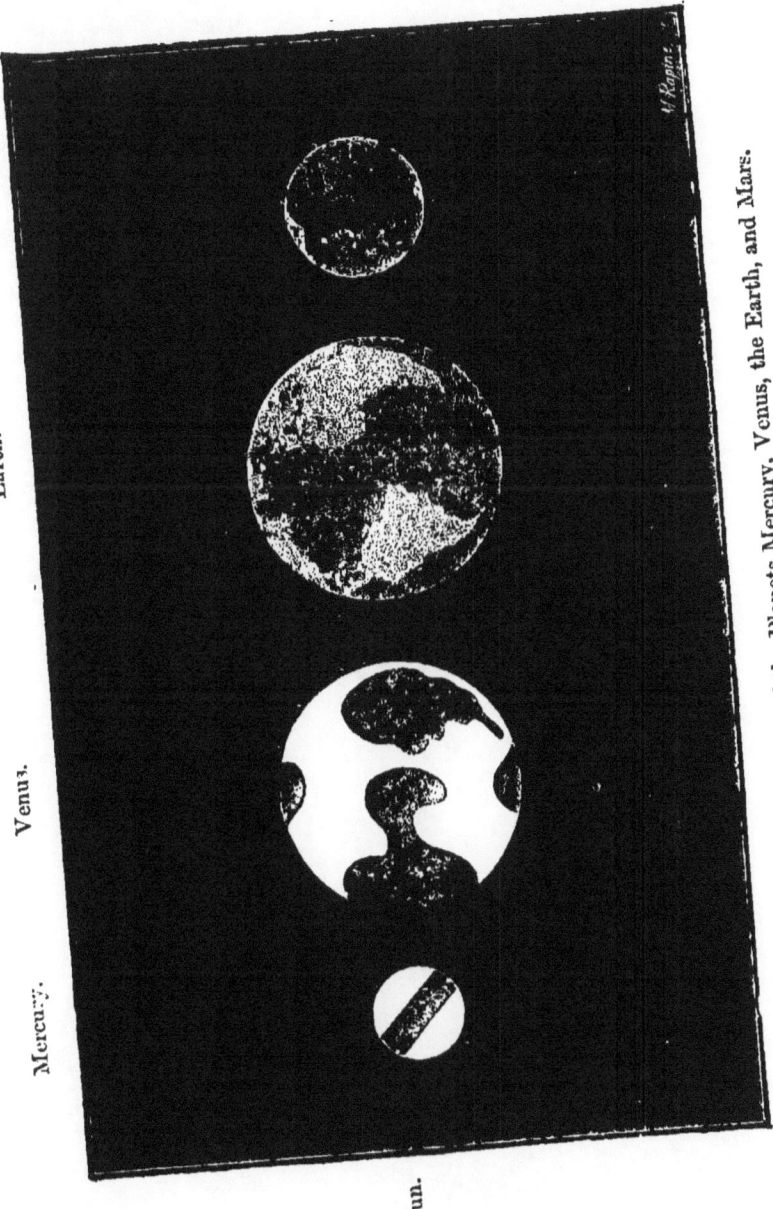

Mercury.   Venus.   Earth.   Mars.

Sun.

Fig. 4.—Comparative Size of the Planets Mercury, Venus, the Earth, and Mars.

Thus the inequality in the length of the days and nights, and the diversity of the four seasons on the same parallel, are accounted for.*

The inclination of the axis of the terrestrial sphere is 23°, which is a considerable deviation, and occasions great differences in the duration of days and of seasons on different points of our globe. The inclination of the axis of the planet Mercury is enormous: it is 70°. This planet bends over itself as if about to fall. Hence results prodigious variation of light and heat on the same parallel, and seasons whose abrupt changes must be painful and hard to bear by the inhabitants of this planet, if such inhabitants exist.

Mercury is five times less than the Earth, as is shown in plate 4. Venus comes after Mercury, according to distance from the Sun.

Venus, which is 27,000,000 of leagues from the Sun,

---

* Milton, in his *Paradise Lost*, says that before the fall of our first parents, perpetual spring reigned upon the Earth, but that as soon as Adam and Eve had eaten the forbidden fruit, angels, with flaming swords, were sent from Heaven to incline the poles of the Earth more than 20 degrees. It is well for us that the angels did not cause them to incline farther, or our seasons would have been still shorter and more defective. Fourier pretends that it would be possible for humanity to produce an effect sufficiently great to set the globe straight upon its axis, and thus restore the equality of the seasons, and perpetual spring. This philosopher forgot to indicate one thing only, the mechanical means by which man is to produce this effect. This theory reminds us of the drowning man who fancied he could save himself by catching hold of his own hair, while he was struggling in the water.

receives twice as much light and heat as our globe.   Its days
are of nearly the same length as ours (23 hours, 21 minutes),
but its year, necessarily shorter than that of the Earth, since
it is nearer to the Sun, lasts only 224 days.   Its seasons last
two months each.   Its globe is nearly of the same bulk as
that of the Earth.   Venus is almost always wrapped in
clouds, which must fall in rain, forming rivers and seas.
These waters refresh the plains, which must be scorched by
the heat of the burning sun.   The seasons are still shorter
and more unequal in Venus than in Mercury ; its axis is, in
fact, inclined at 75°.

After Venus comes the Earth, which is almost of the same
bulk, but 28,000,000 of leagues from the Sun.   Its diameter
is nearly 3000 leagues.   It accomplishes its revolution on its
axis in 24 hours (23 hours, 56 minutes, 4 seconds), and in
365 days, 5 hours its revolution around the sun.

The inclination of the Earth's axis is 23°, which produces
the differences of days and nights, and the inequality of the
seasons, according to latitude.   The Earth possesses a privilege denied to the planets Mercury, Venus, and Mars ; she
has a secondary star, or satellite, called the Moon.   Placed at
a distance of only 90,000 leagues from the Earth, the Moon
accomplishes her revolution around it in 27 days.   It is not
the object of this work to give any description of our globe.
We will suppose our readers to be sufficiently acquainted with
it, and pass on to the planet which comes next to it in the
scale of distance from the Sun.   This is the planet Mars.

An extraordinary resemblance exists between Mars and the

Earth. Physical, geographical, and climatological conditions, days and nights, seasons, celestial perspectives, all are alike in these two planets, with the sole difference that the globe of Mars is half as small again as that of the Earth; so that, if a man were transported to Mars, he might believe himself to be, not in a strange planet, but in a little known corner of the Earth, such as Australia or Polynesia.

As we pursue our journey through the heavens, ever increasing our distance from the Sun, we shall find, after Mars, the group of the Asteroïds. We shall not linger before this cluster of small stars, which is no doubt nothing but a collection of the dismembered fragments of a planet, which formerly existed in this particular point of space, and was dashed to pieces by some formidable accident in the universe. These little stars, like the important planets, have each their names, such as *Vesta, Pallas, Circe,* &c., &c. *Maximiliana,* and *Feronia* are placed at the two extremities, with respect to distance from the Sun. These remains of a broken star continue to circulate around the Sun, like the planet which they formerly composed.

After the Asteroïds comes great Jupiter.

Jupiter is the largest planetary sphere in our solar system, being 1400 times greater than the Earth. Its distance from the Sun is 200,000,000 miles. In consequence of this distance, its year is as long as twelve of our years. Notwithstanding its colossal dimensions, Jupiter turns with such rapidity upon its axis, that it accomplishes an entire revolution in twelve hours, so that its day and night are respectively only

ten hours long.   The shortness of Jupiter's nights are com-
pensated by the existence of four moons, or satellites, which
revolve around this planet, and give it permanent light. This
illumination by reflection, added to very long twilights,
must make Jupiter's nights nearly equal to the day in
brightness.

Though Jupiter suffers under the disadvantage of very
short days, it has on the other hand the inappreciable advantage of perfect equality in the length of its days and
nights, and of that of the four seasons over all its parallels.
The axis of Jupiter is hardly at all oblique, and therefore
Jupiter, like the planet Saturn, enjoys a sort of perpetual
spring, that is to say, an equable distribution of solar heat and
light along the same degrees of latitude. Jupiter, unlike Mars
and Venus, has no vicissitudes of seasons, no sudden and painful transitions from cold to heat in the same place. The climates are invariable in each latitude, and the seasons are
hardly discernible.

The globe of Saturn is 734 times larger than that of the
Earth, and is 364,000,000 leagues from the Sun.   It takes
thirty years to perform its revolution around the central star,
and its year is therefore thirty times as long as ours.

Saturn, like Jupiter, has very short days.   It revolves on
its axis in ten hours, so that its day and night respectively are
but five hours.   But it has eight moons, or satellites, which
accompany it, and give it light, thus, as in the case of Jupiter,
supplementing the shortness of its days. There is hardly any
obliquity of the axis of Saturn, so that its days and nights

are always equal. There is a perpetual *equinox*, and the climates are invariable, while variation of seasons hardly exists. In Saturn, as in Jupiter, perpetual spring reigns. Saturn has one peculiarity which does not belong to any other body in our solar system. It is placed in the centre of a ring, of the same nature as its own, and which surrounds it on every side. This ring (see plate 5), is surrounded by a second, and the second by a third, and the whole are called the rings of Saturn. This circular envelope is exceedingly thin—only ten leagues in thickness—but very wide; its width is 12,000 leagues. It is not motionless, but it revolves with the globe which it surrounds.

The strange disposition of the rings of Saturn affords a proof of the inexhaustible riches of nature, and the variety of forms which the Creator has called into being in the vast universe. It ought to guard us against our constant tendency to model all the worlds which we do not know, upon the type of the earth.

Hardly anything is known about the peculiarities of Uranus, a planet which is only eighty-two times larger than the earth, but which is 732,000,000 of miles from the sun, and takes eighty-four years to accomplish its revolution around the central star.

Plate 5 shows the relative proportions of Uranus and the earth. The prodigious distance of Uranus from our globe, added to its small size, renders it almost inaccessible to observation.

For the same reason, nothing can be ascertained respecting

the physical and geographical conditions of Neptune, the last planet of our solar system, which was discovered in our time by M. Le Verrier, thanks to the simple force of calculation, thereby affording the most brilliant proof ever given of the utility of the mathematical sciences. Neptune is so small and so far from us, that it is probable mere observation of the heavens would never have detected its existence. In this case mathematical analysis was more powerful than the telescope. It would be impossible to give particulars analogous to those which we have supplied concerning the foregoing planets, in reference to a star only 105 times larger than the earth, which revolves at the distance of *one milliard* 150 *millions of leagues* from the sun, and the duration of whose year is 164 times that of the terrestrial year, so that if the ages of the Christian era were counted according to the Neptunian chronology, instead of being in the 19th century, we should be in the 12th year of that era. All we can say about Neptune, therefore, is that it forms the boundary of the domain of our visible world.

We cannot, however, state positively that our solar world terminates at this limit. No doubt the range of our astronomical glasses goes no farther, but assuredly they do not sweep the boundaries of the empire of the sun. It is known, in fact, that comets return to us after having (as indicated by their geometrical curve), swept over the depths of space to a distance of thirty-two *milliards of leagues.* Thus the distance of one milliard 150 millions of leagues, which is that of Neptune from the sun, by **no means** represents the confines of our

Asteroids.　Jupiter.　Saturn.　Uranus.　Neptune.

Size of
the Earth.

Fig. 5.—Size of the Planets Jupiter, Saturn, Uranus, and Neptune, compared with the Earth.

solar world, but simply defines the limits of the range of our telescopes.

This rapid glance at our solar system in its entirety, proves that the earth is not in possession of any privilege. The part which she plays in the economy of the universe is equally fulfilled by other stars, and there is nothing to justify the pre-eminence assigned to her by the ancients. She is not the largest, the warmest, or the brightest of the planets. She simply forms a portion of a group of stars, and is but one individual of that group.

These considerations tend to lead us to a very important deduction. Since the earth is in no way distinguished from the other planets of our solar system, there must exist in other planets the things which are found on our globe ; air, water, a hard soil, rivers and seas, mountains and valleys. Even vegetation and forests ought to be there, regions covered with verdure and with shade. So there surely ought to exist in the other planets, animals, and even men, or at least creatures superior to animals, corresponding to our human type.

But is this possible ? is it true ? are the planets which, like the earth, and together with it, turn round the sun, consti-tuted physically as the earth is ? Are they covered with vegetable growth ? are they tenanted by animals and by beings belonging to the human type ?

This grave question has been profoundly discussed by M. Camille Flammarion, in a work entitled *Pluralité des Mondes Habités*, and in a later publication, *Les Mondes Ima-*

ginaires et les Mondes Réels. It would be outside the province of this book to follow the author through the various scientific considerations, from which he reasons that the planets which form a portion of our solar system, are, like the earth, the scene of life, organization, thought, and feeling. In the 17th century, Fontenelle and Huygens had successfully approached this successful problem, which M. Camille Flammarion has lately treated with especial care and development, invoking the lessons of contemporaneous astronomy and physics, which refer to the subject. We therefore refer the reader, who wishes to be instructed upon the question of the possibility of the planets being inhabited, to M. Flammarion's works.

CHAPTER THE FOURTEENTH.

THAT WHICH HAS TAKEN PLACE UPON THE EARTH WITH RE-
GARD TO THE CREATION OF ORGANIZED BEINGS HAS PRO-
BABLY ALSO TAKEN PLACE IN THE OTHER PLANETS.—THE
SUCCESSIVE ORDER OF THE APPEARANCE OF LIVING BEINGS
ON OUR GLOBE.—THIS SAME SUCCESSION HAS PROBABLY
TAKEN PLACE IN EACH OF THE PLANETS.—PLANETARY MAN.
—THE PLANETARY, LIKE THE TERRESTRIAL MAN, IS TRANS-
FORMED, AFTER DEATH, INTO A SUPERHUMAN BEING, AND
PASSES INTO THE ETHER.

E believe, with M. Camille Flammarion, that
organized beings exist in all the planets. But
are these beings who live in the distant worlds
accompanied, like terrestrial man, by a superior
type? This is the subject which we now propose to examine.
In the absence of observation analogy is our only means of
investigation, and, guided by analogy, we must admit that the
processes which have taken place upon the earth, since the
epoch of its formation, must have similarly taken place upon
all the other planets, the earth's congeners.

We are now perfectly acquainted with the manner in
which the vegetable and animal creations have appeared, and
succeeded each other upon our globe since its origin. At first

the earth was simply a collection of gas, and burning vapour
which revolved round the sun.   This mass of gas and vapour
grew cold by degrees in its passage through space, and first
becoming liquid, afterwards assumed the consistency of paste,
and ultimately became solid, by a gradual process of refrigeration.   Consolidation began on the surface, because the cir-
cumference of a sphere is more exposed than the remainder
of the mass to refrigerating influences.   Then the water and
the vapours which still flowed upon the consolidated globe
became condensed, and, falling in burning showers upon the
hard soil, they formed the first seas.

The proof that the earth's primitive condition was like to
a liquid or half paste, is, that if we take a plastic sphere, for
instance a slightly fluid ball of quicksilver, and make it turn
rapidly upon its axis, we observe that it swells out in the
middle, and becomes flat at the two poles, or the extremities
of the axis ; this is the effect of the centrifugal force engendered by the rotatory motion.   Now the earth is depressed
at the poles, and slightly swelled out at the equator.

The other planets must have been formed by the same process
as the earth.   They were, no doubt, composed of a collection of
gas and vapours, which became liquid, pasty, and eventually
solid, by a process of refrigeration.   This process, taking
effect especially upon their surface, they began to put forth a
skin, or exterior and solid covering, which was the soil of
the planet.   On this resisting soil fell the liquids resulting
from the condensation of the water vapour, and thus the first
seas of the planets were formed.

We would remind those who doubt the correctness of this theory that the poles of the globe of Saturn and that of Jupiter are much more flat than those of the Earth ; which is explained by the greater velocity of the rotation of each upon its axis. Our days are 24 hours long, whereas those of Jupiter and Saturn are only 10 hours. Greater rapidity of rotation produces a correspondingly increased depression at the extremities of the axis. This geometrical result demonstrates the justice of the assimilation in their respective origin which we maintain between the Earth and the other planets.

In the warm waters of the basin of the seas the first living beings which existed upon our globe appeared. Animal life commenced in the waters, in the primitive forms of zoophytes and mollusca, as we know, because zoophytes and mollusca, with the addition of a few articulates, composed the animal remains found in the transition strata which come after the primary formations. The first vegetables are found in the same transition strata, they are mosses, algæ, and ferns.

When the earth had become somewhat cooler, phanerogamous vegetables appeared upon the continents. Numerous vegetable species were simultaneously created, for the flora of the secondary formations is extremely rich and varied.

It was the same in the case of animals. So the zoophytes, mollusca, and fish which existed in the transition period succeeded reptiles, in the secondary formation, which inhabited both land and sea. At this period appeared those monstrous saurian reptiles, whose formidable shapes, and collossal dimensions fill us with surprise and almost with dismay. Then

the gigantic mososaurus ravaged the seas, the terrible ichthyosaurus spread terror among the inhabitants of the waters,
and the gigantic iguanodon laid waste the forests. The
secondary formation, which is filled with their remains,
shows us that at that period reptiles held the first rank in
creation.

At a later date, the atmosphere having become purer, birds
began to traverse the air. In the tertiary deposit we find the
remains of several kinds of birds, and these remains, which
do not exist in the earlier formations, sufficiently prove that
it was in the tertiary period that birds made their first appearance upon the terrestrial globe.

Still later, at a more advanced period of the tertiary epoch,
mammifers appear upon the scene. We must observe that
these animal species do not replace each other, that the one
does not exclude the other. Several of the ancient animal
species continue to exist after the appearance of entirely
novel kinds. We might quote as instances whole groups of
animals, such as the lingulæ (mollusca), the coral (zoophyte)
among animals, and among vegetables, the algæ, ferns, and
lycopodes, which appeared on our globe in the earliest period
of the reign of organization, and have never ceased to exist.
It was not until the last epoch in the history of the Earth,
during the quaternary epoch, that man appeared, the highest product of living creation, the ultimate term of organic,
intellectual, and moral progress, the crowning upon our earth
of the visible edifice of nature.

At present, man lives together with the animals which be-

gan to exist during the quaternary epoch, and a great number
of other kinds of mammifers which were created during the
tertiary epoch.

The various phases of the development of the animal and
vegetable kingdoms on our globe, these perfected organized
species each succeeding the other, and finally reaching the
superior type which we call man, must, in our opinion, have
been produced in the selfsame order, upon the other planets
of our solar world. M. Flammarion proves, in the work
which we have already quoted, that the physical and climatological constitution of the planets is similar to that of our globe.
There is therefore no reason why things should have taken
place otherwise in Mercury, Jupiter, or Venus, than in the
Earth, in respect to the successive order of the creation and
appearance of living beings, and, in our belief a precisely
similar successive appearance of vegetables and animals, has
taken place in these planets. The plants and animals of Mercury, Jupiter, Saturn, &c., were certainly not identical with
those species which have had existence on the Earth, and
perhaps no resemblance could be traced between them, but
all, in their successive appearance, obeyed the principle of
progress and perfecting. Life, commencing in the burning
waves of the primitive seas, subsequently manifested itself
upon the continents. Animals of aërial organization have
lived upon these continents, their species have by degrees
reached the perfection of their type, at length, and finally, a
creature appeared in these planets more complete, superior in
organization, intelligence, and sensibility to all the animal

creation which formed the population of each particular globe.

This superior being, this last step of the ascending scale of living creation proper to the planetary worlds, the corresponding analogous creature to terrestrial man, we shall take leave to call *planetary man.*

In all the planets, then, there exist *men,* as on the earth, just as there exist animals which are inferior to that noble and privileged type.

According to the views which we have explained at the commencement of this work, terrestrial man undergoes, after his death, a glorious metamorphosis. Leaving his miserable material covering here below, his soul springs upward into space, and becomes incarnate in a new being, whose type is infinitely superior, by reason of its moral perfection, to that of our poor humanity. He becomes that which we have called the *superhuman being.* If this be true of the terrestrial man, it must be equally true of the planetary man. So that the superhuman being must proceed, not only from the earth, but from all the other planets.

Superhuman beings come from the human souls who have lived either upon the Earth, or upon Mercury, Jupiter, Venus, Saturn, &c. And precisely as the superhuman being, who comes from the Earth passes into the surrounding ether, so the planetary man, leaving Mars, Mercury, Jupiter, &c., passes into the ether, which surrounds his own planet, becomes incarnate in a superhuman being, and lives in the ethereal plains adjoining the planet which he has quitted.

All these superhuman beings float in the clouds of ether which, in the case of every planet, succeed to its atmosphere.

Thus, the principles upon which we have based terrestrial humanity, are general, and apply to all planetary humanity. Not from the Earth only do those souls proceed who are incarnate in new creatures in the bosom of the ethereal spaces, these souls proceed from all the globes which, together with the Earth, form the attendant court of the royal Sun.

CHAPTER THE FIFTEENTH.

PROOFS OF THE PLURALITY OF HUMAN EXISTENCES, AND OF RE-INCARNATIONS.—APART FROM THIS DOCTRINE IT IS IMPOSSIBLE TO EXPLAIN THE PRESENCE OF MAN UPON THE EARTH, THE SAD AND UNEQUAL CONDITIONS OF HUMAN LIFE, AND THE FATE OF CHILDREN WHO DIE IN INFANCY.

THE doctrine of the plurality of existences, and of re-incarnations, which bind together, like so many links of the same chain, all living creatures, from the most minute animal, even to those blessed beings to whom it is given to behold God in His glory; which gives brethren in the different planets to terrestrial humanity; which makes of the inhabitants of our globe a nation of the universe; which sees but one family in all the population of the worlds—a planetary family—whose every member may raise himself by his merits and his struggles, in the hierarchy of happiness, is supported by so many proofs. So many, indeed, that we are puzzled to choose among all the methods of demonstration which offer themselves in aid of it. To enumerate them all would unduly enlarge the dimensions of this work, so that we shall content ourselves with bringing forward the most striking.

Why are we on the earth? We did not ask to be placed there, we did not express a wish to be born. If we had been consulted, we should probably have objected to coming into this world at all, or at least we should have wished to appear there at some other epoch. We should probably have asked to be permitted to sojourn in some other planet than the Earth. Our globe is, indeed, a very disagreeable habitation. In consequence of its inclination on its axis, climate is very unpleasantly distributed. Either we must succumb to cold, if we are not artificially protected against it, or we must be terribly incommoded with heat. Regarded from the moral point of view, the conditions of humanity are very sad. Evil predominates in the world; vice is held almost everywhere in honour, and virtue is so ill-treated, that to be honest is, in this life, to be tolerably certain of evil fortune. Our affections are causes of anguish and tears. If, for a while, we enjoy the happiness of paternity, of love, of friendship, it is only to see the objects of our love torn from us by death, or separated from us by the accidents of a miserable life. The organs given us to be exercised in this life are heavy, coarse, subject to maladies. We are nailed to the earth, and our heavy mass can be moved only by fatiguing exertion. If there are men of powerful organization, gifted with a good constitution and robust health, how many are there who are infirm, idiots, deaf and dumb, blind from their birth, ricketty, and mad! My brother is handsome and well made, and I am ugly, feeble, ricketty, and hump-backed; nevertheless, we are both sons of the same mother. Some are born in opu-

lence, others in the most hideous destitution. Why am I
not a prince and a great lord, instead of being a poor toiler of
the rebellious and ungrateful earth? Why was I born in
Europe and in France, where, by means of art and civilization,
life is rendered easy and endurable, instead of being born
under the burning skies of the tropics, where, with a bestial
snout, a black and oily skin, and woolly hair, I should have
been exposed to the double torments of a deadly climate and
social barbarism? Why is not one of the unfortunate African
negroes in my place, comfortable and well off? We have
done nothing, he and I, that our respective places on the
earth should have been assigned to us.   I have not merited
the favour, he has not incurred the disgrace.   What is the
cause of this unequal division of frightful evils which fall
heavily upon certain persons, and spare others?   How have
they who live in happy countries deserved this partiality of
fate, while so many of their brethren are suffering and weeping in other regions of the world?

Certain men are endowed with all the gifts of the intellect;
others, on the contrary, are devoid of intelligence, penetration,
and memory.   They stumble at every step in the difficult
journey of life.   Their narrow minds, their incomplete faculties, expose them to every kind of failure and misfortune.
They cannot succeed in anything, and destiny seems to select
them for the chosen victims of its most fatal blows.   There
are beings whose whole life, from their birth to their death,
is a prolonged cry of suffering and despair.   What crime have
they committed?   Why are they upon the earth?   They

have not asked to be born, and if they had been free, they would have entreated that this bitter cup might be removed from their lips. They are here below in spite of themselves, against their will. This is so true that some, in an excess of despair, sever the thread of their own life. They tear themselves away with their own hands from an existence which terrible suffering has rendered insupportable to them.

God would be unjust and wicked to impose so miserable a life upon beings who have done nothing to incur it, and who have not solicited it. But God is neither unjust nor wicked; the opposite qualities are the attribute of His perfect essence. Consequently, the presence of man on certain portions of the earth, and the unequal distribution of evil over our globe, are not to be explained. If any of my readers can show me a doctrine, a philosophy, a religion by which these difficulties can be resolved, I will tear up this book, and confess myself vanquished.

If, on the contrary, you admit the plurality of human existences and *re-incarnations,* that is to say the passage of the same soul into several different bodies, everything is wonderfully easily explained. Our presence in certain portions of the globe is no longer the effect of a caprice of fate, or the result of chance ; it is simply a station of the long journey which we are taking throughout the worlds. Previous to our birth in this world we have lived either in the condition of superior animals, or that of man. Our actual existence is only the consequence of another, whether it be that we bear within ourselves the soul of a superior animal, which we must

purify, perfect, and ennoble, during our sojourn on earth ; or
that, having already fulfilled an imperfect and evil existence,
we are condemned to re-commence it under new obligations.
In the latter case, the career of the man re-commences, because
his soul is not yet sufficiently pure to rise to the rank of a
superhuman being.

Our sojourn upon earth is then only a kind of trial, imposed upon us by nature, during which we must refine our
souls, free them from earthly bonds, rid them of the defects
which weigh them down, and hinder them from rising, in
radiance, towards the ethereal spheres. Every ill-fulfilled
human existence has to be recommenced. Thus, the school-
boy who has worked hard, who has studied well, goes into a
higher class at the end of the year; but if he has made no
progress in his studies, he must go through his class again.
Perverse men are, in our opinion, vicious beings who have
had a previous life, and are obliged to live it over again.
They must go through it again and again, until the day comes
when their souls shall be fit to take higher rank in the hierarchy of creatures, that is to say, until they shall be fit to
pass, after their death, into the condition of superhuman
beings.

In proportion as the cause of our existence here below is
obscure and even inexplicable according to ordinary ideas, it
is simple and luminous in the light of the doctrine of the
plurality of existences. We must add that this doctrine is
conformable to the justice of God. In making earthly life a
trial for man, God is equitable and good, like an earthly

father. Is it not better to subject a soul to a trial which may begin over again if it have an unfortunate result, than to bind it to one condition, failure in which must involve the condemnation of the guilty person? It is better to offer the possibility of rehabilitation by his own efforts, by his personal struggles, to a fallen creature, than to utterly crush him, stained by his crimes and imperfections. The justice and the goodness of God are manifest in this paternal arrangement, much more than in the severe jurisdiction which would irretrievably condemn a soul after one single trial had resulted unfavourably.

If human life be a trial, if it be a period during which we are preparing for a new and happier existence, there is no need to look beyond that truth for an explanation of why we are on the earth, why we are living to-day rather than to-morrow, and in one latitute of our globe rather than in another; there is no need to ask why we are born in the earth, and not in Mercury, Saturn, or Mars. Whether we are living now, or are to live later, whether we have been born in the earth, in Mercury, or in Mars, whether we inhabit Europe or Africa,—all these things are utterly unimportant to our destiny. We are undergoing a period of preparation indispensably necessary to be accomplished before we pass into the superhuman condition; and the place, the moment of our transit, the country in which we sojourn, the planet which is assigned to us as the scene of this trial, are without any importance in the part which we have to play in accordance with the intentions of nature. We are making an im-

mense journey through the worlds, and a short sojourn on
the Earth makes a part of our vast itinerary.   Whatever may
be the corner of the universe in which we find ourselves we
cannot escape the trial imposed upon us by God, a trial by
strife and suffering, a period of moral and physical pain to
which we must submit before we can be promoted in the
hierarchy of creatures.   The time, the place, the good or evil
moral conditions ought therefore to be indifferent to us.
What is needful for us is a brief sojourn on a planet in which
this trial may be accomplished, and it may be accomplished
on the Earth, or in Mars, or in Mercury, and on any spot of
the Earth's surface one chooses to think of.

If, during the course of this trial, we meet with moral evil,
if we see vice triumphant and virtue persecuted, if we see
the innocent victims of the injustice, the cruelty, or the ignorance of man, we have no right to murmur against Providence,
we have no right to utter maledictions against pain, to de-
plore the scandal of successful and triumphant crime, and of
suffering and weeping virtue.   We have no right to regret
our bodily infirmities, the diseases which lay hold upon us on
the Earth, and which afflict us all our lives, or to complain of
the weakness of our minds, the decay of our faculties.   All
these conditions, which are inimical to earthly happiness, are
a portion of the series of trials which we have to undergo
here below.   We ought to bless those evils, and be grateful
to those sufferings, for they are the instruments of our eternal
redemption, and the more piercing and bitter they are the
sooner will come the hour of our deliverance, the happy mo-

ment when we shall leave this impure and filthy world which our feet have trodden for a while. Besides, justice will speedily be done. With brief delay the wicked shall be punished for his evil deeds by having to recommence a new existence here, while the good shall be elevated to the upper world, where a new, wide-ranging life awaits him, far more happy and more wise, in truer harmony with the aspirations of our nature than his previous and miserable existence here. Then we shall be born again, radiant and strong, with our memory, our feelings, and our liberty complete.

Thus difficulties vanish, and problems are solved : thus uncertainty vanishes away, and mysteries which no doctrine, no religion, no philosophy, could dissipate, and which almost made us doubt the justice of God, are cleared up. The doctrine of re-incarnations and prior existences explains everything, answers everything.

We pass on to one of the most interesting questions of the doctrine of the pre-existence of souls, the question of children who have died in infancy. What becomes of children who die at a few days old, or at the age of eight or ten months, or at their birth? Until after all these periods the human soul remains quite undeveloped; it is in almost the same rudimentary state as at the hour of its birth. What, then, is the fate of young children after their death? The doctrine of the plurality of existences simplifies this question. It admits that when an infant dies before it has lived one year (the period of dentition), its soul remains upon the earth, and does not pass, like that of a grown man, into the state of a superhuman

14

being. The soul of an infant a year old is still in a rudimentary condition, almost as much so as at the moment of its
birth. The soul of a child who dies at that age has to begin
life over again, disengaging itself from the little corpse, it
incarnates itself in another newly-born body, and after this
fresh incarnation, it begins a second life.

If the new incarnation does not last more than a year,
there is no reason why the soul should not undergo a third
incarnation in the body of a child, and so on until it shall
have accomplished the period of admission to the conditions
common to all.

It is impossible that the soul of a child, which is as yet
undeveloped, which has added nothing to that which it has
received, should be treated as perfected souls, purified by the
experience of life, by physical and moral sufferings, who have
used their sojourn upon earth as a period of preparation and
training. An infant child cannot therefore be admitted to
the super-terrestrial dwellings, he simply recommences an
interrupted trial. The mortality of children between the day
of their birth and the age of one year is so considerable, that
nature must have reserved to herself the means of annulling
this cause of disarrangement in the sequence and order of her
operations.

This explanation of the destiny of young children is conformable to the economy which is observed in the operations
of nature. Nature wills that nothing which is created should
be lost. The soul of a criminal is evil, but it is a soul, it
exists, and it is eternal : it must not be lost. But it must be

corrected and perfected, which is done by means of the new existences to which nature consigns that imperfect soul, in order that it may enjoy the means of restoration. Thus the principle of the soul is preserved, and nothing is lost of that which was created. The soul of the child dying in infancy must not be lost either. A second incarnation in another child will permit it to resume the course of its evolution, accidentally interrupted by death. Thus the soul will be preserved, and nothing will be lost.

Chemistry, since Lavoisier's time, has brought to light a great truth: it is, that nothing of the elements of matter is lost; bodies change their form, but the material element, the simple body, is imperishable, indestructible, and always to be found intact, notwithstanding its numerous transformations. If it is true that in the material world nothing is lost, it is equally certain that neither is anything lost in the spiritual world; that only transformation takes place. Thus, nothing is lost, either of immaterial or material beings, and we may lay down this new principle of moral philosophy by the side of the principle of chemical philosophy established by the genius of Lavoisier.

CHAPTER THE SIXTEENTH.

FACULTIES PECULIAR TO CERTAIN CHILDREN, APTITUDES AND
VOCATIONS AMONG MEN, ARE ADDITIONAL PROOFS OF RE-IN-
CARNATIONS.—EXPLANATION OF PHRENOLOGY.—DESCARTES'
INNATE IDEAS, AND DUGALD STEWART'S PRINCIPLE OF
CAUSALITY CAN ONLY BE EXPLAINED BY THE PLURALITY
OF LIVES. — VAGUE RECOLLECTIONS OF OUR ANTERIOR
EXISTENCES.

F there are no re-incarnations, if our actual existence is, as modern philosophy and the ordinary
creeds maintain it to be, a solitary fact, not to
be repeated, it follows that the soul must be
formed at the same time as the body, and that at each birth
of a human being, a new soul must be created, to animate
this body. We would ask, then, why are not all these souls
of the same type? Why, when all human bodies are alike,
is there so great a diversity in souls, that is to say, in the
intellectual and moral faculties which constitute them? We
would ask why natural tendencies are so diverse and so
strongly marked, that they frequently resist all the efforts of
education to reform, or repress them, or to direct them into
any other line? Whence come those instincts of vice and
virtue which are to be observed in children, those instincts of

pride or of baseness, which are often seen in such striking
contrast with the social position of their families? Why do
some children delight in the contemplation of pain, and take
pleasure in torturing animals, while others are vehemently
moved, turn pale, and tremble at the sight or even the
thought of a living creature's pain? Why, if the soul in all
men be cast in the same mould, does not education produce
an identical effect upon young people? Two brothers follow
the same classes at the same school, they have the same
masters, and the same examples are before their eyes. Nevertheless, the one profits to the utmost by the lessons which he
receives, and in manners, education, and conduct, he is irreproachable. His brother, on the contrary, remains ignorant
and uncouth. If the same seed sown in these two soils has
produced such different fruit, must it not be that the soil
which has received the seed, *i.e.*, the soul, is different in the
case of each?

Natural dispositions, vocations, manifest themselves from
the earliest period of life. This extreme diversity in natural
aptitudes would not exist if souls were all created of the same
type. The bodies of animals, the human body, the leaves of
trees, are fabricated after the same type, because we can
observe but few and slight differences among them. The
skeleton of one man is always like the skeleton of another
man; the heart, the stomach, the ribs, the intestines are
formed alike in every man. It is otherwise with souls; they
differ considerably in individuals. We hear it said every
day that such an one's child has a taste for arithmetic, a
second for music, a third for drawing. In the case of others

evil, violent, even criminal instincts are remarked, and these dispositions break out in the earliest years of life.

That these natural aptitudes are carried to a very high degree and unusual extent, we have celebrated examples recorded in history, and frequently cited. We have Pascal, at twelve years old, discovering the greater portion of plane geometry, and without having been taught anything whatever of arithmetic, drawing all the figures of the first book of Euclid's geometry on the floor of his room, exactly estimating the mathematical relations of all these figures to each other; that is to say, constructing descriptive geometry for himself. We have the shepherd, Mangiamelo, calculating as an arithmetical machine, at five years old. We have Mozart executing a sonata with his four-years-old fingers, and composing an opera at eight. We have Theresa Milanollo playing the violin with such art and skill, at four years old, that Baillot said she must have played the violin before she was born. We have Rembrandt drawing like a master of the art, before he could read. Etc., etc.

Every one remembers these examples, but it must be borne in mind that they do not constitute exceptions. They only represent a general fact, which in these particular cases was so prominent as to attract public attention. They are valuable as exponents to the public of a fundamental law of nature, the diversity of natural faculties and aptitudes, and the predominance of particular faculties among certain children. Children endowed with these extraordinary and precocious vocations are called *little prodigies.* This qualification is sometimes used in a depreciatory sense, for the little prodi-

gies are accused of failing to carry out the promises of their
childhood ; it is observed that the brilliant abilities of their
early years have not been guarantees of extraordinary success
in their careers as grown men. A child, whose drawings
were wonderful at four years old, has become a wretched
dauber, as an established artist. A musician, who enchanted
his audience at eight years old, has grown up a very mediocre
performer.

This remark is just, and the fact is explicable thus : If
the little prodigies have not become great men, it is because
they have not cultivated their faculties ; because they have
allowed sloth and disuse to extinguish their talents. It does
not suffice to possess natural abilities for a science, or an art,
work and study must strengthen and develop them. Little
prodigies are outstripped in their career by hard workers, as
is natural. They have come upon earth with remarkable
faculties which they had acquired during a previous life, but
they have done nothing to develop those faculties, which
have remained as they were at the moment of terrestrial birth.
The man of genius is the man who unceasingly cultivates and
perfects such great natural aptitudes and faculties as he has
been endowed with at his birth.

The predominance of particular faculties in certain children
is not to be explained according to the common philosophy
which discerns the creation of a new soul in the birth of every
infant. They are, on the contrary, easily explicable according
to the doctrine of re-incarnations, indeed they are no more than
a corollary of that doctrine. Everything is comprehensible if
a life, anterior to the present, be admitted. The individual

brings to his life here, the intuition which is the result of the
knowledge he has acquired during his first existence. Men
are of more or less advanced intelligence and morality, according to the life which they have led before they come into
this world to play the parts which we can see. This is self-
evident in the case of a man who recommences his life. This
man had acquired certain faculties during his first, which are
profitable to him in his second existence. Perhaps he does
not possess all the faculties with which his first life was
endowed, in their full and perfect integrity, but he has what
mathematicians call the *resultant* of those faculties, and this
resultant is a special aptitude, it is *vocation*. He is a calcu-
lator, a painter, or a musician by vocation, because, in his
former human career he has had the faculty of calculation,
drawing, or music. We believe that it is impossible to find
any other explanation of our natural aptitudes. It will be
objected to this, that it is strange that aptitude and faculties
should be the resultant of a prior existence, of which we
have, nevertheless, no recollection. We reply to this objection that it is quite possible to lose all remembrance of events
which have happened, and yet to preserve certain faculties of
the soul which are independent of particular and concrete
facts, especially when those faculties are powerful. We constantly see old men who have lost all recollection of the
events of their life, who no longer know anything of the history of their time, nor indeed, of their own history, but who,
nevertheless, have not lost their faculties, or aptitudes.
Linnæus, in his old age, took pleasure in reading his own
works, but forgot that he was their author, and frequently

exclaimed : "How interesting ! How beautiful ! I wish I had written that !"

There is no reason to doubt that a child, after its re-incarnation, may preserve the aptitudes of its previous existence, though it has entirely lost the remembrance of the facts which took place and which it witnessed during that period. These faculties reappear and become active in the child, just as the half-extinguished flame of a fire is rekindled by the breath of the wind. The breath which fans the smouldering flame of human faculties is that of a second existence.

The absence of memory may be urged as an objection to re-incarnations in the body of a child, but this argument does not apply to the incarnation of the soul of an animal in a human body. The animal, being almost without the faculty of memory, it is easy to understand that its aptitudes only pass into the condition of man. The good or evil, gentle or fierce instincts which human souls manifest so early, are explained by the species of the animal through which the soul has been transmitted. A child who has a faculty for music may have received the soul of a nightingale, the sweet songster of our woods. A child who is an architect by vocation may have inherited the soul of a beaver, the architect of the woods and waters.

In short, the various aptitudes, the natural faculties, the vocations of human beings, are easily explained by the doctrine of the transmigration of souls. If we reject this system, we must charge God with injustice, because we must believe that He has granted to certain men useful faculties which He has refused to others, and made an unequal distribution of intelligence and morality, these foundations of the conduct and direction of life.

This reasoning appears to us to be beyond attack, for it does not rest upon an hypothesis, but upon a fact : namely, the inequality of the faculties among men, and of their intelligence and morality.   This fact, inexplicable by any theory of any received philosophy, is only to be explained by the doctrine of re-incarnations, and forms the basis of our reasoning.

Discussion for and against phrenology has been plentiful, and has ended in the abandonment of the inquiry, because the ideas of ordinary philosophy do not supply a sound theory on the subject.   It has been found more convenient to ignore the labours of Gall than to endeavour to explain them.   The truth is, that Gall has committed some errors of detail, which is always the case with every founder of a new doctrine, who cannot bring an unprecedented work to perfection by himself alone ; but his successors have rectified the errors of the system, and we are now obliged to acknowledge that Gall's theory is correct.   It is indeed simply composed of observations which everyone may repeat for himself.

When Gall's theory, or *phrenology*, is applied to animals, the evidence in its favour is astonishing.   In the case of man the facts are almost always confirmatory of the theory. It is certain that the skull of an assassin does exhibit the abnormal developments indicated by Gall, and that, according to the doctrine of the German anatomist, the sentiments of affection, love, cupidity, discernment, &c., may be recognised externally by the bumps in the human skull.   It rarely happens that the phrenologist, on examining the skull of a Troppmann, or a Papavoine, fails to trace the hideous indications of evil passions and brutality.

Unfortunately, many of our moralists find themselves seriously embarrassed by philosophy, because their views are limited by the commonplace philosophy of the day. Classic moralists ask themselves whether a man with the bump of murder in his skull is responsible for his crime, whether he is a free agent, whether he is so guilty as he is held to be, when he yields to the cruel instincts with which nature, in his case a wicked step-mother, has endowed him. Is it just to be pitiless towards a man who has only obeyed his physical conformation, almost as a madman obeys the impulses of his diseased mind? It would seem that the punishment of assassination is an injustice, and men ask themselves whether the criminal courts and the scaffold ought not to be abolished, and whether the judge who condemns to death an individual, who is not responsible for his actions, is not the real criminal?

The same reasoning, the same uncertainty apply to virtuous deeds. Is much commendation due to the man who fulfils his duties exactly, to the conscientious and faithful citizen, the honest and kindly individual, if his wise and respectable conduct be simply obedience to the good impulses communicated to him by his physical organization?

These results of phrenology were, it is evident, very embarrassing, and almost immoral. Barbarity on the part of society which punishes the guilty;—absence of merit in the well-behaved man! these consequences were difficult and painful to admit, so the world got out of the difficulty by rejecting phrenology.

It is quite unnecessary to reject phrenology ; we may retain it, and congratulate ourselves on a fresh conquest in the sphere of the sciences of observation, if we hold the doctrine of previous existences. Phrenology is most naturally explained, in fact, by that doctrine. When it enters on the occupation of a human body, the soul lends to the cerebral matter, which is the seat of thought, a certain modification, a predominance in harmony with the faculties which that soul possesses at the period of its birth, and which it has acquired in an anterior animal or human existence. The brain is moulded by the soul into conformity with its proper aptitudes, its acquired faculties ; then the bony covering of the skull, which moulds itself upon the cerebral substance within its cavity, reproduces and gives expression to our predominant faculties. The ancients who said, *Corpus cordis opus* (the body is the work of the soul, or the soul makes its body), expressed this same idea with energetic conciseness.

There is, therefore, no need to excuse a murderer, there is no need to deny his free will, there is no need to spare him the just chastisement of his crime. It is not because there are certain protuberances on his skull that the murderer dips his hands in the blood of his victims. These protuberances are only the external indications of the evil and vicious propensities with which he was born, by which he might have been warned and corrected, and which he might have conquered by the strength of his will, by a real and ardent desire to restore his deformed and vicious soul to rectitude. It is always possible, by adequate effort, to surmount the evil inclinations of one's nature; every one of us can resist pride, idleness, and envy. The man who has not corrected these bad impulses is guilty, and nothing can render a crime committed in all the plenitude of his free will excusable. Thus, neither God nor society is implicated in this question, if we accept the doctrine of the plurality of existences.

Descartes and Leibnitz have demonstrated that the human understanding possesses ideas called *innate*, that is to say, ideas which we bring with us to our birth. This fact is certain. In our time, the Scotch philosopher, Dugald Stewart, has put Descartes' theory into a more precise form, by proving that the only real *innate* idea, that which has universal existence in the human mind after birth, is the idea, or the *principle of causality*, a principle which makes us say and think that there is no effect without cause, which is the beginning of reason. In France, Laromiguière and Damiron have popularized this discovery of the Scotch philosopher. Thus the classics of philosophy record this proposition as a truth beyond the reach of doubt. We unreservedly admit the principle of causality as the *innate* idea *par excellence,* and we take account of the fact. But we ask the fashionable philosophy how it can explain it? In our minds there are *innate ideas,* as Descartes has said ; and the *principle of causality,* which invincibly obliges us to refer from the effect to the cause, is the most evident of those ideas which seem to make a part of ourselves ; but why have we innate ideas, where do they come from, and how did they get into our minds? The classical philosophy, the philosophy of Descartes, which reigns in France, at the Normal School, and among the professors of the University of Paris, cannot teach us that. It will be said, perhaps, to use the favourite argument of Descartes, that we have innate ideas because it is the will of God, who has created the soul. But such a reply is at once commonplace and arbitrary, it may be used on all occasions—it is so used in fact—and it is not a logical argument.

Innate ideas and the principle of causality are explained very simply by the doctrine of the plurality of existences; they are, indeed, merely deductions from that doctrine. A man's soul, having already existed, either in the body of an animal or that of another man, has preserved the trace of the impressions received during that existence. It has lost, it is true, the recollection of actions performed during its first incarnation; but the abstract principle of causality, being independent of the particular facts, being only the general result of the practice of life, must remain in the soul at its second incarnation.

Thus, the principle of causality, of which French philosophy cannot offer any satisfactory theory, is explained in the simplest possible manner, by the hypothesis of re-incarnations and of the plurality of existences.

We have previously alluded to memory, and explained its relation to re-incarnations, and the reasons why we are born without any consciousness of a previous life. We have said, that if we come from an animal, we have no memory, because the animal has none, or has very little. We must now add, that if we come from a human soul, reopening to the light of life, we are destitute of memory, because it would disturb the trial of our terrestrial life, and even render it impossible, as it is the intention of nature that we should recommence the experience of existence without any trace, present to our minds, of previous actions which might limit or embarrass our free will.

We cannot pass from this portion of our subject without calling attention to the fact that the remembrance of a previous existence is not always absolutely wanting to us. Who is there, who, in his hours of solitary contemplation, has not seen a hidden world come forth before his eyes from the far distance of a mysterious past? When, wrapped in profound reverie, we let ourselves float on the stream of imagination, into the ocean of the vague, and the infinite, do we not see magic pictures which are not absolutely unknown to our eyes? do we not hear celestial harmonies which have already enchanted our ears? These secret imaginings, these involuntary contemplations, to which each of us can testify, are they not the real recollections of an existence anterior to our life here below?

Might we not also attribute to a vague remembrance, to an unconscious sympathy, the real and profound pleasure which we derive from the mere sight of plants, flowers, and vegetation? The aspect of a forest, of a beautiful meadow, of green hills, touches us, moves us, sometimes even to tears. Great masses of verdure, and the humble field daisy, alike speak to our hearts. Each of us has a favourite plant, the flower whose perfume he loves to inhale, or the tree whose shade he prefers. Rousseau was moved by the sight of a yew tree, and Alfred de Musset loved the willows so much, that he expressed a wish, piously fulfilled, that a willow might overshadow his grave.

This love of the vegetable world has a mysterious root in

our hearts. May we not recognize in so natural a sentiment, a sort of vague remembrance of our original country, a secret and involuntary evocation of the scene in which the germ of our soul was first loosed to the light of the sun, the powerful promoter of life?

Besides the undecided and dim remembrance of pictures which seem to belong to our anterior existences upon the globe, we sometimes feel keen aspirations towards a kinder and calmer destiny than that which is allotted to us here below. No doubt coarse beings, entirely attached to material appetites and interests, do not feel these secret longings for an unknown and happier destiny, but poetical and tender souls, those who suffer from the wretched conditions of which human nature is the slave and the martyr, take a vague pleasure in such melancholy aspirations. In the radiant infinite they foresee celestial dwellings, where they shall one day reside, and they are impatient to break the ties which bind them to earth. Read the episode in Goethe's *Mignon*, in which Mignon, wandering and exiled, pours out her young soul in aspirations to heaven, in sublime longings for an unknown and blessed future, which she feels drawing her towards itself, and ask yourself whether the beautiful verses of the great poet, who was also a great naturalist, do not interpret a truth of nature, *i.e.*, the new life which awaits us in the plains of ether. Why do all men, among all peoples, raise their eyes to heaven in solemn moments, in the impulses of passion, and the anguish of grief or pain? Does any one, under such circumstances, contemplate the earth on which he stands? Our eyes and our hearts turn towards the skies.

The dying raise their fallen orbs to heaven, and we look towards the celestial spaces in those vague reveries which we have been describing. It is permitted to us to believe that this universal tendency is an intuition of that which awaits us after our terrestrial life, a natural revelation of the domain which shall be ours one day, and which extends over the celestial empyrean, to the bosom of ethereal space.

CHAPTER THE SEVENTEENTH.

E propose now to collect, within a few summary propositions, the principal features of the system of nature which we have defined.

1. The sun is the primary agent of life and organization.

2. In the primitive time of our globe, life began to appear in aquatic and aërial plants, as well as in zoophytes. The same order reproduces itself at present, in the point of departure, and in the development of life and of souls. The solar rays, falling on the earth, and into the waters, produce the formation of plants and that of zoophytes. The rays of the sun by depositing in the waters and on the earth, *animated germs*, emanating from the spiritualized beings who inhabit the sun, bring about the birth of plants and zoophytes.

3. Plants and zoophytes are endowed with sensation. They enclose an animal germ, just as a seed encloses an embryo.

4. The animal germ contained in the plant and in the zoophyte, passes, at the death of each animal, into the body of the animal which comes next to it in the ascending scale of organic perfection. From the zoophyte the animated germ

passes into the mollusc, from thence into the articulated animal, the fish, or the reptile. From the body of the reptile, it passes into that of the bird, and then into the mammifers.

In the inferior beings, for instance zoophytes, several ani-mated germs may be united to form the soul of a single being of a superior order.

5. In passing through the entire series of animals, this ru-dimentary soul becomes perfected and acquires the beginnings of faculties. Conscience, will, and judgment succeed to sen-sation. When the soul has attained the body of a mammi-fer, it has acquired a certain number of faculties. In addi-tion to feeling, it has the basis of reason, *i.e.*, the *principle of causation*. From the body of a mammiferous animal belong-ing to the superior species, the soul passes into the body of a newly-born infant.

6. The child is born without memory, like the superior animal whence it has proceeded. At a year old it acquires this faculty, and gradually obtains others; imagination and thought develop themselves, reason grows strong, memory becomes firm and extensive.

7. If the child dies before the age of twelve months, his soul, still very imperfect, and devoid of active faculties, passes into the body of another newly-born child, and recommences a new existence.

8. When a man dies, his body remains upon the earth, his soul rises through the atmosphere to the ether which sur-rounds all the planets, and enters into the body of the angel, or *superhuman being*.

9. If, during its sojourn upon the earth, the soul has not undergone a sufficient amount of purification and ennobling, it recommences a second existence, passing into the body of a newly-born child, and losing the remembrance of its first life. Only when the soul has attained the suitable degree of perfection, and, after having been re-incarnate once, or many times, is empowered to leave our globe, to assume a new body in the bosom of the ethereal plains, and thus become a superhuman being, can it recover the recollection of its past existences.

10. That which occurs upon the Earth also takes place in the other planets of our solar system. In these planets vegetables, or beings analogous to vegetables are produced by the action of the sun. By means of his rays animated germs are carried into these globes, and plants and inferior animals are produced. Then these animated germs contained in the plants and inferior animals, passing successively through the whole series of animals, end by producing a being, superior, in intelligence and sensibility, to all the other living creatures. This superior being, the analogue of the human being, we call planetary man.

11. The planetary man, who inhabits Mercury, Mars, Venus, &c., being dead, his material form remains upon the planetary globe, and his soul, provided it has acquired the necessary degree of purity, passes into the surrounding ether, is incarnate in a new body, and produces a superhuman being.

12. Phalanxes of these superhuman beings float in the planetary ether. It witnesses the reunion of all the purified souls which have come from our globe and from the other

planets. The organic types of these beings is the same, whatever may be their planetary abode.

13. The superhuman being is provided with special attributes, he is endowed with mighty faculties which raise him to a height infinitely above terrestrial or planetary humanity. In this being, matter, in comparison with the spiritual principle, is reduced to a much smaller proportion than in man. His body is light and vaporous. He possesses senses which are unknown to us, and the senses which he possesses in common with us, are prodigiously intensified, subtilised, and perfected. He can transport himself, in a short space of time, to any distance, he can travel, without fatigue, from one point in space to another. His vision is of immeasurable extent. He has intuitive knowledge of many facts of nature which are hidden by an impenetrable veil from feeble human perception.

14. The superhuman being who comes from the earth can place himself in communication with men who are worthy of the privilege. He directs their conduct, watches over their actions, enlightens their understanding, inspires their hearts. When, in their turn, they too reach the celestial dwellings, he receives them on the threshold of their new abode, and initiates them into the life of blessedness beyond the tomb.

15. The superhuman being is mortal. When he has terminated the normal course of his existence in the ethereal spaces, he dies, and his spiritual principle enters into a new body, that of the *archangel*, or *arch-human being*, in whom the proportion of spiritual principle predominates still more strongly, in proportion to matter.

16. These re-incarnations, in the depths of the ethereal spaces, are reproduced more frequently than can be defined, and give us a series of creatures of ever-increasing activity and power of thought and action. At each promotion in the hierarchy of space these sublime beings find the energy of their moral and intellectual faculties, their power of feeling, and of loving, and their induction into the most profound mysteries of the Universe, undergoing augmentation.

17. When he has arrived at the highest degree of the celestial hierarchy, the *spiritualized being* is absolutely perfect ; in strength and in intelligence. He is entirely freed from all material alloy, he has no longer a body, he is a pure spirit. In this condition he passes into the sun.

18. The sun, the king-star, is then the final and common sojourn of all the *spiritualized beings* who have come from the other planets, after having passed through the long series of existences which have rolled away in the plains of ether.

19. The *spiritualized beings* gathered together in the sun, send down upon the earth and upon the planets emanations from their essence, that is to say, *animated germs.* These *animated germs* are carried by the sunbeams, which distribute organization, feeling, and life over all the planets, at the same time that they preside at all the great physical and mechanical operations which take place on the earth, and on the other planets of our solar world.

20. The formation of the aërial and aquatic plants, and the birth of inferior animals or zoophytes, are, as we have said, the result of the action of the sun's rays on our globe. Then commences the series of the transmigrations of souls through

the bodies of various animals, which results in man, in the superhuman being, and in all the succession of celestial metempsychoses, whose ultimate term is the spiritualized being or the dweller in the sun.

Thus does the great chain of nature close and complete itself;—that uninterrupted chain of vital activity, which has neither beginning nor end, and which links all created beings into one family, the universal family of the worlds.

Nature is not a straight line, but a circle, and we cannot say where this wonderful circle begins or ends. The wisdom of the Egyptians, which represented the world as a serpent coiled around itself, was the symbol of a great truth which the science of our time has once more brought to light.

CHAPTER THE EIGHTEENTH.

REPLIES TO SOME OBJECTIONS.—FIRST : THE IMMORTALITY OF
THE SOUL, WHICH IS THE BASIS OF THIS SYSTEM, IS NOT DE-
MONSTRATED.— SECOND : WE HAVE NOT ANY RECOLLECTION
OF ANTERIOR EXISTENCES.—THIRD : THIS SYSTEM IS NO OTHER
THAN THE METEMPSYCHOSIS OF THE ANCIENTS.—FOURTH : THIS
SYSTEM IS CONFOUNDED WITH DARWINISM.

HAVING brought into relief, by the preceding summary, the entire doctrine of successive lives and of re-incarnations, we must now meet some objections which will have been provoked by these propositions, and reply to them in a way which has the advantage of still more distinctly explaining our ideas on several points.

First objection. It will be said : The existence of an immortal soul in man forms the basis of all this reasoning. Now, the fact of the existence of an immortal soul is not demonstrated in the course of this work, and, besides, it could not be demonstrated.

The following is our reply to this first objection.

We are composed of two elements, or of two substances; one which thinks—the soul, or the immaterial substance; the other, which does not think—the body, or the material substance. This truth is self-evident. Thought is a fact, certain in itself; and it is another fact, equally certain, that my arms, my nails or beard, do not think. Here, then, is the proof of the immortality of the soul, or thinking principle.

Matter does not perish; observation and science prove that material bodies are never annihilated, that they merely change their condition, their form, and their place; but are always to be found somewhere intact as to their substance. Our bodies decompose, and are dissolved, but the matter of which they were formed is never destroyed, it is dispersed in the air, the fire, and the water, in which it produces new material combinations, but it is not destroyed for all that. Now, if matter does not perish, but only becomes transformed, all the more certainly must the soul be indestructible and imperishable. Like matter, it must be transformed, without being destroyed.

Descartes has said, *I think, therefore I am.* This reasoning, so much admired in the schools, has always appeared to us rather weak. To give force to the syllogism, he should have said, *I think, therefore I am immortal.* My soul is immortal, because it exists, and it does exist since I think. Thus the fact of the immortality of the spiritual principle which we bear within us is self-evident, and we do not need any of the demonstrations which abound in philosophical works, and have been put forth from antiquity until our own time; we need no *Treatises on the Soul* to establish its existence.

The difficulty does not consist in proving that a spiritual principle exists within us, that is to say, a principle which resists death, because, in order to contest the existence of this principle, it would be necessary to contest thought. The real problem is to find out whether this spiritual and immortal principle which we bear within us, is to live again, after our death, in ourselves or in others. The question is, whether the immortal soul will be born again in the same individual, physically transformed, in the same person, in the *ego,* or whether it will pass into the possession of a being strange to that person.

We may remark here that on this all the interest of the question for us turns. It would be of very little importance to us, in reality, whether the soul were immortal or not, if the soul of each of us, being really indestructible and immortal, should pass to another than ourselves, or if, reviving in us, it did not possess the memory of our past existence, The resurrection of the soul without the memory of the past would be a real annihilation, this would be the nothingness of the materialists. It must be, then, that the soul lives again after our death, in ourselves, and that this soul, then, has clear remembrance of all the actions which took place in its previous existences. It behoves us, in short, to know, not whether our souls are immortal—that fact is self-evident—but whether they will belong to us in the other life, whether, after our death, we shall have identity, individuality, *personality.* It is to the study of this question that the present work is devoted. We are endeavouring to prove that the soul of the man remains always the same, in spite of its numerous peregrinations, notwithstanding the variety of form of the bodies in which it is successively lodged, when it passes from the animal to the man, from the man to the superhuman being, and from the superhuman being, after other celestial transmigrations, to the spiritualized being who inhabits the sun. We are endeavouring to establish that the soul, notwithstanding all its journeys, in the midst of its incarnations and various metamorphoses, remains always identical with itself, doing nothing more in each metempsychosis, in each metamorphosis of the exterior being, than perfect and purify itself, growing in power and in intellectual grasp. We are endeavouring to prove, that, notwithstanding the shadows of death, our individuality is never destroyed, and that we shall be born again in the heavens, with the same moral personality which was ours here below ; in other words, that the human *person* is imperishable. It is for the reader to say whether we have attained our object, whether we have established the truth of this doctrine conformably with the laws of reasoning and the facts of science.

If an absolute demonstration of the existence of an immaterial principle in us be insisted upon, we must reply, that philosophy, like geometry, has its axioms, that is to say, its self-evident truths, which need not, or, if we choose to say so, which cannot be mathematically demonstrated. The existence of the soul is one of those axioms of philosophy. Diogenes answered a rhetorician who denied movement by walking in his presence. By expressing any thought, by saying "yes," or "no," we may prove the existence of the immortal soul to the sophists who would attempt to contest it.

We have just said that geometry has its axioms. Let us remember that an entire school of geometricians amused themselves by disputing the axioms, under the pretext that it was impossible to demonstrate them. We were present, in December, 1866, at a curious sitting of the Institute, during which M. Liouville, a celebrated mathematician, and professor at the Sorbonne, explained this strange polemic with great skill.

In attempting to demonstrate the propositions of geometry, certain axioms, *i.e.*, self-evident truths, must be admitted in the first place. Otherwise, the primary reasoning will have no basis. But, among the numerous propositions of this kind which present themselves to the mind, and which result from the admission of one of their number, which is the most evident? That depends on the nature of the mind of each of us, and therefore it is that there is not, and that there never will be, an argument on this question.

There is a school of geometry which pretends to demonstrate everything. There is another, the true and good school, which, recognizing that the human mind has limits, and that everything is not accessible by our thoughts, lays down, under the name of axioms, certain truths which do not require proof, or, which is often the same thing, are incapable of proof.

Among the number of self-evident truths, or truths difficult of demonstration, we find the question of parallel lines. What are two parallels? Two lines which never meet each other. But how can we prove this property of two lines by reasoning? That is not, exactly speaking, possible, since the notion of the infinite is not admitted, or not understood by everybody, and cannot, therefore, serve as the basis of an absolutely rigorous argument.

It was for this reason that Euclid, the founder of geometry in ancient times, laid down this truth as a simple axiom, requiring (hence the *postulates* of Euclid, from the Latin verb *postulare,* to demand), that the truth of this principle, which he acknowledged himself unable to prove by logical demonstration, should be granted.

A hundred geometricians, since Euclid, who renounced the attempt to demonstrate it, have tried to prove this theory of parallels, but not one has succeeded. It was on the occasion of a fresh attempt at demonstration by a mathematician in the provinces, that M. Lionville spoke before the Academy, to recall the principles almost unanimously professed by geometricians on this subject.

The question is, in reality, thoroughly understood; it is treated on all works on geometry, and has been for a long time a settled matter. But certain minds are tempted by the subtlety of certain subjects, and the question of the *postulatum* turns up periodically before the learned societies, as it does in the conversations between the teachers of mathematics.

M. Lionville reminded his audience that many demonstrations of this celebrated proposition had been attempted, but had not succeeded, because there are limits within which human reason ceases to be accepted by all. M. Lionville even proposed that the question of the *postulatum* should be classed among those whose examination is interdicted by the Academy, such as the quadrature of the circle, and the trisection of the angle. On this point M. Lionville quoted an anecdote relative to Lagrange. That great mathematician, believing that he had found an absolute solution of the *postulatum,* went to the Academy to read his demonstration, but on reflection, he changed his mind, and decided that it would be better not to publish it. He put his manuscript in his pocket, and it never came out.

Several geometricians spoke on this occasion, and confirmed the views of M. Lionville; and when the demonstration submitted by the professor was examined, it was found to be false. We must therefore recognize and proclaim that, in geometry, the axioms cannot be demonstrated.

Many people endeavour to derive an argument from that discussion against the certainty of geometry. Among them is M. Bouillaud, a learned physician and member of the Institute, who declared that he could not get over his astonishment at hearing it said that there were several geometries, and that even the bases of that science were doubtful. Reassure yourself, great and good physician, geometry has nothing to lose and nothing to hide, and the certainty of its methods is not imperilled in this question. That which really was at stake was the methodical, classical teaching of geometry. That which was discussed was the best means of instilling the principles of science into the mind. But, as to the truths of geometry, as to the facts themselves, they are secure from all uncertainty, all these disputes upon the truth which must be recognized as axioms, or demonstrated as theorems, are only fancies of the rhetoricians, as vain as they are subtle. No trace of them remains when they are transported into the practice of facts and of mathematical deductions. Ask the astronomers who calculate the orbit of the stars, who fix the moment of an eclipse with unerring precision, ask those who have calculated the parallaxes, whether they trouble themselves by inquiring how it may be demonstrated that the angles of a triangle are equal to two right angles. All the scholastic subtleties are gotten rid of in the course of practical work.

If we may lay aside, without occupying ourselves with them, the mathematicians who amuse themselves by disputing the axioms of geometry, we may do the same with the few sophists who desire to dispute the axioms of philosophy and reason, and especially the principle of the existence of an immortal soul in man. Let us leave them to their disputations, and go on our way.

Second objection :—We have no recollection of having existed prior to our entrance into this world.

This is, we acknowledge the greatest and most serious argument against our system. But we must hasten to add, that if this difficulty did not exist, if the remembrance of a life anterior to our present existence were always before us, the doctrine of plurality of lives would need no reinforcement from the proofs for which we appeal to argument, to the facts of observation, and to logical induction. It would be plain before our eyes, it would be self-evident. All our merit, all our task in this work, is to endeavour to procure admission of the plurality of existences, though we have no remembrance of our past lives.

We have already treated this question incidentally, and we will now summarize all that has been advanced in former chapters to explain the absence of recollection of our past existences.

The soul in its first human incarnation, if it proceeds from a superior animal, could not possess memory, because in animals that faculty has a small range, and brief duration. If a second or third human incarnation is in question, the difficulty is serious, because it implies that the man who has lived and who is born again, has forgotten his previous life.

But, in the first place, this forgetfulness is not absolute. We have remarked before that in the human soul certain results of impressions received prior to the terrestrial life always linger. Natural aptitudes, special faculties, vocations, are the traces of impressions formerly received, of knowledge already acquired, and, being revealed from the cradle, cannot be explained otherwise than by a life gone by. We have lost the remembrance of the facts, but there remains the moral consequence, the *resultant*, the philosophy, so to speak, and thus the *innate ideas* indicated by Descartes, which exist in the soul from its birth, and also the *principle of causality*, which teaches us that every effect has a cause, are explained. This principle can only be derived from facts, because an abstraction can only be based upon concrete facts, upon accomplished events, and this abstraction, or this metaphysical idea, which we have from our birth, implies anterior facts, which must belong to a past life.

We have already said that when the soul gives free course to reverie, it beholds mysterious and undefined spectacles, which seem to belong to worlds which are not quite unknown to us, but in no wise resembling this earth. In this vague contemplation there is something like a confused remembrance of an anterior life. The love which we bear to flowers, plants, and all vegetation, may be as we have already pointed out, a grateful recollection of our first origin.

If, however, these considerations be not accepted as valid, there is another, which, to our mind, perfectly explains the absence of a remembrance of our former existences. It is we believe, by a premeditated decree of nature, that the

memory of our past lives is denied to us while we are on the
earth. M. André Pezzani, the author of an excellent book
called "*Pluralité des existences de l'âme*," replies to the argument of oblivion, thus :

" Our terrestrial sojourn is only a new trial, as Dupont de
Nemours, that wonderful writer of the eighteenth century,
who outstripped all modern beliefs, has said. If this be so,
can we not perceive that the remembrance of past lives would
embarrass these trials by removing the greater part of their
difficulties, and, in proportion, of their merit, and destroying
their spontaneity? We live in a world in which free-will is
all powerful, the inviolable law of the advancement and the
progressive initiation of men. If past existences were known,
the soul would know the meaning and the bearing of the trials
reserved for it here below; indolent and idle, it would harden
itself against the designs of Providence, and would be either
paralyzed by its despair of overcoming them, or, if better disposed and more virile, it would accept and accomplish them
unfailingly. But neither one nor the other of these positions
is fitting. Our efforts must be free, voluntary, sheltered from
the influences of the past; the field of strife must be seemingly
untrodden, so that the athlete shall show and exercise his
virtue. Previously gained experience, the energies which he
has acquired, help him in the new strife, but in a latent way
of which he is unconscious, for the imperfect soul undergoes
these re-incarnations, in order to develop its previously
manifested qualities, and to strip itself of those vices and
defects which oppose themselves to the law of its ascension.
What would happen if all men remembered their previous
lives? The order of the earth would be overturned, or at
least, it would not remain in its present condition. *Léthé*, like
free-will, is a law of the world as it is."*

* "*La Pluralité des existences de l'âme*," Paris, p. 450.

16

To this it will be objected that there is destruction of identity where memory does not exist, and that expiation, in order to be profitable to the guilty soul, must co-exist with the remembrance of faults committed in the previous existence, for the man is not punished who does not know that he is punished. We may remark here that we do not use the word "expiation" precisely as theologians employ it, but rather as a new dwelling conferred on the soul, in order that it may resume the interrupted course of its advance towards perfection. We believe that the remembrance of our previous life, forbidden to us during our terrestrial sojourn, will come back when we shall have attained the happy realms of ether, in which we shall pass through the existences which are to succeed our life on earth. Among the number of the perfections and moral faculties forming the attributes of the superhuman being, the memory of his anterior lives will be included. Identity will be born again for him. Having suffered a momentary collapse, his individuality will be restored to him, with his conscience and his liberty.

Let us hearken awhile to Jean Reynaud, as he tells us in his fine book, *Terre et Ciel,* the marvels of that memory which shall be restored to man after his being shall have undergone a series of changes.

"The integral restitution of our recollections," says Jean Reynaud, "seems to us one of the inherent principal conditions of our future happiness. We cannot fully enjoy life, until we become, like Janus, kings of time, until we know how to concentrate in us, not only the sentiment of the present, but that of the future and the past. Then, if perfect life be one day given to us, perfect memory must also be given

to us. And now, let us try to think of the infinite treasures
of a mind enriched by the recollections of an innumerable
series of existences, entirely different from each other, and yet
admirably linked together by a continual dependence. To
this marvellous garland of metempsychoses, encircling the
universe, let us add, if the perspective seem worthy of our
ambition, a clear perception of the particular influence of our
life upon the ulterior changes of each of the worlds which
we shall have successively inhabited ; let us aggrandize our
life in immortalizing it, and wed our history grandly with the
history of the heavens. Let us confidently collect together
every material of happiness, since thus the all-powerful
bounty of the Creator wills it, and let us construct the existence which the future reserves for virtuous souls ; let us
plunge into the past by our faith, while we are waiting for
more light, even as by our faith we plunge into the future.
Let us banish the idea of disorder from the earth, by opening
the gates of time beyond our birth, as we have banished the
idea of injustice by opening other gates beyond the tomb ;
let us stretch duration in every direction, and, notwithstanding
the obscurity which rests upon our two horizons, let us
glorify the Creator in glorifying ourselves, who are God's
ministers on earth, let us remember, with pious pride, that we
are the younger brethren of the angels."

Under what condition does the soul regain the remembrance
of its entire past? Jean Reynaud specifies two periods.
1. That which is fulfilled, as the Druids hold, in the world of
journeys and trials, of which the earth forms a part. 2. The
period during which the soul, set free from the miseries and
vicissitudes of the terrestrial life, pursues its destinies in the
ever widening and progressive circle of happiness ; a period
which passes outside of the earth. In the first period there

is an eclipse of the memory at each passage into a new sphere; in the second period, whatever may be the displacements and transfigurations of the person, the memory is preserved full and entire.   This theory of Reynaud's is admitted by M. Pezzani.

With the exception of that *eclipse of the memory at each passage into a new sphere,* which seems to us incomprehensible and useless, we think, with Jean Reynaud, that the complete remembrance of our previous existences will return to the soul when it shall inhabit the ethereal regions, the sojourn of the superhuman being.   In this manner only, in our opinion, can the defect of man's memory, concerning his previous existences, be explained.   Thus, the argument from that defect of memory does not remain without reply.   Writers who have preceded us, and have meditated on this question, had already found the solution which we offer.   This objection is not, then, of a nature to throw doubt on the doctrine of plurality of existences.   Let us conclude, with M. Pezzani, that it is by a design of nature, that man, during this life, loses the remembrance of what he formerly was.   If we retained the recollection of our anterior existences, if we had before our eyes, as if seen in a mirror, all that we had done during our former lives, we should be much troubled by the remembrance, which would harass the greater part of our actions, and deprive us of our complete free will.

Why is an invincible dread of death common to all men? Death is not, in reality, very dreadful, since it is not a termination, but a simple change of condition.   If man feels terror of death to such an extent, we may be sure that nature imposes that sentiment upon him, in the interests of the pre-

servation of his species. Thus, in our belief, the fear of death
and the absence of memory of our former lives are referable
to the same cause. The first is a salutary illusion imposed by
God upon the weakness of humanity ; the second is a means
of securing to man full liberty of action.

Another objection will be made to our doctrine. It will
be said : The re-incarnation of souls is not a new idea ; it is,
on the contrary, an idea as old as humanity itself. It is the
metempsychosis, which from the Indians passed to the
Egyptians, from the Egyptians to the Greeks, and which
was afterwards professed by the Druids.

The metempsychosis is, in fact, the most ancient of philosophical conceptions ; it is the first theory imagined by men,
in order to explain the origin and the destiny of our race.
We do not recognize an argument against our system of nature
in this remark, but rather indeed a confirmation of it. An
idea does not pass down from age to age, and find acceptance
during five or six centuries, by the picked men of successive
generations, unless it rests upon some serious foundation. We
are not called upon to defend ourselves because our opinions
harmonize with the philosophical ideas which date from the
most distant time in the history of the peoples. The first
observers, and the oriental philosophers in particular, who are
the most ancient thinkers of all whose writings we possess,
had not, like us, their minds warped, prejudiced, turned aside
by routine, or trammelled by the words of teachers. They
were placed very close to nature, and they beheld its realities,
without any preconceived ideas, derived from education in
particular schools. We cannot, therefore, but applaud our·

selves when we find that the logical deduction of our ideas has led us back to the antique conception of Indian wisdom.

There is, however, a profound difference between our system of the plurality of lives, and the oriental dogma of the metempsychosis. The Indian philosophers, the Egyptians, and the Greeks, who inherited the maxims of Pythagoras, admitted that the soul, on leaving a human body, enters into that of an animal, to undergo punishment. We entirely reject this useless step backward. Our metempsychosis is upward and onward, it never steps down, or back.

A brief sketch of the dogma of the animal metempsychosis, such as it was professed by the different philosophical sects of antiquity will not be out of place here. We shall explain in what particulars the oriental dogma differs from our system, and show, at the same time, how popular the metempsychosis was among the peoples of antiquity, in Europe as well as in Asia.

The most ancient known book is that of the *Védas*, which contains the religious principles of the Indians or Hindoos. In this code of the primary religions of Asia is found the general dogma of the final absorption of souls in God. But, before it reaches its final fusion with the great All, it is necessary that the human soul should have traversed all the active orders of life. The soul, therefore, performed a series of transmigrations and journeys, in various places, in different worlds, and passed through the bodies of several different animals. Men who had not done good works went into the moon or the sun; or else they came back to the earth, and assumed the bodies of certain animals, such as dogs, butter-

flies, adders, &c. There were also intermediary places between the earth and the sun, whither souls who had only
been partly faulty, went to pass a period of expiation. We
find the following in the *Védas :—*

"If a man has done works which lead to the world of the
sun, his soul repairs to the world of the sun ; if he has done
works which lead to the world of the Creator, his soul goes to
the world of the Creator."

The book of the *Védas* says, very distinctly, that the
animal, as well as the man, has the right of passing to other
worlds, as a recompense for his good works. The oriental
wisdom felt none of that uncalled-for contempt for animals
which is characteristic of modern philosophy and religion.

"All animals, according to the degree of knowledge and
intelligence which they have had in this world, go into other
worlds. The man whose object was the recompense of his
good works, being dead, goes into the world of the moon.
There he is at the service of the overseers of the half of the
moon in its crescent. They welcome him joyfully, but he is
not tranquil, he is not happy ; all his recompense is to have
attained for a while to the world of the moon. On the ex-
piration of this time, the servant of the overseers of the moon
descends again into hell ; and is born as a worm, a butterfly, lion, fish, dog, or under any other form (even under a
human form)."*

" At the last stages of his descent, if one asks, who are you ?
he replies : I come from the world of the moon, the wages of
the deeds done during my life merely for the sake of reward.
I am again invested with a body ; I have suffered in the womb

---

* "*La Religion des Hindous selon les Védas,*" par Lanjuinais,
Paris, p. 286.

of my mother, and in leaving it; I hope finally to acquire the knowledge of Him who is all things, to enter into the right way of worship and of meditation without any consideration of reward.

"In the world of the moon, one receives the reward of good works which are done without renunciation of their fruits, of their merits; but this reward has only a fixed time, after which one is born again in an inferior world, a wicked world, a world which is the recompense of evil.

"By the renunciation of all pleasure, and of all reward by seeking God only, with unshaken faith, we reach the sun which has no end, the great world, whence we return no more to a world which is the recompense of evil."*

The Egyptians, having borrowed this doctrine from the Hindoos, made it the basis of their religious worship. Herodotus informs us,† that, according to the Egyptians, the human soul, on issuing from a completely decomposed body, enters into that of some animal. The soul takes three thousand years to pass from this body through a series of others, and at the conclusion of this interval, the same soul returns to the human species, entering the form of a newly-born infant.

The Egyptians employed excessive caution in the preservation of human bodies. They embalmed the corpses of their relatives or of personages of importance to the state, and thus prepared the mummies which are to be seen in all our museums. The universal practice of embalming was not

* "*La Religion des Hindous selon les Védas,*" pp. 324, 325.
† "*Histoires,*" Vol. II. ch. cxxiii. (translated by M. Larcher.

intended, as has been supposed, to keep the human body ready to receive the soul, returning at the end of three thousand years, to seek its primitive abode. It had another object. It was supposed that the soul did not commence its migrations after the death of the human body, while any portion of the corpse remained entire. Hence the efforts made by the Egyptians, to retard the moment of separation by the preservation of the corpse as long as possible. Servius says :

"The Egyptians, renowned for their wisdom, prolonged the duration of corpses, that the existence of the soul, attached to that of the body, might be preserved, and might not pass away quickly to others. The Romans, on the contrary, burn corpses, so that the soul, resuming its liberty, might immediately re-enter nature."

The most ancient and remarkable of the Greek philosophers, Pythagoras, found out the doctrine of the metempsychosis, in his travels in Egypt. He adopted it in his school, and the whole of the Greek philosophy held, with Pythagoras, that the souls of the wicked pass into the bodies of animals. Hence the abstinence from flesh meat, prescribed by Pythagoras to his disciples, a precept which he also derived from Egypt, where respect for animals was due to the general persuasion that the bodies of beasts were tenanted by human souls, and, consequently, that by ill-treating animals, one ran the risk of injuring one's own ancestors. Empedocles, the philosopher, adopted the Pythagorean system. He says, in lines quoted by Clement of Alexandria :—

> "I, too, have been a young maiden,
> A tree, a bird, a mute fish in the seas."

Plato, the most illustrious of the philosophers of Greece, accords a large place to the views of Pythagoras, even amid his most sublime conceptions of the soul, and of immortality. He held that the human soul passes into the body of animals, in expiation of its crimes. Plato said that on earth we remember what we have done during our previous existences, and that to learn is to remember one's self.

"Cowards," he says, "are changed into women, vain and frivolous men into birds, the ignorant into wild beasts, lower in kind and crawling upon the earth, in proportion as their idleness has been more degrading ; stained and corrupt souls animate fishes and aquatic reptiles." Again, he says : "Those who have abandoned themselves to intemperance and gluttony enter into the bodies of animals with like propensities. They who have loved injustice, cruelty, and rapine assume the bodies of wolves, hawks, and falcons. The destiny of souls has relation to the lives which they have led."

Plato held that the soul took only one thousand years to complete its journey through the bodies of animals ; but he believed that this journey repeated itself ten times over, which gives a total of 10,000 years for the completion of the entire circle of existences. Between each of these periods the soul made a brief sojourn in Hades. During this sojourn it drank of the waters of the river Lethe, in order to lose the recollection of its previous existence, before re-commencing its new life.

Plato exalted the dogma of the animal metempsychosis by his grand views upon spiritual immortality and the liberty of man, ideas which even at the present time are quoted with admiration, but for whose recapitulation we have not space.

The metempsychosis holds less rank in the Platonic doctrine than in the Pythagorean and Egyptian systems. All its importance was resumed among the philosophers of the Alexandrian school, who continued, in Egypt, the traditions of the Platonic philosophy, and revived the days of the schools of Athens on the soil of the Pharaohs. Plotinus, the commentator of Plato, says, concerning the doctrine of the transmigration of souls :

" It is a dogma recognized from the utmost antiquity, that if the soul commits errors, it is condemned to expiate them by undergoing punishment in the Shades, and then it passes into new bodies to begin its trials over again."

This passage proves that the ancients held the sojourn of the soul in hell to be only temporary, and that it was always followed by fresh trials, terrible and painful in proportion to the errors which were to be repaired.

"When," says Plotinus, "we have gone astray in the multiplicity of our corporal passions, we are punished, first by the straying itself, and afterwards, when we resume a body, by finding ourselves in worse conditions. The soul, on leaving the body, becomes that power which it has most developed. Let us, then, fly from base things here below, and raise ourselves to the intelligent world, so that we may not fall into the purely sensational life, by following images which are merely of the senses, or into the vegetative life, by indulging in mere physical pleasure and gluttony ; let us raise ourselves to the intelligent world, to intelligence, to God.

"Those who have exercised human faculties are born again as men. Those who have used their senses only pass into the bodies of brutes, and especially into the bodies of wild beasts, if they have been accustomed to yield to violent impulses of anger ; so that the different bodies which they animate are conformable to their various propensities. Those who have done nothing but indulge their appetites pass into the bodies of luxurious and gluttonous animals. Others, who, instead of indulging concupiscence or anger, have degraded their senses by sloth, are reduced to vegetate in the plants, because in their previous existences they have exercised nothing but vegetative power, and have only worked to become trees. Those who have loved the enjoyment of music over much, but have led lives otherwise pure, pass into the bodies of melodious birds. Those who have governed tyrannically, but have no other vice, become eagles. Those who have spoken lightly of celestial things are changed into birds which fly towards the higher regions of the air. He who has acquired civil virtues becomes a man again, but if he does not possess these virtues to a sufficient extent, he is transformed into a sociable creature, such as the bee, or some other being of that species."

Every one knows that among our own ancestors, and the Druids or high-priests of the Gauls, the metempsychosis was held almost in the same sense as among the Egyptians and the Greeks. It is, so to speak, a national faith to us, for it has been held in honour, its dogmas have flourished, in the same countries in which we now dwell. We have recalled these facts, and collected these passages from ancient writers, only in order to define the manner in which the Egyptians, as well as the Greeks, and, in later times, the Gauls, under-stood the metempsychosis. Our system differs from the old oriental conception, which was embraced by the Egyptians, the Greeks, and the Druids, in our denial that the human soul can ever return to the body of an animal. We believe that the human soul has already passed through this probation, and that it never can be renewed. In nature, in fact, the animal has a part inferior to that of man ; it is below our species in its degree of intelligence, and it cannot have either merit or demerit. Its faculties do not invest it with the entire responsibility of its actions. It is but an intermediate link between the plant and man ; it has certain faculties, but we cannot pretend that those faculties assimilate it to moral man.

Thus, we reject this doctrine of the return of the human soul to conditions through which it has already passed. Retrogression has no place in our system. The soul, in its progressive march, may pause for an instant, but it never turns back. We admit that man is condemned to re-commence an ill-fulfilled existence, but this new experience is made in a human body, in a new covering of the same living type, and not in the form of an inferior being. The oriental dogma of the metempsychosis misapprehended the great law of progress, which is, on the contrary, the foundation of our doctrine.

Fourth objection. It will be said to us : You maintain that our souls have already existed in the bodies of animals ; do you, then, share the belief of those naturalists who derive man from the monkey ?

No, certainly not. The French and German naturalists, who, applying Darwin's theory of the transformation of species to man, have declared man to be derived from the monkey, rely entirely on anatomical considerations. Vogt, Bruchner, Huxley, and Broca compare the skeleton of the monkey with that of primitive man ; they study the form of the skull of each respectively, they measure the width and the prominence of the jaws, &c., &c. From the results, they draw the conclusion that man is anatomically derived from a species of quadrumane. The soul is not taken into any consideration by these men of science, who argue precisely as if nothing of the thinking kind existed in the anatomical cavities which they explore and measure. It is, on the contrary, by comparing the faculties of the human soul with the faculties of animals that we arrive at our conclusion. The animal forms signify nothing to us ; the spirit, in its various manifestations, is our chief object. Why, indeed, should we seek to derive man from the monkey, rather than from any other mammiferous animal, rather than from the wolf, or the fox ? Is there much difference between the skeleton of the monkey and that of the wolf, the fox, or any other carnivorous beast ? Put three or four of those skeletons together, and you will not find it easy to distinguish one from the other, if, instead of selecting a monkey of a superior species, you take an inferior quadrumane, a striated monkey, a lemur, or a macao.

Interrogate the physiological functions of the monkey. You will find them, and the organs which serve those functions, perfectly similar in all animals, and those organs identical in their structure. Why, then, should you derive man from the monkey, rather than from the wolf or the fox ? Is it because the monkeys in our menageries have a distant resemblance to man, in their occasional vertical attitude, and in certain features which are caricatures of those of the human face? How many of the species among the immense simial family of the two hemispheres present this resemblance ? Hardly five or six. All the others have the bestial snout in its fullest development, and are very inferior in intelligence to most of the other mammifers. If it be from the organic point of view that you derive man from the monkey, because certain species of quadrumanes are caricatures of men in their physiognomy, why may he not be derived as reasonably from the parrot, which emits articulate sounds, the caricature of the human voice, or even the nightingale, because that melodious songster of the woods modulates his notes like our singers?

The consideration of animal forms is of very little importance in our estimation, when the matter in hand is to determine the place occupied by a living being in the scale of creation, for these forms are similar in type among all the superior animals, the body varying very slightly in structure in all the great class of mammifers; and also because the physiological functions are discharged in a similar manner by all. The basis on which we ground our researches is quite different, it is the spiritual basis; we ask the faculties of the mind to supply our materials of comparison.

It must not be supposed, therefore, that we espouse the doctrines of Darwin and those who agree with him, because we hold that the soul has a previous dwelling in the bodies of several animals, before it reaches the human body; because we admit that the spiritual principle begins in the germ of plants, and that this germ grows and develops itself in passing through the bodies of a progressive series of animal species, to issue at length in man, the end of its elaboration and perfection. The Darwinists take into consideration only the anatomical structure, and put aside the soul. We consider its faculties only. We are guided, not by the materialistic idea which directs and inspires these men of science, but on the contrary, on a reasoned-out spiritualism.

Our system of nature may be criticised, or rejected. We offer it merely as a personal view, and would not impose it on any reader. The merit of this philosophical and scientific conception, if it has any, consists in the vast synthesis by which it binds together all the living creatures which people the solar world, from the minute plant in which the germ of organization first appears, to the animal; from the animal to the man; and from the man to the series of superhuman and archhuman beings who inhabit the ethereal spheres; and finally, from them to the radiant dwellers in the solar star. In collecting together, on the one hand, all that modern chemistry has learned of the composition of plants, and the physical phenomena of their respiration, and on the other hand, everything which is known of the physical and chemical properties of solar light, the idea struck us that the rays of the sun form the vehicle by whose means the animated germs are placed in the plants. While meditating upon what has been written by the philosophers Charles Bonnet, Dupont de Nemours, and Jean Reynaud, upon the physical condition of resuscitated human beings, and dwelling upon the destiny of men beyond the formidable barrier of the tomb, in short, while drinking at the most various springs of philosophical and scientific knowledge, we have composed this attempt at a new philosophy of the universe.

This system may be erroneous, and another, more logical and more learned, may be substituted for it. But there will remain, we may hope, the synthesis which we have established from all the facts of the physical and moral order which we have collected together, the links by which we attach all the beings of creation one to another, which comprehends both the moral and organic attributes of these beings;—a vast ladder of nature, on whose steps we place everything that has life ; the endless circle, in which we link all the rings of the chain of living beings. The theoretic explanation of all these facts, thus grouped, may not perhaps be accepted, but we believe that they are correctly placed in juxtaposition, and that any theory which pretends to explain the universe must be established upon the basis of that grouping. If our explanation be contested, we hope that our synthesis of facts will remain.

Besides it is only thus, *i.e.,* by creating a system, that the sciences, exact as well as moral, are made to progress. Chemistry was not, as some have pretended, created by Lavoisier; it was founded by Stahl, it was not the pneumatic theory of Lavoisier, but really the *system of phlogiston* devised by Stahl, which instituted chemistry in the last century. Stahl, it is well known, had the immense merit of collecting all the facts known up to his time, into a general theoretical explanation of composing a summary of them, and of creating the *system of phlogiston.* This system was, undeniably, incorrect, but the facts which had been collected towards its construction had been perfectly well selected, and included every useful element of information or research. Thus, when ten years later than Stahl, came Lavoisier, he had only, so to speak, to turn the system of his predecessor inside out, as one turns a coat. For phlogiston Lavoisier substituted oxygen;

17

he preserved all the facts, and changed only the explanation. Thus chemistry was founded.

A well constructed synthesis must necessarily precede every theory of nature. Descartes, when working out his system of whirlwinds, formulated a conception which was certainly very inexact; but the facts upon which this theory rested were so well selected, they responded so exactly to the requirements of science, that when Newton came, with his *system of attraction*, it only remained to apply the new hypothesis to the facts collected by Descartes for his *whirlwinds*, and there was real astronomy, the true physics. When Linnæus created his *system of botany*, he made an undeniably artificial distribution of the vegetables, and Linnæus himself perfectly understood the defects of his system. But, owing to this artificial method, he succeeded in grouping all the plants into a methodical catalogue. If the principle of classification was bad, the service rendered to botany by this catalogue was immense. It was not, in fact, until after Linnæus' time that the immense mass of facts which he collected could be put in order, and the study of the vegetable world made to progress from those data. Botany dates from the publication of the *systema naturæ* of the immortal botanist of Upsal.

We do not pretend to put forward an irreproachable theory of the universe in this work, but simply to collect together and methodically group the facts upon which such a theory ought to rest, facts physical, metaphysical, and moral.

CHAPTER THE NINETEENTH.

UR system of nature may be met with the following final objection. It will be said, how can the rays of the sun, being material bodies, convey animated germs which are immaterial substances? These terms exclude each other.

We find, in the Scriptures, a magnificent comparison, of which we shall avail ourselves in order to answer this objection, or rather, this question.

Saint Matthew speaks of a grain of mustard seed, that is to say, of a tree germ, which, cast into the earth, produces a herbaceous plant, then a tree with majestic branches, and he is astonished to behold the imposing lord of the forests, which, laden with flowers and fruit, towers aloft in majestic beauty, and gives shelter under its shadow to the weary birds, springing from a humble little seed. Not only, says the evangelist, is there no resemblance between the tree and its original seed, but there does not exist in the tree a single atom of the matter of which the seed was primarily composed.

17—2

To our mind, this grain of mustard-seed is an image of
the sun, which, falling upon the earth, sows animated germs
in its bosom, which produce plants that afterwards give birth
to animals, and later still to man, and thus to the entire
series of creatures, invisible to us, which succeed him in the
domain of the heavens.

The little cold, colourless, scentless seed is nothing to look
at, nothing distinguishes it apparently from the neighbouring
dust.   Nevertheless, it contains that mysterious leaven, that
sacred being, so to speak, which we call a germ.   And what
wonderful things are to be born from that sacred being !
In the obscurity of the cold, damp earth the germ transforms
itself, it becomes a new body without any resemblance to the
seed which contained it.   It produces a plantlet, a subterranean, but perfectly organized creature, possessing a root
which fastens itself into the soil, and a stalk which takes the
opposite direction.   Between the two portions lies the seed,
split, gutted, having allowed the germ to escape, its part in
the matter ended.

The subterranean plantlet is a new being ; it has no longer
anything in common with the seed from whence it came.
The plantlet is dull and colourless, but it breathes, it has
channels, in which liquids and gases are circulating.

In a little while the plantlet comes up above the earth, it
greets the daylight, it appears to our eyes, and then it is a
very different being from the subterranean creature.   The
new-born vegetable is no longer as it was when in the bosom
of the earth, dull and grey ; it is green, it breathes like other
vegetables, producing oxygen under the influence of life,

whereas in the bosom of the earth it gave out carbonic acid. Instead of the dull and sombre subterranean plantlet, you have a green and tender shoot, provided with special organs. Where is the grain of mustard seed ?

Presently our shoot grows, and becomes a young plant. It is still weak and hidden under the grass, but nevertheless the young plant has its complete individuality. It resembles neither the shoot nor the plantlet, its subterranean ancestor.

The shoot grows, and becomes a twig, that is to say, the adolescent of the vegetable kingdom, with the ardour and the energy of the young among herbaceous creatures.

In this state the plant has already renewed its substance several times, and nothing remains of the organic and mineral elements which existed in the different beings that have preceded it on the same little corner of the earth which have witnessed the changing phases of its curious metamorphoses. Wait a while, and you will see the twig growing long and large. Its respiration becomes active, its leaves spread out, and vigorously exhale the carbonic acid gas of the air. The exhalation of watery vapour over all the surface takes place, and a young and vigorous tree is there, which day by day grows more robust and more beautiful.

During this growth, during this transition from the shrub to the young tree, with a separate and upright stem, a new being has been formed. Organs which it had not have come to it, and have made it a separate individual. It has flowers, it has branches, it has new vessels for the circulation of the sap, and the juices which were not previously elaborated. The structure of the surface of its leaves has been

changed, so that absorption may be more successfully accomplished.

Where is the shoot, from which our vigorous young shrub
sprung ?   What relation, what resemblance is there between
these two beings ?   We can only discern differences.   One
individual has succeeded to another individual.   The vegetable has been renewed, not only in matter, which is changed,
but in the form of its organs.   A series of new forms have
succeeded each other in the shrub, since it was a simple shoot,
just peeping above the soil.

It is still the history of change, when the young tree has
become adult, when, in the progress of years, its trunk has
grown hard, and become incrusted with layers of accumulated
bark, when its branches have multiplied, and flowering and
fruitage have modified all its internal and external parts.   It
is then a grand cedar tree, whose majestic and imposing shade
covers a considerable extent of the soil; or a superb oak,
whose robust and gnarled branches spread far and wide ; or a
flexible chestnut, which flings about its polished and shining
arms.   The organs of these luxuriant vegetables, the pride of
our forests, have no relation to those which belonged to them
in the first years of their life.   Their flowery crowns in spring-
tide, the fruits which succeed to them, the seeds shut up in
the protecting shelter of those fruits, these are all peculiarities
of organization, belonging to these noble trees, without any
analogy in nature.

Where is the grain of mustard seed which formerly sucked
the juice of the earth in darkness ?   Everything is changed ;
the place of habitation, which is no longer the earth, but the

air; the form, and the physiological functions. Not only has all this changed, but it has changed a great number of times. Not only does nothing remain of the matter of which the tree was composed in the earlier stages of its life, but nothing has been retained of the organic forms which were proper to the infancy of the vegetable.

Nevertheless, O great mystery of Nature, in the midst of all these changes, notwithstanding this continual succession of beings, which mutually replace each other, there is something which remains immovable, which has never changed, which has preserved a constant individuality,—it is the secret force which produced all these changes, which presided over all these organic mutations. In our belief, this force is the animated germ which the young plant has received from the seed, whence it has proceeded. In the midst of all the transformations which the vegetable creature has undergone, in spite of the numerous phases through which it has passed, and which have produced a series of different beings succeeding each other in its material substance, the spiritual principle, cause and agent of all this long activity, has remained the same. This animated germ which now exists in the adult vegetable is the same which was there during its growth, the same which was there when it was a shoot, the same which slept in the seed which was thrown into the bosom of the cold and humid earth. In that majestic tree which, coming forth from an imperceptibly minute seed, has had a whole genealogy of successive beings, replacing each other, differing in form and size, and has preserved, throughout its incessant development, the sole and immutable principle of its activity, we behold the faithful image of the persistent, indestructible soul, in the midst of the beings or different bodies which it has animated in succession. Issuing from a germ, it has never ceased to grow, to develop, to become amplified, still remaining itself.

The grain of mustard seed, or the seed of the tree, is according to us, the plant or inferior animal into which the sun has thrown the animated germ. The subterranean plantlet corresponds to the animal whose mission it is to perfect the germ transmitted by the plant, and which develops and amplifies this germ; for example, to the fish or the reptile, perfecting the spiritual principle which they have received from the zoophyte or the mollusc. The shoot which, having burst out of the earth, grows in the shade of the grass, and tries its air organs, corresponds to the animal somewhat more elevated in the organic scale, such as the bird, in which the animating principle—derived from the reptile or the fish—increases in intellectual power. The young vegetable, arrived at the condition of the twig, which lives a completely aërial life, corresponds to the mammifer. The tree, grown tall, and pushing out its young boughs, corresponds to man, perfecting the soul which he has received from a mammifer. Finally, the powerful and vigorous forest lord, overtopping all the neighbouring trees in size and majesty, with mighty girth of stem, and noble crest, with wide-spreading branches and splendid flowers, this grand creature corresponds to the superhuman being who lives in the bosom of the ethereal fluid, and who is himself destined to be replaced by a series of superior creatures, who shall climb from stage to

stage, from height to height, even to the radiant kingdom of
the sun, where those absolutely spiritual beings, whose essence
is entire and perfect immateriality are enthroned.

Thus, the animating principle remains immutable and
identical with itself, during all the transformations undergone
by the beings who are successively charged to receive this
precious deposit. From the vegetable, in which it had its
first domicile as a germ, and through the whole series of
living creatures, from the plant and the zoophyte to the man
and the superhuman being, the same spiritual principle
is preserved in its identity, perfecting and amplifying itself
without cessation.

Let us complete the comparison. When the forest tree has
ripened its fruits, the fruits burst open, the seeds escape from
it, and fall into the soil, or are dispersed by the caprice of the
winds. If the seeds fall into damp earth, they germinate,
and, according to the laws of nature, young vegetables are
produced, as we have previously explained. Multitudes of
similar vegetables are produced by a single oak, a single cedar,
a single chestnut tree. Just as the majestic adult tree lets
fall from its thousand branches upon the soil the countless
seeds which are to germinate there, so the spiritualized beings
who dwell in the sun shed their emanations, their *animated
germs*, upon all the planets. These germs, carried to the earth
by the sunbeams, and falling upon our globe, produce the
vegetables which afterwards give birth to the various animals,
by the effect of the successive transmigrations of the same soul
into the bodies of these creatures.

We can now reply to the objection which we have placed

at the beginning of this chapter : "How can the solar rays, being material substances, convey animated germs, which are immaterial substances?

When the physicists professed Newton's theory of the nature of light, in the theory of *emission*, it was necessary to regard light, and, consequently the solar rays, which produce it, as material bodies.

But science has now rejected this theory, and replaced it by the theory of *undulation*, founded by Malus, Fresnel, Ampère, and all the constellation of great physicists and mathematicians of the commencement of this century. Facts, collected on every side, prove that the solar rays are not matter which transports itself from the sun to the earth, but that light, like heat, results from a primitive disturbance produced by the sun upon the ether, which is spread over all space. This disturbance communicates itself from molecule to molecule, from the planetary ether down to us, and produces the phenomena of light and heat. We cannot here develop at greater length, or explain more scientifically, the theory of undulations, which will be found sufficiently demonstrated in works on physics. We merely desire to prove that, according to the principles of modern science, the solar rays are not material bodies, but that they result from a simple vibration of the planetary ether. If, then, the rays of the sun are not material substances, there can be no difficulty in admitting that these rays (immaterial substance) are the bearers of the animated germs, which are immaterial substance.

If we be driven to a closer definition of the problem, if we be asked to explain with greater precision how these immaterial germs journey through space, we reply that we must guard against the mania for insisting on everything being explained. Absolute explanation is forbidden to the limit of our intelligence. We are forced to confess our powerlessness whenever we try to explain the phenomena of nature rigorously. What is the true cause of the fall of bodies, of the gravitation of the stars, of electricity, of heat? What is the cause of the circulation of our blood, of the beating of our hearts? The deepest obscurity veils the primary causes of these phenomena, which we all behold every day; and the more earnestly we desire to penetrate the secret essence, the more the darkness deepens in our minds. Since the time of Newton, the physicists have laid down a wise and excellent principle. They have agreed to study the laws of physical phenomena with sedulous care, to measure with exactness the effects of heat, weight, electricity, or light, but, also, never to disquiet themselves by researches into the causes of these phenomena. The more we learn, the further we advance in the knowledge of the universe and its laws, the more we become convinced that man knows absolutely nothing about first causes, that he ought to esteem himself happy in knowing the laws according to which the effects of these first causes manifest themselves ; that is to say, the physical and vital actions which are visible to us, but that he ought, in the interests of his own peace of mind, to lay down a rule that he would never seek to know the wherefore of things. Pliny, speaking of first causes, said : "*Latent in majestate mundi*," ("They are hidden in the majesty of the world.") The thought is as fine as the phrase is eloquent. Let us, then, leave to nature her secrets, and, if we are led to believe that the sun sheds animated germs upon the earth and the planets, let us not try to penetrate further into the essence of this mysterious phenomenon. Let us not ask of the earth why she turns, the stone why it falls, the tree why it grows, our hearts why they beat—nor the rays of the sun why they produce life on earth, and immortality in the heavens.

CHAPTER THE TWENTIETH.

PRACTICAL RULES RESULTING FROM THE FACTS AND PRINCI-
PLES DEVELOPED IN THIS WORK.—THE ENNOBLING OF THE
SOUL BY THE PRACTICE OF VIRTUE, BY SEEKING TO KNOW,
THROUGH SCIENCE, NATURE AND ITS LAWS.—THE RENDER-
ING OF PUBLIC WORSHIP TO THE DIVINITY.—THE MEMORY
OF THE DEAD TO BE RETAINED.—WE OUGHT NOT TO FEAR
DEATH.—DEATH IS ONLY AN UNFELT TRANSITION FROM ONE
STATE TO ANOTHER, IT IS NOT A TERMINATION, BUT A
METAMORPHOSIS.—THE IMPRESSIONS OF THE DYING.—THEY
WHOM THE GODS LOVE DIE YOUNG.—REUNION WITH THOSE
WHO HAVE GONE BEFORE.

 E will conclude our work by laying down certain
practical rules which result from the facts and
the principles that have been explained in its
course.

Since man can raise himself to the range of a superhuman
being only when his soul has acquired the necessary degree of
purification in this life, it is evidently his interest to apply
himself to the culture of his soul, to preserve it from every
stain, to keep it from falling. Be good, generous, and com-
passionate; grateful for benefits, accessible to the suffering,
the friend of the oppressed. Console those who suffer and

who weep. Practise every form of charity. Endeavour to raise your thoughts above terrestrial things. Strive against those material instincts, which are the stigmata of human existence. Aspire to the good and the beautiful. Live in the most elevated spheres, those which are the least bound to lower things. It is only thus that you can elevate and ennoble your soul, and render it fit to enjoy the higher existence which awaits it in the ethereal spheres. For, if your soul be vicious and corrupt, if, during all your terrestrial life, you have been sunk in material interests, exclusively given up to purely physical occupations and enjoyments, which make you the fellow of the animals ; if your heart has been hard, your conscience dumb, your instincts low and evil, you will be condemned to recommence a second existence on the earth. Once, or many times again you will have to bear the burthen of life on this disinherited globe, where physical suffering and moral evil have taken up their abode, where happiness is unknown, and unhappiness is the universal law.

There is another motive for our careful cultivation of the faculties of the soul, and for our constantly purifying ourselves by the practice of good. Noble and generous persons, elect souls, are, as we have said, the only ones capable of communicating with the dead, with the beloved beings whom they have lost. If, therefore, we be stained with moral evil, we shall not receive any communication, any succour from the beings who have left us, and whom we loved. This is a powerful motive for our constant striving towards perfection.

One of the most effectual means of perfecting and ennobling the soul, of raising it above terrestrial conditions, and bringing

it near the higher spheres, is science. Study, labour to learn
of nature, to comprehend the plans and the phenomena which
surround you, to explain to yourselves the universe of which
you form a portion, and your soul will grow in strength and
wisdom. It is very sad to contemplate the shameful ignorance in which almost all humanity is sunk. The population
of our globe numbers 1,300,000,000, and of all this multitude
hardly 10,000,000 can be said to have studied the sciences,
and really cultivated their minds. All the rest of mankind
are abandoned to an intellectual passiveness, which almost
reduces them to the level of the animals. The earth is but a
vast field of ignorance. As far as knowledge is concerned,
almost all men die as they were born, they have not added a
single idea, a single branch of knowledge to those which their
parents—themselves ignorant—have inculcated in their youth.
Nevertheless, thanks to the labours of some few men of
uncommon mind and energy, the knowledge we possess at
the present time is immense, we have made great progress in
the study of nature and its laws.

We understand the mechanism and the regulation of the
universe, we have learned to reject the fallacious testimony
of our senses, we have discerned the courses of the different
stars, which look so much alike, when they shine in the
firmament by night. We know that the sun is motionless in
the centre of our world, and that a company of planets,
among which the earth figures, revolve around him, in an orbit
whose mathematical curve has been precisely fixed. We
know the cause of the days and nights, as well as that of the
seasons ; we can predict almost to a second the return of the

stars to a certain point of their orbit, their meetings, eclipses, and occultations.   The globe which we inhabit has been surveyed and explored with care which has hardly missed a nook of it.   We know the causes of the winds and of the rains, we can point out the exact course of the sea-currents, and foretell the hour and the height of the tides all over the globe.   We know why glaciers exist at the northern and southern extremities of the earth, and why other glaciers crown the great mountain heights.   The movements of the earth, which formerly produced chains of mountains, and which at present occasion volcanic eruptions and earthquakes, are quite comprehensible to us.   The composition of all the bodies which exist on the surface, or are hidden in the depths of the earth, has been fixed with certainty.

We know what air contains, and what water is composed of.   There is not a mineral, not a particle of earth to which we cannot assign its composition.   More than that, we can tell what is the composition of the soil of the planets, and of their satellites, those stars which roll at incalculable distances above our heads, and which we can reach only with our eyes. Science has performed this miracle, the chemical analysis of bodies which it cannot touch, and which it can only see across millions of miles in space.

We have studied, classified, demonstrated all the living beings, animals and plants which people the earth.   There is not an insect hidden in the grass of the fields which has not been described, which has not had its just place in creation assigned to it; there is not a blade of grass which has not been reproduced by the pencil of the naturalist.

Beyond all this, science has penetrated far beyond the reach of our vision. It has invented a marvellous instrument which has unveiled an entire world to our astonished gaze, a world whose existence we never should have suspected without its aid. The world thus revealed to us is that of infinitely little things. We know that myriads of living creatures, both animals and plants, exist in a drop of water; that those creatures, in all their prodigious littleness, have a complete existence, and are as well organized as those of great size which are analogous to them, and that the physiological functions of all these imperceptible beings are fulfilled as perfectly as our own.

Just as we have penetrated into the life of infinite littleness, so we have pierced the depths of celestial space, and scrutinized with our eyes the magnified image of the stars which revolve at an incalculable distance above us. The telescope shows us the surface of the moon, the depths of its ravines, and the rough serrated edges of its enormous mountains, furrowed with deep circular crevasses. We can cast our eyes over the lunar disc as if it were a distant landscape of our own globe. We can even, thanks to the magnifying powers of the telescope, form an idea of the aspect of the surfaces of those planets which are almost lost in the infinite distances of the heavens.

After this faint and incomplete sketch of that which human science has been able to accomplish, it might be supposed that every inhabitant of the earth is impatient to make all this knowledge his own, that every one must desire to fill his mind with its treasures. Alas! the great majority of the

18

human species is ignorant of even the elements of all this. Take away the ten millions of individuals to whom we have already alluded, and who, numerically, are hardly to be counted in considering the population of the globe, all people imagine that the earth is a flat surface which extends to the limits of the horizon, and is covered with a blue cupola, called *heaven.* If you assert that the earth revolves, they laugh, and point to the motionless earth, and the sun which *rises* on the right hand and *sets* on the left, a manifest proof that the sun comes and goes. The poets will have it that the sun rises from his bed in the morning, and returns to it in the evening. People believe that the stars which shine by night, in the celestial vault, are simply ornaments, an agreeable spectacle, made to please our eyes, and that the moon is a beacon. Nobody inquires into the causes of the rain or fine weather, of heat or cold, of the winds or the tides. Every one shuts his eyes to natural phenomena, so as to avoid the trouble of explaining them. Nature is a shut book for the majority of mankind, who live in the midst of the most curious and various phenomena, but who occupy themselves in eating and drinking, and trying to harm their fellows.

It is a sorrowful spectacle to behold humanity thus preoccupied by its more material necessities, and utterly without interest in any mental exertion, and one grieves to think that such is the condition of almost all the inhabitants of the globe. How far is he superior to the great mass of his fellows, who has cultivated his mind, enriched it with various and useful ideas, and appropriated to himself at least one branch of the varied tree of the exact sciences. What breadth and power must be acquired by a mind thus fortified ! Strive, O my reader, to study and to learn.   Initiate yourself into the secrets of nature, try to understand all that surrounds you, the universe and its infinite productions, admire the power of God in learning the wonders of His works.   Then shall you not approach the tomb with your soul void as on the day of your birth.   At the supreme hour of death you will be wise, instructed, and, finding yourself nearer to the sublime essence of superhuman beings, you will be eager to follow them into the ethereal spheres.

In order to elevate and perfect the soul, it is not sufficient only to apply ourselves to the practice of moral virtues and to learning ; we must also endeavour to understand God, the Author of the universe.   Therefore, let men enter into the temples, and prostrate themselves before God according to the forms and rites of worship in which they have been reared. All religions are good, and ought to be respected, because they permit us to pay the homage of gratitude and heartfelt submission to the Author of nature.

The Christian religion is good, because it is a religion. The religion of Mahomet is good, because it is a religion. For the same reason Buddhism and Judaism are good, and the religion of the wild Indians who worship the sun in the depths of their forests.

The fourth practical rule which we derive from the principles and theories which we have laid down, is that the remembrance and commemoration of the dead should be preserved.   Let us not efface from our hearts the memory of those whom death has snatched from us.   To forget them is

18—2

to cause them the most cruel anguish, and to deprive ourselves of the aid and guidance which they can give us here below.

The ancients sedulously kept up the memory of the dead. They did not put the idea of death away from them with terror, like the modern peoples; on the contrary, they loved to invoke it. Among the Greeks and Romans the cemeteries were places of meeting, used for festivals and promenades. The Orientals of our days preserve this ancient tradition. Their cemeteries are perfectly kept gardens, whither festive crowds resort on festal occasions. They visit the relatives and friends who are buried in the shrubberies and the flower-beds, and revel in the pleasures of life amid the pretty dwelling-places of the dead.

In Europe we know nothing of this wholesome philosophy. But we may remark, that peasants, unlike dwellers in cities, who are not brought into familiar daily contact with nature, are far from shunning the idea of death, or avoiding the cemeteries where their relatives and friends rest. They recall the remembrance of their dead, they speak to them, they question them, they consult them, as though they were still seated by the family fireside.

The custom of funeral repasts, which dates from the time of primitive man, is still observed in several countries. On returning from the cemetery the company seat themselves before a well-spread table, in the house of the deceased, and wish him a happy journey to the land of shadows. In our cities, it is "*the people*" who hold it a duty to carry flowers to the graves of their relatives. Among the higher classes of society people hold themselves exempt, in general, from this pious care, and they are wrong. Piety towards the dead, and reverent commemoration of them, are prescribed by the laws of nature.

Finally, we would impress upon the reader, as a consequence and a practical rule resulting from all that has gone before, that he ought not to fear death. Let him regard with firm heart and tranquil eye that moment which all men dread so much. We have said that death is not a conclusion, but a change, we do not perish, we are transformed. The grub which seems to die, enclosed within a cold shell, does not die, but is born again, a brilliant butterfly, to flutter joyously in the air. Thus it shall be with us. Though our miserable frames remain on earth, and restore their elements to the common reservoir of universal matter, our souls shall not perish. They shall be born again, brilliant creatures of the celestial ether. They shall leave a world in which pain and evil are the constant law, for a blessed domain where every condition of happiness shall be realized. Why, then, should we dread death? If we do not desire it, we ought at least to await it with hope and tranquillity. Death must unite us to those beings whom we have loved, whom we do love, and whom we shall love for ever. What an immense source of consolation during the remainder of our life! What a store of courage for the terrible moment of our own end! The beloved dead, who have never ceased to be present to our memory, have done us the sad, supreme service of softening the anguish of death to us. The sadness of our last moments will be calmed by the thought that they are awaiting our coming, that they are ready to receive us on the threshold of the other life, that they are gone before to lead us into the new domain of existence beyond the tomb !

The fear of death, which is so prevalent among men generally, loses its intensity when the last hour has come. Those who are accustomed to witness death know that the last agony is rarely severe. He who dies after a long and honourable existence knows at that solemn moment that he is going to a new and better world. He is happy, and his words and looks express happiness. The only thought which makes him sorrowful is the grief which his loss must occasion to those whom he loves and is about to leave.

The observations which follow have been made by persons accustomed to observe the dying. But deaths occasioned by maladies which destroy consciousness, or reason, or speech, must not be included in these observations. In order to judge of the thoughts which occupy the dying we must consider those who preserve the integrity of their intellectual faculties until their latest breath. They always die calmly. Consumptive patients, the wounded, those who die from an affection of the stomach or of the intestinal tube, of those slow fevers which consume the strength without impairing the intellectual faculties, these generally remain in the full possession of their intelligence to the last, and die with great tranquillity, even satisfaction. In almost all these cases death is preceded by a gradual decline of strength and sensation, so that the individual has hardly any consciousness of the change he is about to undergo, and looks forward to the moment of death with perfect indifference.

There is a period, which frequently lasts for several hours, during which, life having completely left the body, it is already a corpse which is under the eyes of the spectators, and yet that corpse still moves and speaks. But the soul which survives in the body, really dead, is not the soul of the terrestrial man, but of the superhuman being. The dying person has the consciousness, and perhaps even the prevision of the ineffable happiness which awaits him in that new world upon whose threshold he is standing, and he expresses his happiness by his words and looks. In a sigh of supreme joy he exhales his last breath. This extraordinary state, in which the dying are partly on earth, and partly in the new world to which they are destined, explains the touching eloquence, the sublime words which sometimes come from their feeble lips. An uneducated poor man will express himself upon his death-bed with eloquence incomprehensible to those who are listening to him. It also explains the prophecies, justified by subsequent events, which have been uttered by the dying. They have a knowledge of things of which, in their ordinary condition as belonging to the human species, they could not possibly have had any notion. Therefore, we ought to treasure up their last words with pious care, and scrupulously fulfil the wishes which they express.

In Moldavia, when a peasant has escaped death in a severe illness, after having been on the brink of the grave, his friends press around his bed to ask him what he had seen in the other world, and what news he has for them from their dead relatives. Then the poor invalid interprets his visions for them as well as he can.

A modern writer, who has left some small books on spiritualist philosophy, M. Constant Savy, relates in his " *Pensées et Méditations*," an extraordinary dream which he had when he was, apparently, at the point of death.   We transcribe this curious and interesting document from M. Pezzani's work :—

" I felt very ill," writes Constant Savy, " I had no strength, it seemed to me that my life was making efforts to resist death, but in vain, and that it was about to escape. My soul detached itself little by little from the matter spread all over my frame ; I felt it retiring from all, those parts with which it is so intimately united, and, as it were, concentrating itself upon one single point, the heart, and a thousand obscure, cloudy thoughts about my future life occupied me.   Little by little nature faded from before me, taking irregular and strange forms, I almost lost the faculty of thinking, I only retained that of feeling, and this feeling was all love, love of God and of the beings whom I had most cherished in Him, but I could not manifest this love ; my soul, withdrawn to one single point in my body, had almost ceased to have any relation with it, and could no longer command it.   My soul experienced some distractions still, caused by the pain of the body, and the grief of those who surrounded me, but these distractions were slight, like the pains and the perceptions which caused them.   My life was now attached to matter by one only of the thousand links which had formerly bound it, and I was about to expire.

" Suddenly, no doubt to mark the passage from this life to the other, there came a thick darkness, to which succeeded a brilliant light.   Then, O my God ! I saw Thy day, that daylight I had so much desired !   I saw them, all assembled together, those beings whom I had so dearly loved, who had inspired me during my life in this world after they had left me, and who had seemed to me to dwell in my soul, or float about me. They were all there, full of joy and happiness. They were waiting for me, they welcomed me with delight. It seemed to me that I completed their life and that they completed mine! But what a difference was there in the happiness I now felt from the sensations of the world I left! I cannot describe them! They were penetrating without being impetuous; they were mild, calm, full, unmixed, and yet they admitted the hope of a yet greater happiness!

" I did not see Thee, my God! Who can see Thee? But I loved Thee more than I had loved Thee in this world! I comprehended Thee better, felt Thee more strongly, the traces of Thee which are everywhere, and on everything, appeared more plain and bright to me, I experienced such admiration and astonishment as I had never hitherto known, I saw more distinctly a portion of the wonders of Thy creation. The bowels of the earth hid no more secrets from me, I saw their depths, I saw the insects and other creatures which dwell in them, the mines known to men, and undiscovered by them, the secret ways and channels of the earth. I reckoned its age in its bosom as one counts that of a tree in the heart of its trunk; I saw all the water-courses which feed the seas; I saw the reflux of these waters, and it was like the motion of the blood in a man's body; from the heart to the extremities, from the extremities to the heart; I saw the depths of the volcanoes; I understood the motions of the earth and its relations with the stars, and, just as if the earth had been turned round before my eyes that I might be made to admire Thy greatness, O my God! I saw all countries with their various inhabitants, and their different customs, I saw every variety of my species, and a voice said to me: ' Like thyself, all these men are the image of the Creator; like thyself, they are ever journeying towards God, and conscious of their progress !' The thickness of the forests, the depth of the seas could not hide anything from my eyes; I had power to see everything, to admire all, and I was happy in my happiness, in the happiness of the dear objects of my tender love. Our joys were in common. We felt ourselves united by our former affections which had now become much more deep, and by the love of God: we drew happiness from one and the same source; we were but one, we each and all enjoyed this happiness, which was far too great to be expressed. I am silent now, that I may feel it more deeply."*

It is easy for us to verify to ourselves the fact that men who are condemned by nature to a premature death, are endowed with a great serenity of mind. This moral condition is, in our opinion, an indication that they have the presentiment or even the anticipated possession of the new life which awaits them after death. Why are consumptive people so gentle and sensitive? We believe it is because, being already half out of this world, they are partially endowed with the moral attributes of superhuman beings. They are, as it is well known, always confident in their destinies, they make projects of happiness, and for the future, when their last hour is striking, they feel hope and joy when the bystanders are thinking of their burial. It is customary to explain this anomaly by saying that persons in consumption do not understand the gravity of their illness, but we believe that they have, on the contrary, a confused notion of their state, that nature reveals to them the approach of an existence of cloudless happiness, and that it is this secret conviction which gives them hope and confidence in the future. The future which they foresee is not of this world, but the

* Quoted by M. Pezzani, in his " *Pluralité des Existences de l'âme,*" pp. 261—263.

future of the heavens. This applies not to consumptive persons only. Every man destined to die young seems to be marked with that inner stamp of the soul which lends him now a gentle and charming melancholy, anon vivacity or sensibility which his parents admire, and which is too often only an indication that he is not to remain with them. The charming qualities of many young people are often only the precursors of their death.

"When they have so much intellect, children have brief lives," says Casimir Delavigne. "Whom the gods love, die young," said the Greeks.

Let us, then, not fear death; but await it, not as the end of our existence, but as its transformation. Let us learn by the purity of our life, by our virtues, by the culture of our faculties, by our knowledge, by the exercise of the religion of our ancestors, to prepare ourselves for the critical moment of that natural revolution which shall usher us into a blessed sojourn in the ethereal spheres on the day after death.

EPILOGUE.

THE author now asks his reader's leave to relate a conversation which took place between himself, and a friend named Theophilus, to whom he had confided the manuscript of "The Day After Death," in order to obtain his opinion and impressions of the work. He will allow the interlocutors to express themselves in the ordinary form of dialogue.

Theophilus, (who comes into the Author's study, and lays the manuscript upon the table). I have read your work, and I will tell you presently my impressions of the details, but I must in the first place point out the great deficiency of the book.

The Author. What is wanting in it?

Theophilus. God.

The Author. But——

Theophilus. (Interrupts him.) You are going to remind me that you frequently mention the sacred name, that Providence, the Author of nature, the Creator of the worlds, and so on, are words you constantly employ. That is true, but it is equally true that you restrict yourself to these vague expressions, that you say nothing about the person of God, that you assign to Him no place in the world which you range over in company with more or less spiritualized souls. Why this reserve? Since you tell us that entirely spiritualized souls inhabit the sun, why do you not tell us where your system places God, the sovereign master of those souls! What is your motive for leaving aside a question of such great importance?

The Author. I have several. In the first place, I have everybody's motive. The idea of God which must be formed in order to place Him in harmony with the boundless immensity of this universe which is His work, so far surpasses the limit of the human intellect, it is so overwhelming to our mind, that we stop, powerless and even frightened at our boldness, when we venture to ask ourselves, *what is God?*

Theophilus. Nevertheless, I am surprised at your hesitation. When a system of the universe is to be constructed, one does not pause in the task, and I can hardly believe that when you venture, as you do, to place on the ladder-steps of your theory all the elements of the solar world—the planets and their satellites, stars and asteroïds, plants, men and animals, creatures visible and invisible, bodies and souls, matter and spirit—you have not assigned a place to the Creator. Have you classified everything in this immense edifice of the worlds, except its Sovereign Architect?

The Author. No, my friend, you are not mistaken; God has His place in my system.

Theophilus. Why, then, have you not said so! Why have you kept silence on this point?

The Author. My book contains so many daring assertions, I have already exposed myself so fully to the animosity of both the learned and the ignorant, that I feared to furnish an additional pretext to their diatribes.

Theophilus. That is not a reason. If you dread discussion and fear detraction, why do you take up your pen at all? You were at liberty to keep your ideas on the origin and the destiny of man to yourself, but, when you decided on submitting them to the public, you became bound to explain all your mind on the subject. If you believe in your system, you must explain it without any reserve.

The Author. Your words are wise, and I ought therefore to bow to them, and follow your imperative advice. Nevertheless I cannot make up my mind to do so, absolutely. I am going to propose a middle course to you. In confidence, and between ourselves, I will explain my ideas about God to you, I will tell you in what part of the immense universe I place this dazzling personality. If the idea seems to you absurd, untenable, or even too hazardous, you will frankly tell me so, and thus duly warned, I will keep my theory to myself; if not——

Theophilus. (Interrupting him.) An excellent plan. There can be no objection to that. Go on, I am listening.

(At this point, Theophilus seats himself, his elbow resting on a book, and a cigar in his mouth, and composes himself to listen, with an expression of grave attention, dashed with suspicious severity, suitable to the arbitrator in a literary and philosophical matter.)

The Author. You want to know, my dear Theophilus,

where I place God? I place Him at the centre of the universe, or, I had better say, at the central focus, which must exist somewhere, of all the stars which compose the universe, and which, carried along by a common motion, circulate in concert around this central focus.

Theophilus. Forgive me, but I do not seize your meaning exactly.

The Author. You will understand it presently. Remember, to start from, that I place God at the common focus of the actual motion of the entire universe. But, where is the common focus? In order to know that, we must first of all know the universe, and all the order of its movements.

Theophilus. All that is explained in the course of your work.

The Author. No, my friend, you are mistaken. In my work I have spoken of the solar system only, and a very incomplete and insufficient idea would be gained of the universe by contemplating that system alone. We must not, as is too often done, confound the *world* and the *universe*. The *world* is our world, that is to say, the solar system, of which we form a part; the *universe* is the agglomeration of all the worlds or systems similar to our world, or solar system. In the manuscript which you have just read, I have only been able to expound one little corner, one insignificant fraction of the universe.

Theophilus. You call the solar world a little corner.

The Author. Yes. Our whole solar system, the sun, with its immense following of planets and asteroïds, with the satellites of those planets, with the comets which from time to time come sweeping on, to fall into the burning furnace of the radiant star, all that, compared with the universe, is no more than an ear of corn in a huge granary, than a grain of sand upon the shore, than a drop of water in the ocean. The terrible vastness of the universe is such that it is absolutely inaccessible to our measurement, and it is for us the image of the infinite, or the infinite itself. Now, my friend, attend to me. ˙Most certainly God, as to His nature, is absolutely inconceivable by our minds. His essence escapes us, and always must escape us. We can only affirm that He is infinite in his moral perfections, and in His intellectual power. But if, on the one hand, God is *The Infinite* in the moral order, and if, on the other hand, the universe is *The Infinite* in the physical order; if one is *The Infinite* in spirit, and the other is *The Infinite* in extent, these two ideas, although in themselves inaccessible to human intelligence, are nevertheless of the same order, and may be regarded in contiguity. It is then possible, without laying one's self open to the charge of presumption or absurdity, to place the Infinite, which is called God, in the Infinite which is called the Universe, in other words, to locate the person of God at the common focus of the worlds which compose the Universe.

Theophilus. Your reasoning is just. But you must prove, or, if you prefer the phrase, you must teach me that the universe is truly *The Infinite* by its extent. I could not admit that assertion without very convincing evidence.

The Author. Very well. Lend me your best attention, and excuse me if my demonstration resembles a lecture on astronomy. I have said that our solar system is only a little corner of the universe. When you look at the vault of the sky on a bright clear night, you see it thickly strewn with stars, which, you will at once acknowledge, it would be impossible to count. But all that you see with the naked eye is next to nothing. Take a good telescope, and direct it to any part of the sky. There where a moment before you saw nothing, you will now discern legions of stars, bright spots will come out upon the darkness of space, like diamonds upon the velvet lining of a casket, each of them a star, exactly like those which we see at night in the sky. And now, let me ask you, do you know what a star is?

Theophilus. Yes, I know from your manuscript, and I had already known, that the stars which we see by night, but which the greater light of the sun hides from us in the daytime, are self-luminous orbs, each the centre of attraction and the lamp to the particular world it lights, and which revolves around it. As a whole company of planets, satellites, asteroïds, and comets revolve round our sun, receiving heat, motion, and light from that great central orb, so, the stars dispersed throughout space, communicate motion and activity to a vast aggregate of planets and satellites. These planets, which revolve round the stars, constitute *stellar worlds,* analogous to our solar world. We cannot see the planets, which accompany these stars, by reason of their smallness, and the prodigious distance between us and them, beyond the reach of the most powerful telescopes; we only see the suns which govern them, *i.e.,* the stars. But the existence of the fixed stars, like our sun, implies the existence of planets revolving around them.

19

The Author. Perfectly correct. Thus, our solar world is not unique, it is only one member of the family of stellar worlds, which resemble our world in the disposition and the motions of the stars within them. The universe is composed of the agglomeration of them all. You know all this, but there is one fact which, as it is the result of recent discoveries, you may not be aware of, it is, the great variety of disposition or of physical aspect presented by certain stars, in which a kind of overturn of that which constitutes nature on our globe has taken place. While they remain similar to our world in the order of their movements, certain stars differ widely in the forces which govern nature in them.

Theophilus. Pray explain your meaning.

The Author. While our solar system is governed by a single central star, there are stellar systems which are governed by two, three, and even four suns. It is evident that worlds which have two or three centres of light and heat must present physical and mechanical peculiarities of which we have no idea. There are also other differences proper to many of the stellar worlds. The light of our sun and of the greater number of the stars is constant : it never undergoes either augmentation or diminution. But this is not the case with many of those distant suns which we call stars. We see their light alternately fade and revive ; sometimes they shine brightly, then become almost imperceptible, and anon brilliant again. Some of them become altogether extinct. The decrease in lustre of several stars has been noted by different astronomers.*

Stars which have been observed in other times no longer

* Arago. *"Astronomie Populaire,"* Vol. I., pp. 372—376.

exist.* Others have suddenly appeared, shone with excessive lustre, and at the end of some years have been seen no more.

These successive augmentations and diminutions of luminous brilliance are not uncommon in the stars with which we are acquainted. According to M. Flammarion,† star *o* of the *Whale* varies very much in luminous intensity and the constellation itself frequently disappears. Star χ of the *Swan* passes from the fifth to the tenth size under our eyes, the thirtieth star of the *Hydra*, which is of the fourth size, almost always disappears at intervals of 500 days. These variations must, as M. Flammarion observes, produce strange results. To-day, the radiant star is shedding floods of light and fire upon the planets which it governs, and the soul of that planet is warmed by its burning rays. A few months later, without the least cloud in the sky, the shining of the sun becomes fainter, and then, by degrees, the obscurity increases, until at length the planet is plunged into thick darkness. When the diminution of the light of the sun is periodical, this universal night lasts for a fixed time, at the end of which the light returns, if not, the darkness is dispersed after varying periods. The light grows, little by little, until at length the radiant star reappears in all its primitive brightness. The fine days, the glorious light returns, until the moment when the same fading recommences and the darkness sets in once more.

Can we picture to ourselves the strange alterations which nature undergoes in regions which are subjected to torrid heat and glacial cold by turns? I am convinced that the *glacial*

---

* Arago. "*Astronomie Populaire*," Vol. I., pp. 376—380.
† Flammarion. "*Pluralité des Mondes habités*," page 195.

period which geologists have defined in the history of our
globe, during which an extraordinary and sudden lowering of
the temperature caused the death of multitudes of living
beings, and covered Europe with glaciers from the mountains
—was caused by a momentary weakening of the intensity of
the sun's light. When it resumed its ordinary brightness,
the sun dispersed the ice which had covered the earth with a
death mantle.*

I have said that there are double stars, that is to say, worlds
illuminated by two suns, and sometimes even by three or four.
It is a strange fact that in almost every instance one of these
suns is white, like ours, but the second is coloured, blue, red,
or green. In the constellation *Perseus* for example, a double
star can be distinctly seen by the aid of a good telescope. The
star η is in fact accompanied by a second, which makes part
of the same solar system. Now, this second star is blue. In
the constellation *Ophiochus* there is a similar system of double
stars, one of which is red and the other blue. The same
peculiarity exists in the constellation of the *Dragon*. In a
double star of the constellation of the *Bull*, there is a red sun,
and a blue sun. There are double solar systems red and blue;
such are the constellations *Hercules* and *Cassiopœia*. Other
double solar systems are yellow and green, and sometimes
yellow and blue. In all the worlds which are illuminated by
these coloured suns, the effect of light must be very strange.
No painter could represent them, and indeed we, who know
only the white light of our own sun, cannot form any idea of
them.

* See the Author's work : " *The Earth before the Deluge,*" pp.
'02—440.

Theophilus. These features of the stellar worlds are very interesting, and I am glad to learn them. But are we not straying from our subject?

The Author. No. After having made you understand that the solar system which we inhabit is only a member of an immense family of other solar worlds, only a small fraction of the universe, I wished to show you by the diversity of those worlds, the facility with which nature varies the forces and the physical conditions proper to the stellar worlds, and consequently the living and inanimate types which make a portion of these different stellar worlds. Now that you understand the prodigious diversity of the solar worlds which compose the universe, I will go on to our principal object. I have not lost sight of my intention of proving to you that the universe has no limits, that in its extent it is really the Infinite. I am now approaching this great question. By the consideration of the stars, I am going to bring out into relief the immeasurable vastness of the universe. Let me speak, first, of the appalling distances which separate the stars from the earth, and the figures will show you that on that side we fall into the Infinite, and then I will speak of the numbers of the stars which people space; and on this side also the abyss of the Infinite will yawn before us. First, as to the distances which separate the stars from the earth, from whence we may logically infer the distances which separate these stars from one another. The distance between the earth and the sun is 38,000,000 leagues, and this shall be our unit, our standard of measurement, by which to estimate the distance of the stars.

I do not know, my dear Theophilus, whether you have formed an exact idea of this extent of 38,000,000 leagues, which lie between us and the sun. In general, we can only conceive prodigious distances such as astronomy deals with, by representing them by the interval of time which certain movable bodies known to us would consume in traversing them. Let us then have recourse to comparisons of this kind. A cannon-ball weighing 12 kilogrammes, exploded by 6 kilogrammes of powder, proceeding at a uniform rate of 500 metres a second, would take 10 years to travel from the earth to the sun.

Supposing sound to travel at the same rate as on the surface of the air, and at a uniform rate, it would take 15 years to accomplish this journey. If a railway were laid through space between the earth and the sun, a train travelling at express speed, $12\frac{1}{2}$ leagues an hour, would not arrive at its destination until the end of 338 years. This imaginary train, if dispatched from the earth in January, 1872, would arrive at the sun in the year 2210. The light from the sun, which travels 77,000 leagues in a second, takes 7 minutes 13 seconds to reach the earth.

Theophilus. The distance between the earth and the sun is, then, 38,000,000 miles—that is our unit of measurement for the distances of the stars. Now let us hear about these distances.

The Author. I will deal first with those stars which are nearest to us. One of these is a star in the constellation of the *Swan.* This star is distant from the earth 551,000 times our unit of measurement, that is to say, that we must multiply 551,000 times the distance of the earth from the sun to represent the distance of the star which we are considering, and yet it is one of the nearest to the earth. If we wish to represent this distance by the time occupied in the transit of light, supposing this light to travel, like that of our sun, 77,000 leagues a second, it would take $9\frac{1}{2}$ years to travel from the star to us.

Now, if you wish to know the distance of other stars, and remember that I only speak of the nearest, look at this table, which I found in an astronomical treatise :

DISTANCE OF CERTAIN STARS FROM THE EARTH.

Names of the Stars.	Distances from the Earth.	Time of transit of light.
a Of the Swan	551,000 times	9 years and a half.
a Of the Lyre	1,330,700	21 years.
a Of the Great Dog	1,375,000	22 years.
a Of the Great Bear	1,550,800	25 years.
Polar Star	3,678,000	50 years.

Thus, the star *a* of the Lyre is distant from us more than 1,330,000 times as far as the earth is from the sun, and its light takes 21 years to reach us. If, by any celestial catastrophe, star *a* of the Lyre were to disappear, to be annihilated, we should still see it for 21 years, as its light takes that time to reach us.

Theophilus. It is then possible that our astronomers are now observing stars which no longer exist, and are only visible to us because the light which they omitted is still travelling towards the earth.

The Author. Just so. But to continue. I have begun with the stars which are nearest to the earth. There are the stars of first and second magnitude. You know, I suppose, the signification of those terms first, second, and third magnitude in astronomy ?

Theophilus. Yes, I know that the word magnitude is only applied to the luminous appearance of the star, and not to its real bulk. A star of the first magnitude is one which forms part of the group of the most luminous stars; a star of the second magnitude is one which comes next in point of brilliancy.

The Author. You must bear in mind that the word *magnitude* signifies in astronomy the opposite of that which it expresses. The more luminous a star appears to us, the nearer it is to us; the paler and less visible, the farther it is away. The brilliance diminishes in proportion as the figure increases. This is an introversion of terms, sufficiently exceptional to be taken note of, and it ought to be remembered, for fear of mistakes. Hitherto we have considered only stars of the first and second magnitudes. Those of the third, fourth, fifth, and sixth, lead us to the contemplation of such immense distances, that the unit which we have adopted, enormous as it is, is no longer of use. The instruments of celestial observation which may be applied to the examination and measurement of stars of the first and second magnitudes, do not serve for stars of the third and following magnitudes, and, because the small visible diameter of those stars make them appear mere specks of light, measuring instruments are equally inapplicable to them. In estimating the distances of the stars after the third magnitude, a method of comparison, based on the amplifying power of the telescopes successively used, is employed. I cannot enter into details of this method, which we owe to Sir William Herschel, but must content myself with explaining its results, which are as follows in the case of stars of the sixth magnitude. From certain stars of that class, light would take 1042 years to reach us : from others it would take 2700. After the sixth magnitude, the stars can only be discerned by the aid of the telescope, and their distances become perfectly stupefying in immensity. Certain of these telescopic stars are so far from the earth, that their light can only reach us in 5000, and even 10,000 years after it leaves the luminous centre. From the stars of the last category (fourteenth magnitude), light would take 100,000 years to reach the earth, supposing it to travel at the same rate as the light of our sun, *i.e.*, 77,000 leagues per second.

Theophilus. But, if we are to accept the results of the labours of recent naturalists, man exists on the earth only within 100,000 years, and some of those stars may have been extinct during all that time, so that the human race may have been contemplating stars no longer in being for 100,000 years. To what strange consequences does such a science lead us !

The Author. Yes, the luminous rays which these stars send us from the deepest depths of space may perhaps be emanations from solar systems no longer in existence. The present shows us only the past. There may be stars so profoundly lost in immensity, that their light has not yet had time to reach us. They exist, but we cannot see them, not because the telescope could not discover them, but because thousands of centuries are required for the journey of their luminous rays to our earth, and those thousands of centuries have not yet elapsed; so that this grand spectacle is reserved, in that awfully remote future, for our descendants.

And now, my friend, will you not acknowledge with me,

that the universe, considered merely by the distances which separate us from the stars, and the stars from each other, is truly the Infinite?

Theophilus. Yes, it is the Infinite which unfolds itself before my eyes. Let me breathe a moment.

The Author. If we contemplate the number of the stars, we shall also have the perspective of the Infinite. It is easy to reckon those of the first magnitude, *i.e,* the nearest to us. They are 20. Those of the second magnitude are 65; of the third, 170. The number of the stars increases as their visibility diminishes, in a very rapid proportion. The number of stars of each class of visibility, in apparent magnitude, is three times greater than that of the stars of the preceding class. There are 500 stars of the fourth, 1500 of the fifth, 4500 of the sixth magnitudes. The stars visible by the naked eye are 6000 in number. A practised eye can succeed in counting the 6000 stars in the two hemispheres.

But the telescope enables us to push the numbering of the suns much farther: it opens up to us the depths of the heavens. Instead of the small number of stars which our eyes

 can see, it shows us a myriad of others, so thickly thronged together that they seem to cover the sky with fine silver sand. Here, for instance (fig. 6), is the aspect which one corner of the constellation of Gemini presents to the naked eye. And here is the same portion of the sky seen by the telescope. By the aid of this wonderful instrument stars of the thirteenth and fourteenth magnitudes have been distinguished.

Fig. 6.—A Corner of the Constellation of Gemini.

The number of stars of the twelfth magnitude is 9,556,000, which, joined to the number of the same stars proper to the preceding categories, gives a total of more than 14,000,000.

Fig. 7.—A Corner of the Constellation of Gemini, seen through the telescope.

In the third magnitude, a total number of 42,000,000 of stars is counted. Thus, reckoning those visible to the naked eye, and by the telescope, we have 56,000,000 of suns, and we stop at this number only because the telescope does not enable us to see smaller stars than those of the fourteenth magnitude. But, let the telescope be brought to greater perfection, and the whole region of the sky will be seen to be covered with this silver sand, with this diamond dust, of which each grain is a sun. And such will be the accumulation of these suns, in the depths of space, that nothing will be seen on the field of the telescope but a luminous network, formed by the agglomeration of the suns, which will appear to touch each other.

Theophilus. The Infinite is beginning again. Let me shut my eyes.

The Author. Wait, I have not said all, I have only begun. I am coming to the nebulæ. Here, indeed, you may expect to grow giddy. The telescope has dispersed all the theories on which the different explanations of the nebulæ were built, and has shown us that they are collections of stars, which, in consequence of their excessive number, and their closeness to each other, appear to form a whole, a single vague and continuous brightness. But, when their dimensions and distances are amplified by the telescope, this diffused light transforms itself into a brilliant point, analogous to that presented by the sky, tapestried with small stars, in the same telescope. These nebulæ are groups of enormous numbers of stars, and even their nearness to each other is only in appearance. They are, in reality, separated by enormous distances, and it must not be supposed that they are all in the same plane; they belong, on the contrary, to very unequal depths in space, and it is only an optical effect which gathers them together on the field of the telescope in the same apparent plane.

The nebula of the *Centaur* is one of the most wonderful. To the naked eye it is but a dimly-lighted point in the sky; but, looked at through a good telescope, it takes the aspect represented by figure 8.

On examination of this figure, it will be seen that a nebula is not the result of a collection of stars simply spread out upon a level in space, but of that of an assemblage of stars all placed

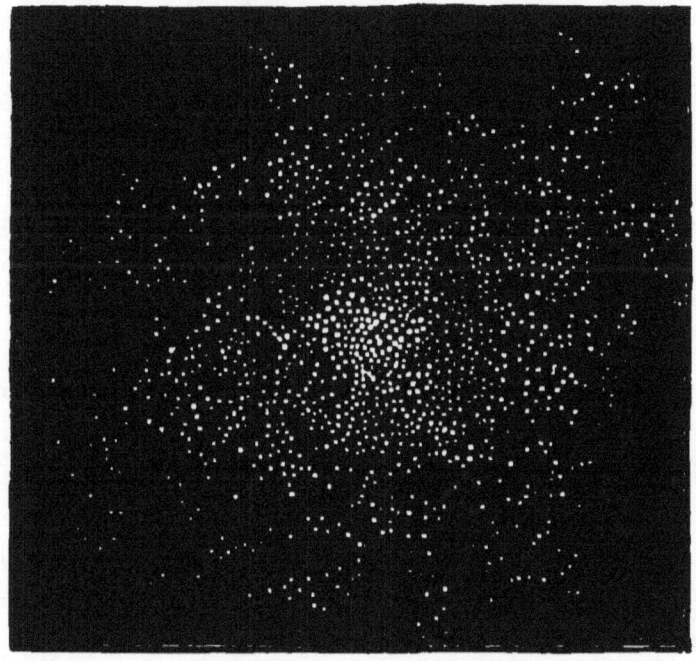

Fig. 8.—The Nebula of the Centaur.

at unequal distances, and forming almost a sphere. In fact the stars are crowded towards the centre, and are, on the contrary, more and more distant from one another as the outer edge is approached. If a spherical assemblage of stars were observed from a distance, it would present a similar aspect. This leads us to believe that the nebula of the *Centaur*, like the greater number of agglomerations of this kind, is spherical.

Is it possible to reckon the stars which form a nebula? Only approximately. Arago estimates the number of stars which form a nebula no larger than the tenth part of the apparent disc of the moon, at twenty thousand, at least. This result may give us an idea of the swarms of suns contained in the nebulæ, for these stellar masses are very numerous in the sky. In the depths of the nebulæ there are luminous points whose nature is as yet unrevealed by the telescope, which cannot be resolved into stars; but analogy leads us to believe that they are other and still more distant nebulæ, which, by reason of their apparent littleness, elude the scope of our instruments. But the time will come, when, thanks to the perfection which our telescopes shall have attained, this theory will be confirmed, and we shall thus see deeper and farther into immensity.

The stars which form the nebulæ are sometimes grouped so as to form regular shapes, spheres, or more or less lengthened ellipses. Sometimes the sphere is hollow in the centre, and so forms a ring. Nothing more varied, nothing more strange can be imagined than the forms of those nebulæ which have hitherto been examined, and which already number more than a million, of which no two are precisely alike. Certain nebulæ seem to be double, or joined. Others are lengthened out, like serpents, as in that of the *Shield of Sobieski*, represented in figure 9.

Lord Rosse was the first to discover that curious disposition of the nebulæ called *spiral.*

Such a form is inexplicable, but it is certain that the suns which compose the nebulæ are often grouped, not around a centre, not in shapeless heaps, but in regular curves, on a system which seems to reveal the existence of some mysterious force acting upon those stars, which are distributed along lines representing spirals of different diameter.

In speaking of the stars, I have said that there are coloured stars or suns. I will add here that nebulæ are observed coloured red, green, and yellow, which is an additional proof

Fig. 9.—The Shield of Sobieski.

that they are only agglomerations of stars. That immense semi-luminous band which traverses the celestial vault, girding it with a silver belt, is not, as it was long supposed to be, a diffused quantity of luminous matter. The telescopic analysis of the Milky Way shows that it consists of a long series of nebulæ. The length of the Milky Way is from 700 to 800 times the distance from Sirius to the sun, a distance which is 1,373,000 times that from the earth to the sun.*

Theophilus. Can any idea be formed of the number of stars comprised in the Milky Way?

* Flammarion. "*Pluralité des Mondes Habités,*" page 203.

The Author. Herschel, having examined the sky of the southern hemisphere from the Cape of Good Hope, in applying his observations to the whole extent of the Milky Way, estimated the number of suns comprised in that immense nebulæ at 18 millions. I have just told you the length of the Milky Way. A ray of light emitted from a star at one of its extremities, and reaching the other, would take 15,000 years to accomplish the transit. So that, when we are looking through the telescope at one of the suns of this nebula, we receive the impression of a ray of light emitted from that star

Fig. 10 —The Milky Way.

7000 or 8000 years ago, *i.e.*, long before the dawn of the historic ages.* The measurement of the Milky Way enables us therefore to measure the extent of other nebulæ, still more distant from us. There are, as I have already said, masses of diffused light in the midst of nebulæ which telescopic analysis has resolved into stars, which are probably much more distant nebulæ. The real distance of these luminous masses can be fixed. If it were asked, to what distance the Milky Way should be removed in order to offer us the aspect of an ordinary nebula, Arago would answer that according to his researches, the Milky Way ought to be removed to a distance equal to 334 times its length. According to this the Milky Way would be seen from the earth at an angle of 10°, and its light would take 5,010,000 years to travel that distance. Thus, light would take *more than five millions of years* to travel from one of the telescopic nebulæ to our earth. Such are the intervals which exist in the universe, and which our instruments can appreciate. It seems to me that we are now on the borders of the Infinite.

Theophilus. We are indeed.

The Author. When we know that those terrible distances, which appal the imagination, are only the results of observations made by our telescopes, and capable of any amount of extension; when we reflect that the innumerable worlds thus revealed to us continue farther and farther, that ever new agglomerations of suns, planetary earths and their satellites add themselves to those which we can measure, without limit and without end, that the imagination cannot err in following

* Flammarion. " *Pluralité des Mondes Habités*," page 203.

20

them to the uttermost limits of its powers ; then, my dear
Theophilus, we comprehend that the universe is truly infinite.
And if you consider that these endless ranks of solar systems
have all their following of planets and satellites, filled with
living beings, plants, animals, men, and superhuman creatures,
that flaming comets traverse the orbit of each world at intervals and plunge into the burning furnace of its sun ; that these
milliards of suns are endlessly various, and that all the complicated motions of these different systems are accomplished
with perfect order, without any mutual disturbance, you will
find that the universe is not only the infinite in extent, but
also in order, harmony, equilibrium of motion, and laws !

Theophilus. The mind loses itself in such thoughts ; for the
idea of the infinite is not made for our feeble intelligence.
Let us go no farther, or our reason will fail us.

The Author. Nevertheless, I must pursue my long argument to the end. I must add that in the midst of this
boundless space, above this immense cortége of stars, which
are the dwelling places of living creatures and sentient souls,
there exists the Supreme Author, the Sovereign Ordainer,
from Whom, as their sacred source, all that our eyes behold,
our souls feel, and our intelligence admires, is derived. He,
whom I bless with all the gratitude of my heart—God !

Theophilus. Thus, then, you have reached the true object
of your discourse. This journey through space is undertaken
to prove that God, being infinite in moral perfections, may be
placed in that infinitude in extent, called the universe. It
only remains now to say in what precise spot you place the
sojourn of the Divinity, for I do not see how there can be a
centre to the Infinite, seeing it has neither beginning nor end.

The Author. I am about to explain myself on this point. The absolute fixity of the sun and the stars was an astronomical principle, which, in the time of Newton, appeared to be indubitable. But science never stands still. Observations made in the present century have proved that the fixity, the immobility of the sun is only relative. The truth is that the sun, and with him the entire system of planets, asteroïds, satellites, and comets, which he carries, in his train, change their places, very slightly no doubt, but still appreciably. Our sun appears to advance slowly, with all the planetary family, towards that part of the sky in which the constellation of *Hercules* is situated, at the rate of 62,000,000 of leagues each year, or two leagues each second, describing an orbit which comprehends millions of centuries. That which is the case with our sun is equally the case with the other suns, that is to say, the stars. This general motion of translation must be common to all the stellar systems, and it is indubitable that the countless millions of solar systems suspended in infinite space, are moving more or less quickly towards an unknown point in the sky. Now, there is nothing to forbid the supposition that all these circles or ellipses traced by myriads of solar systems, have a common centre of attraction, towards which our system and all the others gravitate. Thus, all these celestial bodies, without exception, all this ant-hill of worlds which we have enumerated, may be turning round one point, one centre of attraction. What forbids us to believe that God dwells at this centre of attraction for all the worlds which fill infinite space?

Theophilus. Now I understand your thought, and I am

20 —2

struck by its grandeur. This God, placed at the mathematical centre of the worlds which compose the universe,
this infinite intelligence, throned in the centre of the infinite
universe, and presiding over the movements of all the innumerable phalanxes of heavenly bodies which our imagination
can conceive, responds to the idea which we form of God,
if we venture to face the awful personality of His Omnipo-
tence. You have done well to develop this theory in your
work. It will be in harmony with the kind of religious
spirit which animates it, and which is, besides, the expression of the desires, and the aspirations of the men of our
time.

In the present day a deep and profound need of belief in
Providence makes itself felt. Men want to render homage to
God, in whom they feel there is truth, peace, and safety for
the present and in the future. But the established religions
leave many minds in cruel uncertainty. In "The Day after
Death" you have endeavoured to lay the foundations of *the
religion of science and of nature.* These principles respond, as
I believe, to the prevalent wishes of mankind. They satisfy
the mind and the heart, sentiment and reason; they console
and strengthen; in short, they consecrate the idea of God,
without laying aside either the universe or nature.

The Author. So be it !

THE END.

BILLING AND SONS, PRINTERS, GUILDFORD.

S. & H.

STANDARD WORKS
FOR THE LIBRARY.

PROFESSOR MOMMSEN'S HISTORY OF ROME TO THE TIME OF AUGUSTUS. Translated by Dr. DICKSON. LIBRARY EDITION, in 4 vols., demy 8vo., 75s. The POPULAR EDITION, in 4 vols., crown 8vo., 46s. 6d.
. This last Edition is sold in certain Volumes separately; also Vols. I. and II., 21s.; Vol. III., 10s. 6d.; Vol. IV., 15s.

THE ROMAN PROVINCES: Being the History of Rome from Cæsar to Diocletian. By Professor MOMMSEN. Translated by Rev. P. W. DICKSON. 2 vols., 8vo., 36s.

THE HISTORY OF ANTIQUITY. From the German of Professor MAX DUNCKER. By EVELYN ABBOTT, M.A., LL.D., of Balliol College, Oxford. In 6 vols., demy 8vo. Each volume can be obtained separately, 21s.

ESSAYS: Classical and Theological. By CONNOP THIRLWALL, D.D., late Bishop of St. David's. Demy 8vo., 15s.

THE CHURCH AND ITS ORDINANCES. By the late Dean HOOK. 2 vols., demy 8vo., 10s. 6d.

THE LIVES OF THE ARCHBISHOPS OF CANTERBURY. By WALTER FARQUHAR HOOK, late Dean of Chichester. ST. AUGUSTINE to JUXON. 12 vols., demy 8vo., £9. Each separately (with exception of III., IV., VI., and VII.), 15s. The New Series begins with Vol. VI. Vol. XII. is the Index.

THE HEAVENS. By AMÉDÉE GUILLEMIN. In demy 8vo., with over Two Hundred Illustrations, 12s.

THE HISTORY OF THE THIRTY YEARS' WAR. From the German of ANTON GINDELY. In 2 vols., large crown 8vo., with Maps and Illustrations, 24s.

THE LETTERS OF HORACE WALPOLE, FOURTH EARL OF ORFORD. Edited by PETER CUNNINGHAM. In 9 vols., demy 8vo., with Portraits, 94s. 6d.

THE HISTORY OF THE GREAT FRENCH REVOLUTION. From the French of M. THIERS. By FREDERICK SHOBERL. With Forty-one fine Engravings, and Portraits of the most Celebrated Personages referred to in the Work, engraved on Steel by WILLIAM GREATBACH. 5 vols., demy 8vo., 36s.

THE FIFTEEN DECISIVE BATTLES OF THE WORLD. By Professor CREASY. LIBRARY EDITION, in demy 8vo., 10s. 6d.

MEMOIRS OF NAPOLEON BONAPARTE. By FAUVELET DE BOURRIENNE, Private Secretary to the Emperor. Edited by Colonel PHIPPS. 3 vols., demy 8vo. Map and Thirty-eight fine Illustrations on Steel, 42s.

THE NAVAL HISTORY OF GREAT BRITAIN. By WILLIAM JAMES. In 6 vols., crown 8vo., with Portraits of Distinguished Commanders, on Steel, 42s.

RICHARD BENTLEY & SON, NEW BURLINGTON STREET,

Publishers in Ordinary to Her Majesty the Queen.

MISCELLANEOUS SIX-SHILLING VOLUMES.

*Each Volume to be had separately, with the exceptions
shown, in crown 8vo., cloth, price 6s.*

MME. CAMPAN'S PRIVATE LIFE OF MARIE-ANTOINETTE.† 6s.
RENAN'S STUDIES IN RELIGIOUS HISTORY. 6s.
COOPER'S ISLANDS OF THE PACIFIC.† 6s.
THE AUTOBIOGRAPHY OF EDMUND YATES.† 6s.
THE SPORTING LIFE OF THE REV. 'JACK' RUSSELL.† 6s.
MITFORD'S RECOLLECTIONS OF A LITERARY LIFE.† 6s.
BRINSLEY RICHARDS' SEVEN YEARS AT ETON. 6s.
LOW'S LIFE OF LORD WOLSELEY.† 6s.
BISHOP THIRLWALL'S LETTERS TO A FRIEND.† 6s.
W. H. MALLOCK'S SOCIAL EQUALITY. 6s.
W. H. MALLOCK'S ATHEISM AND THE VALUE OF LIFE. 6s.
ARNOLD'S TURNING POINTS IN LIFE. 6s.
THE INGOLDSBY LEGENDS.† 6s.
ASHLEY'S LIFE OF LORD PALMERSTON.† 2 vols. 12s.
STEPHENS' LIFE OF DEAN HOOK.† 6s.
THE LIFE OF THE REV. R. H. BARHAM (Thomas In-
goldsby).† 6s.
SIR E. CREASY'S FIFTEEN DECISIVE BATTLES. 6s.
SIR E. CREASY'S HISTORY OF THE ENGLISH CONSTITUTION. 6s.
SIR E. CREASY'S HISTORY OF THE OTTOMAN TURKS. 6s.
GUIZOT'S LIFE OF OLIVER CROMWELL.† 6s.
MIGNET'S LIFE OF MARY QUEEN OF SCOTS.† 6s.
BARHAM'S LIFE OF THEODORE HOOK. 6s.
BAKER'S OUR OLD ACTORS.† 6s.
HAVARD'S THE DEAD CITIES OF THE ZUYDER ZEE.† 6s.
TIMBS' LIVES OF PAINTERS.† 6s.
TIMBS' LIVES OF STATESMEN.† 6s.
TIMBS' WITS AND HUMOURISTS.† 2 vols. 12s.
TIMBS' DOCTORS AND PATIENTS. 6s.
THE LETTERS OF RUNNYMEDE. 6s.
THE BENTLEY BALLADS. 6s.
LADY HERBERT'S WIVES AND MOTHERS IN THE OLDEN
TIME. 6s.
THE NEW BOOK OF SPORTS AND GAMES. 6s.
WOOD'S CRUISE OF THE RESERVE SQUADRON.† 6s.
WOOD'S IN THE BLACK FOREST.† 6s.
LETTERS FROM HELL. 6s.

† These volumes contain Portraits, Illustrations, or Maps.

To be obtained at all Booksellers'.

MONTHLY, ONE SHILLING.

THE TEMPLE BAR MAGAZINE.

Serial Stories by the following Writers have appeared in the pages of this Magazine:

The Seven Sons of Mammon, by George Augustus Sala.—For Better, for Worse, edited by Edmund Yates.—Aurora Floyd, by Miss Braddon.—The Adventures of Captain Dangerous, by George Augustus Sala.—The Trials of the Tredgolds.—John Marchmont's Legacy, by Miss Braddon.—Broken to Harness, by Edmund Yates.—Paid in Full, by H. J. Byron.—The Doctor's Wife, by Miss Braddon.—David Chantrey, by W. G. Wills.—Sir Jasper's Tenant, by Miss Braddon.—Land at Last, by Edmund Yates.—Archie Lovell, by Mrs. Annie Edwardes.—Lady Adelaide's Oath, by Mrs. Henry Wood.—A Lost Name, by J. Sheridan Le Fanu.—Steven Lawrence : Yeoman, by Mrs. Annie Edwardes.—Kitty, by M. E. Betham-Edwards.—Vera.—Red as a Rose is She, by Rhoda Broughton.—Susan Fielding, by Mrs. Annie Edwardes.— A Race for a Wife, by Hawley Smart.—The Bird of Passage, by J. Sheridan Le Fanu. — His Brother's Keeper, by Albany de Fonblanque. — The Landlord of the Sun, by W. Gilbert. — The Poison of Asps, by Florence Marryat. — Goodbye, Sweetheart! by Rhoda Broughton.—Ought we to Visit Her ? by Mrs. Annie Edwardes.—The Illustrious Dr. Mathéus, by MM. Erckmann-Chatrian. — The Wooing o't, by 'Mrs. Alexander.'—The Deceased Wife's Sister, by 'Sidney Mostyn.'—The New Magdalen, by Wilkie Collins. — Uncle John, by W. Whyte-Melville. — A Vagabond Heroine, by Mrs. Annie Edwardes. — My Beautiful Neighbour, by W. Clark Russell.—Leah : a Woman of Fashion, by Mrs. Annie Edwardes.—Patricia Kemball, by Mrs. Lynn Linton.—Philip Leigh.—The Frozen Deep, by Wilkie Collins.—Bitter Fruit, by A. W. Dubourg.—Lilith, by W. H. Pollock.—Ralph Wilton's Weird, by 'Mrs. Alexander.'—The Dream Woman, by Wilkie Collins.—Basil's Faith, by A. W. Dubourg. — The American Senator, by Anthony Trollope.—Her Dearest Foe, by 'Mrs. Alexander.'—Vittoria Contarini, by A. W. Dubourg.—The Two Destinies, by Wilkie Collins.—An Old Man's Darling, by A. W. Dubourg.—Cherry Ripe! by Helen Mathers.—A Blue Stocking, by Mrs. Annie Edwardes.—The Ordeal of Fay, by Mrs. Buxton.—The 'First Violin,' by Jessie Fothergill.—Two Handsome People, Two Jealous People, and a Ring, by Miss Lablache.— Jet, her Face or her Fortune, by Mrs. Annie Edwardes.—Auld Robin Gray, by Mrs. Godfrey.—Probation, by Jessie Fothergill.—Ebenezer, by C. G. Leland.—Vivian the Beauty, by Mrs. Annie Edwardes.—Celia, by Mrs. Godfrey.—Adam and Eve, by Mrs. Parr.—The Portrait of a Painter, by Himself, by Lady Pollock.—A Little Bohemian, by Mrs. Godfrey.—The Rebel of the Family, by Mrs. Lynn Linton.—Kith and Kin, by Jessie Fothergill.—The Freres, by 'Mrs. Alexander.'—Marie Dumont, by Lady Pollock.—The Beautiful Miss Roche, by Mrs. Godfrey.—Wild Jack, by Lady Margaret Majendie.—Robin, by Mrs. Parr.—A Ball-room Repentance, by Mrs. Annie Edwardes.—Unspotted from the World, by Mrs. Godfrey.—Belinda, by Rhoda Broughton.—Ione Stewart, by Mrs. Lynn Linton.—Uncle George's Will, by Lady Margaret Majendie.—A Perilous Secret, by Charles Reade.—Zero: a Story of Monte Carlo, by Mrs. Campbell Praed.—Mrs. Forrester's Secret, by Mrs. Godfrey.—Peril, by Jessie Fothergill.—Mitre Court, by Mrs. Riddell.—A Girton Girl, by Mrs. Annie Edwardes.—A Bachelor's Blunder, by W. E. Norris.—Put Asunder, by Mrs. Godfrey. —Paston Carew, Miser and Millionaire, by Mrs. Lynn Linton.—Red Spider, by the Author of ' Mehalah,' etc.—The Danvers Jewels.—Loyalty George, by Mrs. Parr.—A Village Tragedy, by Mrs. M. Woods.—Out of the Fog, by W. M. Hardinge.—Moor Isles, by Jessie Fothergill.—The Rogue, by W. E. Norris.

To be obtained at all Bookstalls.

www.ingramcontent.com/pod-product-compliance
Lightning Source LLC
Chambersburg PA
CBHW060538030726
47498CB00004B/1238